getaway
a novel by
maureen brady

Praise for Maureen Brady's *Getaway*

"A tension-filled yet ultimately humane story about hard-won second chances. Warm and wise, Maureen Brady's *Getaway* takes the reader on a suspenseful and memorable journey to the tenderest corners of the human heart."

—*Aaron Hamburger, author of* The View from Stalin's Head *and* Faith for Beginners

"Suspenseful pages jam-packed with action which carries the reader away into a different yet recognizable world, where likeable and believable characters will linger long in the mind after the book is closed."

— *Sheila Kohler, author of ten novels, including* Cracks *and* Becoming Jane Eyre, *the memoir,* Once We Were Sisters, *and three short story collections*

"Sensitive, sensual, and stirring. *Getaway* is a true page-turner but one with heart and with context. I couldn't put it down until I got to the end, not *just* to find out what happened, but also to discover who these intriguing and complex characters would develop into. An extremely satisfying read!"

— *Danielle Ofri, author of* What Patients Say, What Doctors Hear, *Editor-in-Chief,* Bellevue Literary Review

"Maureen Brady's new novel, *Getaway*, explores wife abuse with surprising delicacy. Her upstate characters have grit and guts. . . *When did your sex last belong to you?* is the question that drives the heroine's pell-mell flight all the way to Canada. A compelling read, especially for those who recognize that those whom we love can be the most dangerous."

— *Terese Svoboda, author of five novels including* Bohemian Girl *and the biography,* Anything That Burns You: A Portrait of Lola Ridge, Radical Poet, *as well as several books of poetry*

getaway

a novel by
maureen brady

Bacon Press Books
Washington, DC

2018

Cover Design: Carol March (www.carolmarch.net)
             Alan Pranke (www.amp13.com)
Editing: Lorraine Fico-White (magnificomanuscripts.com)
Interior Design: Lorie DeWorken (mindthemargins.com)

ISBN: 13: 978-0-9971489-6-1

Library of Congress Control Number: 2017963691

Also by Maureen Brady

FICTION

Ginger's Fire

The Question She Put to Herself

Folly

Give Me Your Good Ear

NONFICTION

Midlife: Meditations for Women

Daybreak: Meditations for Women Survivors of Sexual Abuse

*Beyond Survival: A Writing Journey
for Healing from Childhood Sexual Abuse*

Praise for Maureen Brady's other novels

Ginger's Fire

"Maureen Brady is a marvelous writer and *Ginger's Fire* reads like a dream. Readers will root for Ginger all the way."
> — *Lesléa Newman, author of* I Carry My Mother *and*
> October Mourning: A Song for Matthew Shepard

"Brady is a sensual, sensitive, bold and original writer at the height of her powers."
> — Janice Eidus, author of *The War of the Rosens* and *The Last Jewish Virgin*

"A narrative honesty that invests *Ginger's Fire* with uncommon heft and integrity."
> — *Richard Labonte,* Book Marks

Folly

"*Folly* speaks with an authenticity, a force, a caring that deepens and enlarges us."
> — *Tillie Olsen, author of* Tell Me a Riddle, Yonnondio, *and* Silences

"Maureen Brady is one of our most original voices. *Folly* is riveting and inspirational, a heartwarming testimonial to what a few good women can do to make the world less racist, homophobic and oppressive to women workers."
> — *Karla Jay, author of* Lesbian Texts and Contexts: Radical Revisions

"Shades of *Norma Rae,* but in Brady's scrupulously observed rendition, we meet Folly, Martha, and a love story that juices the rhetoric."
> — *Laurie Stone,* Village Voice

"In this novel about work and passion Maureen Brady shows us the pride that has helped women survive a society that devalues both women and labor. Economic circumstance can't douse the spark that lights each of her characters' lives."
> — *Jewelle Gomez, author of* The Gilda Stories

"*Folly* is a refreshing and skillfully told story of strength and contradiction as ordinary women move through each other's lives. These women are very real to me in their tenderness and their conflicts."

— *Audre Lore, poet and author of* Zami *and* Sister Outsider

Give Me Your Good Ear

"The writing is so good I *heard* it all."

— *Alice Walker, author of Pulitzer Prize winning* The Color Purple, The Cushion in the Road: Meditation and Wandering as the Whole World Awakens to Being in Harm's Way, *and others*

"Violence; daily work; female connections: these are the warp and woof of Maureen Brady's novel. And all are perceived through a woman's eye, in ways largely unavailable to us in fiction. The integrity of Brady's writing never falters."

— *Adrienne Rich, author of* Lies, Secrets and Silences, Of Woman Born *and numerous books of poetry*

"*Give Me Your Good Ear* is a book of enduring value, about violence and silences echoed through generations, about coming to consciousness and learning to heal."

— *Library Journal*

". . . in this strong, short novel by an excellent feminist writer, Francie learns how to break the chains of the woman-relayed behavioral law that woman's life function is to placate man."

— *Maria Kuda, Booklist*

"An excellent novel—Ms. Brady skillfully weaves the past into the present providing it as an explanation/search for why this present. Her characters and settings are rich—drawn with sensitivity and the humor of self-knowledge. A really extraordinary first novel."

— *Women Library Workers*

*To all those in the path of healing
from abuse and addiction
or in search of that path*

Part I

June 2004

Chapter 1

Cookie dove between the tall grasses, jarred with adrenalin. In the gloom, she could barely make out the blue cottage on the other side of the lake, but her eyes clung to it desperately. It was up for sale and she thought, unoccupied. Maybe if she bushwhacked around the lake and found her way there without being seen, she'd be able to hide behind it.

The air sparkled. Everything around her seemed to vibrate with too much life. When a bullfrog glugged in the reeds, she jumped, stood still, then made herself get moving again. This was no time to try to understand what she had done.

She inched along the shoreline, her feet sinking into the mud. Her foot slipped off a root and twisted painfully. Damn weak ankle, she muttered, working it before she pushed on.

A three-quarter moon came up to light the way a bit, but it was getting cold. She stopped to put on her windbreaker, the one thing she'd managed to grab from the hook by the door. A good thing she had, even though it was a bright aqua, too colorful for someone who wanted not to be seen.

Squatting, she buried her face in her hands. Her stomach roiled and she thought she might throw up. *My God, Warren, why did you have to come after me like that?*

She was struck by the sound of twigs breaking underfoot. A

bear or a coyote? Someone coming after her? That got her moving again, making low, humming noises to keep whatever it was at bay.

When she finally came out to the clearing, she scooted through tall tufts of grass in front of the blue cottage and crept around back. The building blocked the moonlight as she huddled against the cinderblock cellar wall, her arms wrapped around her legs, her feet wet and freezing. She stared into the night as the fireflies spit tiny patches of light before flickering out.

As she adjusted to the dark, she noticed a hump a few feet away, a rounded Bilco cellar door. She stood and lifted the handle. Detecting a little give, she lifted again, hard, and one side came up. Three steps down, there was a wooden door. It, too, had been left unlocked, so the knob turned and she was in.

She sunk to the cellar floor and wrapped her windbreaker around her wet pant legs but couldn't stop her teeth from chattering. Trying to still her jaw only made her whole arm shake. She remembered once as a child when her teeth had rattled on this way. It had been fear, not cold that time her father had raised his large square hand but stopped just short of slapping her across the face.

When she finally found the remains of a matchbook in her pocket, the first match she struck crumbled. She stood up and struck another. The light flared up shockingly fast and extinguished itself before she'd seen a thing. She caught a glimpse of a stairway, which she shuffled toward, hands out ahead of her, searching for a light switch.

In the flare of the last match, she spotted a worktable under the stairs. Patting along its surface, she touched something soft and squishy, almost like human skin. She jumped back, horrified. Gathering her courage, she reached out again but she must have turned when she jumped back because, where the squishy thing had been, there was nothing, not even the bench. She made a quarter turn and reached out again. Still nothing! At least it wasn't the squishy thing, but where the hell was she and what was that anyway? Someone's clay? Shakily, she took another step, hand out in front, and finally found a wall.

She followed it around to the stairs—solid, dusty-smelling blocks of wood. Though she didn't expect the door at the top of the stairs to be unlocked, she ascended them with a flutter of hope.

The doorknob didn't turn. Sitting on the cellar stair, cradling her face in her hands, her thoughts muffled everything and created a damped down feeling in her ears. She had to think. She had done something she could not change. It was final.

But suddenly Warren was crowding in to corral her like he had at the counter, and when she sprang to her feet to shake the image out of her head, she gave the door a solid kick, and it flew open. Moonlight illuminated the front room with a silvery glow. She stood transfixed and listened to the silence of the empty house.

Beyond the living room, there was a small kitchen. The fridge was empty except for a carton of orange juice, which she grabbed and looked at the last sale date. Only a week away. Might someone be living here? She listened for any possible noise but heard only her breath.

She rooted around the kitchen drawers until she found a flashlight, closed the fridge door, and shone the small light around. Someone had obviously moved out, leaving only a sofa, two chairs, and a square butcher block table. Along the back wall was a bathroom with a door slightly ajar. Beyond that, a closet with a few men's shirts and jackets hanging in it, and when she separated the hangers, she found a two-drawer chest pushed against the back wall. She held up a pair of jeans—size 32—changed into them and shortened the legs by rolling up large cuffs. They hung on her hips, which sent her searching for a belt. She found one as well as a plaid flannel shirt and some clean T-shirts. All men's clothes but she clutched them to her chest gladly.

Glancing up at the second story loft, she suddenly got spooked, imagining someone up there, someone whose clothes she might just have donned.

"Hello," she ventured in a small voice, but no one answered. In spite of that, she scrambled up the ladder to find only a mattress on the floor. For now, she was alone, but someone might be coming back. She'd better rest a while and figure out where to go.

Not until she draped her own damp pants and shirt over two kitchen chairs to dry did she discover the tangy, rank odor she'd been smelling had not been in her imagination; it was the blood on her shirt. It was almost a relief to see it. But once she had, the odor grew stronger and stronger until she had to throw the T-shirt down the cellar steps to get the smell away from her.

Her shoes were hopelessly sopped from making her way around the lake. She found a towel and sponged them, then put on a pair of wool socks big enough to fit Warren, lay down, spread out the afghan that had been draped over the back of the sofa. and curled into herself, waiting for warmth to infuse her body. As she warmed her hands between her legs, a tingle of life arose there, and with it came the thought, *When did your sex last belong to you?*

She shut her eyes, and without wanting to be there, was back on the other side of the lake, hearing the *vroom, vroom* of Warren's truck from the last shot of acceleration he gave it just before he cut the engine, which always set her heart to pounding. She'd done her best to pull a mask down over her face to keep him from seeing how scared she was as he'd clambered up the porch steps.

"I let your supper go cold," she mumbled as he came in. She had kept it warm and waited supper for him a good two hours before she'd given up and eaten hers.

He'd lurched toward her, shaking his head as if to warn her she'd done something bad, grabbed her by the ponytail and turned her around, pushing her up against the counter, as if she were a horse he was about to mount or a sheep that needed shearing. He lifted her ponytail and slobbered on the back of her neck, saying, "That don't matter. You're gonna be my hot supper tonight." Then he pressed her into the counter and rubbed roughly against her, like he'd done a dozen times before when he'd pulled down her pants, bent her over and pushed into her while she begged him not to.

But this time, as his hand clawed at her jeans, something in her bucked top to bottom, and there lay the knife right in front of her— she'd sharpened it just before to cut the fat off the pork chops. She picked it up and whirled around with a shocking animal strength, and it went into him so easily, right below the diaphragm. Even though his chest was thick and hard, she knew exactly where his breastbone ended because he had many times pressed his thumb into that spot on her, saying, *Shut up, no more lip from you*—the pressure of his thumb making her gag.

Then she was bushwhacking around the lake and all she could remember was how Warren had stared at her in shock as he'd slid to the floor.

———

She woke under the thin afghan to the chirping of birds and a new day rushed at her with the sun rising pink and a mist wafting off the lake. After a moment of gathering her wits to comprehend where she was, she went out and sat on the floor of the porch, so the rail would hide her from early morning joggers or cars going by. Her eyes wouldn't stop leaping to the opposite side of the lake, to the dense brush and tall reeds she had made her way through, and beyond that, the path to her home. Had Warren been found? The only one who ever came to their house was her girlfriend, Nita, and Nita never came without calling first. She should have called 911. Should have tried to stop the bleeding! How could she have run out, leaving him lying there?

She put her head back and drew in the sweet, fresh air. She wanted only to stay here. She wished she could live in this cottage and awaken every morning to watch the light come up as it was doing now, making the surface of the lake glisten. She remembered her aunt, her father's sister, who had lived in a modest lake bungalow in Pennsylvania. They'd mocked her because she was a spinster, but Cookie had admired how she'd lived quietly and peacefully, despite a sometimes-acid tongue for her neighbors, filling her bird feeders and tossing scraps to the deer in her backyard. But you can't get lost just sitting here, she warned herself. You must get out of here. Either go far away. Or else walk into the Woodstock Police Station and turn yourself in.

But going to the police was not an option because, besides running his own masonry contracting business, Warren was a bastion of the volunteer emergency squad. He went around ranting about how the town had cowed to the city people—weekenders, other rich people—who'd call if they had a heart attack but had no time to offer the community while working up to it. Buying up all the property and pricing out working-class guys like him.

Warren was one of "Mulley's boys." If Cookie were to walk in and describe how he had pushed her down on the counter, Police Chief Mulligan would not believe it. No one in that town wanted to know Warren had a mean streak that came out at home.

The sun was rising fast now, the shadows disappearing. She rounded up a few things to throw into the empty backpack she'd found in the closet and headed for the main road. She'd wait until the next bus to Kingston came along, then head north from there, to Canada. She walked, searching for a spot out of sight of anyone's house, turning away each time a car passed so no one would see her face or think she was a hitchhiker. But there was a steady string of houses, no good place to stand unnoticed in.

Finally, she reached the pull in where the overseer of the Cooper Lake Reservoir lived. Pretending she was just someone who liked watching the water, she kept her back to the road but positioned herself to be able to flag down the bus. The trouble was, across the lake, just beyond the thick woods where she was looking, stood her home. Where Warren might well be lying on that floor by the counter, lumped up and still—more than still—dead. She covered her mouth with her hand to keep from crying out.

When she spotted the bus coming around the curve, she flagged it down and soon enough was in Kingston. She got a ticket from Lake Hill to give to the bus driver, went across the street and took out as much as she thought possible from the bank, then returned to the bus station and bought a ticket to Montreal. Strange, there'd been times when she'd fantasized living there, where the people spoke French, which she did not, and where, even though she would stand out as different and everything would be alien, she somehow imagined she might feel comfortable having no need to belong.

A couple of hours later, Cookie stared out the window as the bus flew up the Northway past the high peaks of the Adirondacks.

It was a pure, clear day and she was taken, in spite of her current state, by the splendor of the mountains against the deep blue sky. This far north the trees were still filling out with chartreuse green leaves, shimmering against the pewter stone faces that rose up above the tree line.

Breathe in, breathe out, she told herself, remembering her friend saying that after she'd gone to hear one of the Tibetan monks talks on meditation. "You could use this breathing," Nita had told her, "I can see you're stressed." Little did Nita know that Cookie looked ghostly because of the exhaustive make-up job she had to do to cover up the bruises on her face and neck.

Warren had forbidden her to partake of any such breathing nonsense, but if she made it to Canada, she vowed to find a monk to teach her. As she closed her eyes and started to fall asleep, she saw the knife, the length of it slippery and wet with blood. Then she knew how blessed she had been to put this out of her mind for even a few hours' sleep in the little blue cottage last night, because she sensed it was going to haunt her forever.

If only, she thought. If only she had been able to open her mouth and scream at him instead of cowering when he came at her. Or somehow get him to be more like the Warren she had married instead of the Warren whose father would come over him.

Even before they married, Warren had told her about his father's brutality. Like once, when he'd brought home a report card that said, "*Stubborn with a tendency to bully. For a smart boy, he should be farther along. He skims his pages, then is first out to recess, but with no comprehension of what he has read.*" Warren's father had grabbed his wrist and dragged him into the back kitchen, yanked off his belt and pulled Warren down over his lap.

Later, back at the kitchen table, his mother had reminded him. "Eat, eat, eat," while lauding him for getting the teacher to recognize he was smart, while his father chimed in, "I like the stubborn part, too, a chip off the old block."

Warren always laughed when he told Cookie this story, saying he was glad *she* was such a good reader because he had never been able to tame letters, which had sometimes looked backward or upside down to him. Math he'd been able to peg. Good thing, too, as he had to use so many measurements on his jobs. But other times when he was softer because they'd just made love, Warren had buried his face in her breast and come apart, telling her it wasn't just the strap, it was that his father had wanted him to admit fault, even when he had done nothing. *That* had hurt the worst.

The bus zoomed on up the Northway, leaving the mountains behind, replaced with a tall concrete wall mounted with rows and rows of razor wire, surrounding a huge prison. She had heard about that place. She'd seen people at the bus station in Kingston, heading back to the city after visiting their relatives there.

She sat up straighter, alarmed. Was that only a men's prison? Or might she end up there? Murder in the first degree? Premeditated? But did dreaming of finding a way out count as premeditation? Sharpening the best knife you had for cutting up meat?

She told herself to look away from the razor wire but could not. Could she survive in such a place? She'd had to lose most of her feelings to live in the same house with Warren these last few years, which had toughened her, but look where the toughness had led. She craved something like the fairy-tale-like blue cottage, some water to gaze out on. If only she could get far enough away. She had a picture in her mind of Nova Scotia from some photo she had seen in a magazine, of rough surf pounding against a rugged coastline. She wasn't at all clear on how far Nova Scotia was from Montreal. She wasn't even sure it was part of Canada, but if she got through the border, she determined to find her way there.

In Plattsburgh, near the New York–Canada border, there was a short layover, so she rushed to the nearby diner and bought herself a huge turkey sandwich and a large coffee. Back on the bus she discovered her appetite and had to hold herself back from wolfing it down too quickly. Better taste every bite, she told herself; the next food you get may be prison food.

Soon enough, the bus slowed and a line of customs booths appeared ahead. The driver took them over to the far right where there was a police car with its lights flashing. She slid down a bit farther in her seat as the bus inched forward behind a series of trucks, the drivers being questioned at the extra-wide lane booth.

She was on the wrong side of the bus to see the police; she could only see the lights flashing. She imagined they would enter the bus, calling out, "Mrs. Wagner? We need to speak to Passenger Wagner."

She'd bought her ticket with cash, to avoid revealing any identifying information, but when the clerk asked her for her last name, she'd given it automatically—Wagner—Warren's name, which she had taken when she married him at twenty-five. A good thing, too, she realized now, as her only chance of getting across the border without getting picked up was if her driver's license matched the name on her bus ticket. They'd told her at the bus station a driver's license would still do for ID, but only for a few more months, then, because of the September 11th terrorist attacks, one would have to show a passport. She slunk down farther. Maybe being caught would be better; then she'd know for certain Warren was dead. If not dead, she was sure he would search the earth until he found her, and kill her.

She remembered his hard body ramming her, her watching this act as if she were absent, reaching for the memory of when they were young and he had taken her gently, encouraging her to trust him and drawing out a passion she hadn't known was in her.

His strength had made her feel safe then, knowing his hard chest protected a heart that beat for her. But when his father died, at first he went to pieces, as if the old man were his best friend, not the man who had belted him raw. Early in their marriage, she had wanted children, but Warren put them off from having any, until suddenly, after his father's death, he wanted a son, and when Cookie didn't get pregnant and they went for testing and it turned out he had a low sperm count, that's when he started getting meaner. Imposing more restrictions on her like, *Girlie, no ifs, ands, or buts, I want you here with my supper ready to go on the table whenever I get home, whether it's 4:30 or midnight!*

She worked at the bakery then, from 7:00 a.m. to 3:00 p.m., and had to fit in shopping and any errands before she dashed home. And once there, she couldn't leave the house without his permission. When the bakery closed down, he wouldn't let her look for another job. Said her job was to take care of him, *period,* and if she wanted to work, she could work on the accounts for his masonry contracting business, do the billing, stuff like that, which, after a while, she agreed to, to appease him.

"Identification, please." The custom's officer startled her, speaking to someone several seats up the aisle. He wore a strap diagonally across his chest and held an electronic notebook in his hand. Was it possible to do a computer check just by putting in her name?

Her hands were sweating as she rifled through the backpack she had stolen from the blue cottage, in which she'd deposited her rolled up, still damp clothes, as well as the remains of the quart of orange juice, a couple of fresh T-shirts, and the items she'd purchased at the CVS—scissors, toothbrush and toothpaste, underpants and some pretzels. She hadn't been sure why she was buying scissors, but part of her had seen ahead to the need to cut her hair off. When she'd gone to the bank, she'd stood sideways at the drive-up ATM, the oversized baseball cap from the cottage pulled down low because she knew they had a camera spying on her, entered her numbers, drew out $500 from their checking, then $500 from their savings account. Not a lot of money, considering she didn't know when she'd ever be able to get more, but she seemed to remember $500 as the limit for a cash withdrawal. Still, it was more cash than she had ever in her life had, stuffed into her pockets. All in twenties.

The customs officer drew closer. He was taking his time with each person, asking questions which she couldn't make out, until he was only a couple of seats away. "Purpose of your visit," she heard him say. What? What was hers? Escape my dead husband? Visiting a friend in Montreal? But she didn't have a friend in Montreal. Pretend Nita lives there, she told herself. Say it like you mean it.

She sipped the cold dregs of her coffee to wet her throat, and before she looked back up, the officer was beside her, saying, "Your identification, please, ma'am," but the driver's license had disappeared from her sweaty palm. "I just had it in my hand," she said.

She looked up but didn't meet his eyes, fumbled with the backpack.

"In your lap," said the officer, and she looked down and there it was.

She handed it to him as fast as she could before her hand started shaking. This time she did meet his eyes, and he had a squarish face and a kind look to him. He punched something into his handheld notebook, then asked her the purpose of her visit.

"A friend," she sputtered. "Visiting a friend in Montreal." Cookie had a flash of Nita looking for her, a bewildered look clouding her eyes.

"Your first time in Quebec?" he asked.

"Yes," she said, repeating as if rote. "First time ever."

She felt like saying, "I'm forty-three years old and this is nearly the first time I've been away from home without my husband since I married him eighteen years ago," but she sat mute, holding her breath, waiting for him to discover she was the one he was on the lookout for.

"Enjoy your stay then," he said, moving on down the aisle.

Chapter 2

In the Montreal bus station, Cookie stared at herself in the restroom mirror. That look of fright! She had to get rid of it. Her pupils were so huge her eyes had almost lost their color.

Her shoulder-length hair was not quite straight, not quite curly. She went into a stall and ran her fingers over and over it, tucking it behind her ears while other passengers who'd been on the same bus came and went from the restroom. Then she was alone at the mirror, scissors in hand, holding out large clumps of hair and rapidly whacking them off, placing them alongside the sink, a churning in her stomach with each whack. Done, she wrapped the lengths of hair in a paper towel and was about to deposit the whole mess in the trash can when her hand deviated without volition and stuck it into her backpack. It was *her*, that hair! Besides, what if someone were to come along and find it?

Lifting what hair remained to snip along the tops of her fingers the way she'd seen hairdressers do, she couldn't stop studying her face. The dark circles under her eyes, the hard muscles clenching her jaw gave her broad face the look of a lady wrestler at the same time the overly large men's clothes seemed to shrink her stature. She unrolled the sleeves of the too-big flannel shirt and rolled them back up more neatly. One thing was remarkable—she was not black and blue as she'd been so many times when she'd stared into a mirror like this.

The door swung open just as she was slipping the scissors into the backpack. With her fingertips, she tried to fluff up the hair that was left on her head. It looked like hell.

"*Bonjour*," said the woman who had entered.

"What?" asked Cookie, gripping the sink.

"Good day," the woman said, and Cookie's legs gained a little strength. How was it possible a simple French phrase could cause her to nearly faint?

"Oh, *bonjour*," she said before pushing the knob of the hand dryer and rubbing her hands briskly.

It was three in the afternoon when she left the restroom and went to buy a ticket and found out she'd missed the last bus to Cape Breton.

"What's your destination beyond Sydney?" the clerk asked. "All the way out to Cape North? Or will Ingonish do? Or is it Neil's Harbour or Seal Cove you want, eh?"

She turned up her hands and shrugged.

"Doesn't matter. Too late for any bus out there today anyway," he said with a grin, handing her the ticket to Sydney.

She was mute, studying the ticket: 6:00 a.m. Where would she sleep? She headed to the street, pulling her cap lower. It unnerved her to think someone might be looking for her. In a couple of blocks, she found a bench and sat to study the map she had picked up. Botanical garden. Her eye landed on it immediately, and though it might be too far to walk, she saw there was a subway station at the end of the block. Maybe she could find a secluded bench in the garden to sleep on.

In her garden back home, the roses were producing the first round of blossoms. So many years she'd been nourishing the yellow one, and this year it had rewarded her, springing forth heavy with buds . . . was it only yesterday she had given it rose food? A yesterday that seemed like years ago.

She climbed the long uphill to the Botanical Garden from the subway station, sucking air by the time she got to the admission booth, sweat wetting her back under the backpack. Fifteen Canadian dollars—could she afford it? She had changed a bit of her money where the bus stopped at the border, but she'd already spent some on her bus ticket to Sydney. There was no way she could risk using the credit or debit cards, and when her money ran out . . .

She forced her mind to stop, shelled out the $15 and went directly to the rose garden, where rows and rows of roses in every imaginable color were blooming. Pink, yellow, red, orange, lavender. Some aromatic. She breathed them in like an asthmatic pulling on a nebulizer, and the sweet smells, plus the smell of the earth, consoled her. She stooped to one of the tea roses, placed her palm flat on the soil, and breathed in the fertile odor. Maybe grounding herself this way would ease that look of fright. She moved on down the rows, stooping to read the names of the roses she liked best. Over the Moon. Walking on Sunshine. Could you walk on sunshine? Not with what she'd done. She brought her hand to her mouth as the sound came back, of Warren gurgling as she'd run out the door.

By late afternoon, she'd been through the entire garden except for the insectarium, and found a bench hidden away in a far back corner under the canopy of an old oak. Maybe no one would find her here, and she could lie down and sleep when night fell. With that thought, she promptly fell asleep sitting straight up.

When someone touched her shoulder, she let out a yelp and nearly jumped a foot in the air, thinking the man in a blue uniform was a policeman.

He said something in French, which she miraculously recognized as six. He was just a Botanical Garden guard.

"Closing?" she asked, her voice hoarse, and he nodded.

Outside the Botanical Garden fence, she stopped to look at the map again. Still twelve hours until the bus. She was so exhausted, in spite of how deeply she'd napped on the bench. But should she spend her precious dollars on a hotel? It was warm enough to stay outdoors, but would a park be safe? Her eyes kept returning to the wide river. It seemed to beckon her the way the blue cottage had. It would be a shame to waste her bus ticket.

Next thing, hardly realizing she had crossed to the riverfront, at the first boat she came to, she asked if anyone was headed to Cape Breton, and the boatman directed her to a scrappy-looking vessel a few slips down.

"Early for tourists yet, lassie," said the salty captain, "but I have a group wants a historic tour leaving just on the hour, if you want to come aboard." He winked and the lines around his eyes crinkled. "We get up to Quebec City tonight, then tomorrow, on to North Sydney."

"How much?" she inquired.

"Dunno. Group's already paid for the trip. How about a twenty?"

"Okay," she said, handing it over.

"If you've not had your supper, better get something to bring on board," he said, pointing her toward the fish shack. "This here's just my own little operation. Not a cruise ship with a cook or nothing like that."

She looked at her watch.

"Don't you worry, I won't leave without you."

On the boat she found a seat away from the others and tore into her fish and chips. Her last meal had been that turkey sandwich hours ago, just before the US to Canada border. The coffee was good, too. It warmed her as the sun put her into a near trance, even as it began to fade with the onset of evening. Though June, this far north, sunset was still a long way off. There was no wind, the water was not choppy and as the boat pulled full steam ahead into the St. Lawrence, she positioned her body sideways on the bench, her feet still on the floor, her head resting on her backpack and began to nod off.

She had often had trouble sleeping, especially when Warren was beside her, but now it seemed as if she could fall asleep anywhere. There was plenty of air around her here compared to those suffocating nights she'd lain next to Warren, his snore forcing her to breathe in sync with him, then startle whenever he'd either skip a breath or escalate to a loud snort. She'd bring her head to the very edge of the bed, think of how the guest bed lay empty in the other room, but knew Warren would find a way to punish her in the morning if she chose to slink out and go to sleep there. He believed it was part of her marital duty to sleep beside his snoring, and the only time she was allowed to sleep in the other room was when she had a bad cold, and he was afraid he'd catch it.

But now, as the boat swayed, she had no trouble falling into a deep sleep and dreamed she was about to fall off a cliff into a dark chasm. When her fist suddenly came up and slammed hard into her chest, she jerked awake, her heart pounding. Had she pulled the knife out of Warren? She must have. She'd seen the shimmering blood that coated it. She should have tried to stop the bleeding. Called someone. Given him a chance.

She sat up, massaged the muscles in her cheeks, then when her hands ran into her hair, which was standing nearly straight up, it sent an electric shock through her. Whose hair was this? The hair of a complete stranger!

At Quebec City, everybody filed off the boat except for her and the Captain. "I'm not going anywhere, if you want to take a look around and find yourself a room for the night," he said. "Just be back by ten in the morning."

She shrugged and stood there, looking around to memorize where they were to be sure she knew where to return to, as the signs were all in French.

He took a hard, long look at her. "Course if you can't find a room, you can always come back and sleep on one of my benches. Narrow, they are, but long as you don't toss and turn too much, you'd be okay."

How'd he know she didn't want to get herself a room? Was it the hair, her baggy clothes? Did she still have that look of fright? She nodded and thanked him. She'd not realized how far away Nova Scotia was but had learned it by studying the map posted in the boat's narrow passageway to the toilet. Looked like they'd round the Gaspe Peninsula, and then go south to Sydney. She had no idea what she'd do when she got there, but that was too scary to think about, so she just thanked Captain Wayne, as he called himself, as she got off the boat and said she might well come back and take him up on his offer.

The next day he gave her that same careful, casing look when they disembarked at the harbor in North Sydney, as she sauntered up slowly to the gangplank after the others were gone, wanting to thank him for bringing her this far. She avoided his eyes by looking off into the distance where hills rose up—green, so green, their shadows in the water repeating in a darker green.

"You've been very kind," she said. Then, almost like a broken record, she repeated, "You couldn't have been more kind, and I thank you."

"Well, lassie," he said, "I don't like to be nosey, but I saw that you came back to sleep on my hard bench last night, and I fear you must be in some sort of trouble." He raised his bushy eyebrows. "Are you gonna be okay?"

No words came. She didn't want to be rude but, needing to get away from him before a flush of tears flooded out of her, she brought her hand to her forehead and gave him a silly, childlike salute and stepped onto the gangplank.

In the center of the town, the tourist office was located next to the small bus station. She sat on the grass under a large maple and tried to breathe like Nita had taught her. No one knows, she told herself. Captain Wayne saw something was wrong with you, but he doesn't know what you did. But you better make up a story before you go another step. Someone else will not let it go so easily.

She had never been a good liar, but she was going to have to learn to lie if she didn't want to land in a stark concrete building like she'd seen as the bus shot up the Northway, with rows and rows of barbed wire strung atop its walls.

Annie had been a good liar, even advocated lying at times, big-sister explaining to Cookie that there was sometimes a kindness in lying. For instance, if you didn't like someone, you didn't have to tell him to his face. Or if you deviated from their father's strict and often arbitrary rules, it was the only way to protect your-self. Yet Cookie had somehow gotten the role of truth teller in her family. She needed to keep track of exactly what was going down, and she had a good memory, so she usually remembered who had said what. Mom said, *bla, bla, bla*; then Dad said, *No, bla, bla, bla;* then Mom said, *I don't want to argue about it.* Leading to Dad saying, *Well, for Christ's sake, then why'd you start with me.*

But if Cookie repeated back what they had said, making it pos-sible for them to analyze logically where they had gone off track, nobody wanted to hear it. It always puzzled her why tracking what was being said was of great import to her but not to them.

She looked around and saw a series of plain houses, two-story, nothing fancy, mostly painted gray or yellow. They were close together, not spread out like where she had grown up, or Bears-ville, where she and Warren lived. *Used to live.* What must be going down back home hit her full force. Warren was dead, and who else might have stabbed him but his missing wife. Police heli-copters would be flying low over the woods, and the cops would be stopping traffic on her road, asking people who passed if they'd heard or seen anything. She knew the things they did because Warren always had that damn CB radio crackling in the dining room and she'd been forced to hear any bit of local drama, major or minor, that ever went on.

Like the Bank of America robbery in Woodstock. The robber stole a car not a mile up the road from them in Bearsville, from the old man who used to own the Woodstock Bakery. The old baker always left the keys in his car so they'd be there when he was ready to drive to town for the paper. Only that morning his car was missing. And he suddenly found himself the chief suspect, because someone had recognized the getaway car as his. But someone else identified the robber as a woman. Cookie silently crowed about that: good for the woman robber. Bank of America had all the money in the world. Though, generally, she was in favor of a lawful world.

It would be easy for them to find out she'd gotten on that bus to Montreal. Thank God she hadn't shown up 6:00 a.m. at the Mon-treal Bus Station but taken Captain Wayne's boat instead. Even so, the clerk knew she was headed to Sydney, so they might well be looking for her right now. Suddenly self-conscious, she ducked her head and inched sideways until she was hidden from the street by the trunk of a large maple and continued studying the map she'd picked up in the Nova Scotia tourist office.

A place called Seal Cove was far out in the Highlands on the Cabot Trail, whatever that was. She remembered the name Henry Cabot from school. Had he discovered Cape Breton? The idea of going to the Cabot Trail made her feel like a pioneer. But how could she get there? Grab a takeout sandwich and go back down to the harbor and see if someone was going in that direction? Or if she found the right road out from town, chance hitchhiking? It didn't look that far, maybe a couple of hours.

But still she needed a story and a name. Lassie, the Captain had called her, not asking her name. She touched the strange, blunt ends of her hair again. Her name before she'd married Warren was Carol Molloy, but everyone called her Cookie. She remembered a time she and Annie played with renaming themselves, passing time on a car trip. "Molly," she'd said.

"Are you kidding? Too close to Molloy," her sister had replied.

"That's why I chose it, on purpose," she said. "Molly Carol. It's almost my name backwards."

"Carol can't be spelled that way as a last name," Annie stubbornly asserted. "It's C A R R E L." She spelled it out.

"Okay, then, what's yours?" Cookie asked.

Annie had thought a moment, then turned to furrow her brow into a monster face, and spreading her fingers to look like claws, pounced on Cookie, saying, "Frankenstein."

Now it occurred to her, since Annie was all the family she had left, the police might seek her out in North Carolina to ask the whereabouts of her sister.

Even if it felt like cutting off an arm or a leg, no way Cookie would contact Annie and tell her; she didn't trust her. Too many times when they were little her sister had put her front and center when it came time for someone to end up over their father's knees. Annie would hover beside the frame of the garage door, listening to the thwack of their father's hand, almost as if she were spanking Cookie along with their father.

"Okay," she silently spoke to herself. "You're Molly Carrel," but she spelled it Annie's way.

Walking down the hill to the docks, she spotted Captain Wayne and picked up her pace, trying to pass by his boat quickly; she didn't want to ask anything more of him after she'd walked off earlier without answering his question. But when he stepped forward and asked where she was heading next, she met his kind eyes for a second. The words stuck in her throat, but finally she cleared it enough to get out, "Seal Cove," and sure enough, he knew which boat to direct her to—a small wooden vessel a few slips down, loading for a run of fish and scallops to some markets and restaurants up in the Highlands. And soon as she pointed out who had sent her, they signaled her to come aboard.

"Seal Cove," she sputtered out, "is where I want to get off."

She wolfed down her sandwich but no sooner had she eaten it than they launched the boat and she lost it. The seasickness grew even worse once her stomach was empty, and she just heaved and heaved. One scruffy bearded fellow handed her a cup of coffee but she had the shakes so bad it spilled before she could get it to her mouth.

"Not got your sea legs," he commented languidly out the side of his mouth, rolling his eyes toward the other hands, as if to say, "We got ourselves a flimsy lass on board," before consigning her to the lowest part of the boat.

"Seal Cove," she said again.

"We'll unload you with the fish there then," he said, "if you make it." He must have seen a flash of terror in her eyes because he added, "Not to worry." But she did worry because, unlike Captain Wayne, he did not seem like anyone she should trust.

It seemed like hours later when one of the hands came to tell her they were approaching Seal Cove, and as she gratefully climbed up to the deck, the fresh air blasting into her face revived her. So, too, did the glimpse of the coast. Bronze rocks curved up to form cliffs, making a frame for the harbor. The captain cut the motor and the boat rocked with the waves. She had to hold on tight, although she didn't feel sick any longer, just as if her insides had been carved out and left behind.

Someone held her elbow as she stepped off along with a stooped old man. Her backpack thrown over one shoulder, she called out to thank the boatmen and then followed the old man up the hill. When he turned up a side street instead of continuing on the main street, she stopped and looked each way. There were houses and stores back from the sidewalk, shabby white and yellow boxes, almost deserted looking, low scrubby bushes, no grass. No color. She thought she might faint from the wave of lost feeling that overtook her. She had made it to her destination but that now seemed not so much a victory as a wreckage. A cold wind blew off the ocean, and she stopped to zip up her windbreaker. She wished she had a sweater. It was June, but this place was rugged and seemed not to know it. Just who lived here in such desolation? She walked another block, passing a boarded-up gas station and a closed antique shop, and came to an old, silver diner, the only thing she'd yet seen that looked alive.

A bell tinkled as she entered.

"Coffee, please," she ordered, and then practically sprinted to the restroom. Washing up, brushing her teeth and rinsing out her rancid mouth, she accidentally looked in the mirror and, once again, didn't know who she was looking at. Her skin had a greenish tinge. Her pupils had narrowed, but she looked lost. Like nobody. And that hair! She sniffed at her armpit and wrinkled her nose with disgust.

Walking back by the counter, the pies looked so good she ordered a piece of apple when the waitress came with her coffee. After she devoured the pie, she sat squeezing her forehead, trying to calm the headache that had grown to a steady beat over her right eye.

The compact, orderly-looking woman facing her in the next booth suddenly made a gesture. Was it to her? She looked over her shoulder to see if someone was behind her, but no, no one was there. The woman was actually waving her small hand at her, and then called out, "Do you need an aspirin?"

"I sure could use one," Cookie said.

The woman rooted around in her purse until she found a little pillbox and held it up for Cookie to come get it, and when she did, the older woman invited her to sit down.

"I don't want to bother you," Cookie said, but the woman said she wasn't bothering her, just to bring her coffee and her water so she could take the aspirin.

What could she do? She obeyed, grabbing her stuff and moving into the woman's booth.

"Edith," the woman said. "Edith Biddle."

Cookie paused. "Molly," she finally eked out. Then she added, "Carrel, Molly Carrel." A good half of the headache left her right then, enough to make her sit up straighter for the next question.

"What brings you to Cape Breton?" Edith asked.

"I once saw some pictures in a magazine of the waves crashing in on the coast. I love water, so I always wanted to come up here."

Edith nodded. "We do have those waves in abundance. But you've arrived a bit early. It doesn't really warm up until July."

The woman's eyes appraised her. She appeared to be waiting for Cookie to say more, but Cookie was stuck. She hadn't really come up with a story. But then the waitress spared her, returning to offer refills of the coffee and asking if they'd like something else. Edith still had three sections of a neatly quartered corn muffin on her plate. It looked so appetizing Cookie ordered one.

When Cookie next looked up, the woman still had that inquiring look squared upon her, her mouth pursed, her brow wrinkled, yet nothing came to Cookie to say, to explain her sudden appearance here in this godforsaken place, so she asked the woman if she had always lived here.

"I grew up in Montreal but met my husband when he went there for medical school. He wanted to come back here to practice, though, so that's how I got here."

"Oh," said Cookie, wondering where the doctor was now.

As if a mind reader, Edith went on to tell her he was dead two years, of a heart attack.

"Oh my," said Cookie, her hand coming up to her mouth as if she had asked the wrong question.

"It's okay," the woman said, "but it's taking me a while to get used to it."

Cookie stared at her hands resting on the table until she noticed that she had a slight ring mark from tanning where she'd removed her wedding ring. She moved her hands quickly down into her lap and squeezed them nervously together. "I'm sorry," she said.

"It's okay," the woman repeated, and once again, Cookie clammed up, not knowing what to say. But she felt her chest tightening because soon enough the woman would get up and leave her alone again, and she remembered the bleakness of the street outside, and the way the wind had blown right through her jacket.

When Edith finished the third quarter of her corn muffin, seeing her plate nearly empty finally drove the words out of Cookie. "Um, is there a motel here, or someplace I can rent a room?"

"You don't have a place to stay?"

"Not yet," Cookie said, hoping to sound as if that was only a matter of choice.

"There's a B&B over in Neil's Harbour, up at the top of the hill."

"Where's that?" Cookie asked. "Just down the road?"

"Maybe six kilometers."

Damn, they didn't use miles here even though they spoke English, not French. How far was six kilometers? She didn't want to ask but guessed it must be at least a few miles.

"Okay, thanks," she said, watching Mrs. Biddle consume the last of her corn muffin.

As Mrs. Biddle left, she pointed Cookie in the direction of Neil's Harbour and told her there was just one street beside the main street that went off to the right, straight up the hill. "Will you be able to get yourself over there?" she asked.

"Oh, sure, I should be able to," Cookie mumbled. Then more clearly, "Thank you so much for the aspirin. My headache's much better."

"You're quite welcome." Mrs. Biddle swung her purse strap up over her shoulder. "Well, if you stay around for long, I'm sure we'll meet again. We're nothing but a little hamlet here. And except for the tourist season, everybody knows everybody, so you'll be the talk of the town."

Cookie cringed but tried not to show it. She raised her head up to meet this kind woman's eyes. "Thank you, again. Thanks for everything."

And then, with one last appraising look, Mrs. Biddle was gone. A few others came into the diner and chatted with the waitress, whom Mrs. Biddle had called Muriel. Cookie stayed in Mrs. Biddle's booth and ordered a bowl of soup, thinking to delay having to go back out in the cold and trying to figure out where was she going to spend the night so that she wouldn't be the talk of the town. If she walked to Neil's Harbour, wouldn't the police be more likely to find her if she signed in to a B&B? And, dog-tired as she was, she didn't think she could walk anywhere.

She picked up a copy of the local paper someone had left on the booth behind her, thinking to look through the classifieds, in case someone was renting a room. But the front-page story fully distracted her. A teenage girl who'd hauled her sleeping bag outside her parent's tent had been mauled by a coyote biting a large chunk out of her scalp. Holy mackerel! Cookie put both hands up to her scalp. There wasn't a lot of meat there. Had he bitten through her skull? The girl was going to survive but was in the hospital. They'd been camping in the interior, inland from the Cabot Trail.

At quarter to eight, the waitress threw vinegar on the grill and started scraping it down. She'd already taken all the sugars, napkins, and salt and pepper shakers from the booths and lined them up on the counter to give them a thorough washing down, so Cookie knew closing time was near. She went to the bathroom and emptied her bladder and pocketed some extra toilet paper. She was on automatic, not at all sure what she was going to do. No real plan had formulated in her mind. But she took off her shirt and put on the three T-shirts she had in the back pack, then added back the long-sleeved shirt, buttoned it up to the neck, put on the fleece, and covered her now bulky torso with her windbreaker.

She paid her bill and stepped out into the buffeting wind. The Atlantic Ocean was right there in all its vastness just across the street. Half a block down, white caps slapped the shore, and the

fierce wind came right through all her layers, chilling her immediately. She walked in the direction of Neil's Harbour; maybe it
would be best to search for that B&B, even if it meant the police
finding her. Better than freezing to death or risk having an encounter with a coyote.

Lucky for her, it was still light out, nearing the longest day of
the year. She walked at a brisk pace. She was warming up and
feeling hopeful that Neil's Harbour might appear around the next
curve when she approached a setback house and heard the low
growl of a dog. She stopped and held her breath as a silky black
Doberman charged out at her. She clutched her hands together
and brought them up to her chest. When she tried to take a small
step forward, he bared his teeth and growled deeper, sending her
heart into her throat. Finally, she turned around and took a step
back toward Seal Cove, first very slowly, then speeding up, com-
manding in the gruffest voice she could summon. "Git! Go home!
Git!" until he finally dropped back and stopped trailing her, though
she took little peeks over her shoulder for a very long time, fearing
he might charge her again.

By the time she got back to the place where the boat had
dropped her off in the afternoon, the light was dusky, and she had
grown dangerously cold. It helped that she had not stopped moving, but now she was so tired she could no longer force herself to
put one foot in front of the other. Yet she feared she might freeze to
death if she stopped walking.

At the boarded-up antique shop, she looked up and down the
street to make sure no one was watching, then snuck across the
yard and went around to the backyard. There she grabbed an old
tarp lying across a mostly used up woodpile. The tarp had holes in
it and smelled of humus and mold, but she beat it flat and folded it
as well as she could and, holding it under one arm, fighting against
the wind that wanted to tear it out of her hands, she dragged it
down toward the shore, where the boatmen had delivered her
earlier. No one was out now. It was dark and cold. Few houses
even had any light peeking from behind the blinds. She walked the
shore until she came upon a tiny cove back from the water, created

by a few huge boulders, and using the tarp partly as a blanket to lie on and partly to pull over her, with her nearly empty backpack as a pillow, she lay down and curled up. Her hands were icicles and her whole body shivered. Her rough nest felt damp, but at least it protected her against the wind.

All night she drifted, falling off into frightening dreams of the coyote coming to take a bite out of her head. Waking to rub her arms and legs, warming her icicle fingers between her thighs, cupping her nose and blowing warm breath up to it. Then falling off into a void again. A dark bottomless chasm. Then suddenly there was Warren, legs splayed, blood spurting out of him, standing over her, saying, "I'll get you for this!"

How could she have done it? It was not like her. She was docile. She remembered Miss Crosslin, her high school track coach, how she had to call out to her, "Go, go, you can do it!" coaxing her to pass the other girls as they neared the finish line, urging her on when her instinct was to hold back rather than letting herself out, full throttle. Well, this time she had let herself out full throttle.

Never was she more grateful for a dawn. The sky flamed red before it grew lighter and lighter. It seemed as if sunrise brought the wind up even stronger, so the tide lapped nearly to her feet, but somehow she had stopped shivering. She sat up and rubbed her hands, curled the tarp over them, pulled her knees up to her chest, and watched the sky. None of her worries had gone, but the day was alive.

And so was she.

———————

Edith Biddle also woke at dawn and marveled at the red sky. School was in session for another week, and she had time to go back to sleep for an hour, yet once she drew open the curtains and saw the splendor of the sunrise, she thought of the lonely girl in the diner again. She lay back down but was suddenly jolted to full awareness. What on earth was the matter with her? She was nothing if not strongly intuitive, prided herself on that. Others described her that way, too. It came in handy in her work as a guidance counselor, getting a handle on her problem kids. But last night, she had gone off and left the poor girl to fend for herself, despite sensing she was in deep trouble. Well, she was not exactly a girl, maybe late 30s? A mature woman, but she didn't look it. She looked like a runaway. Haunting expression on her face and chopped-up hairdo. Come to think of it, she'd not seen a car she didn't recognize outside the diner when she'd left. So how was she—whoever she was—going to get to Neil's Harbour? She should have gone back and offered her a ride.

God, where was her humanity? Was it buried in her grief over Martin's death? How grief made one preoccupied! If Martin were alive and she had called him, he'd have simply said, "Why don't you bring her on home with you?" Oh, Martin, she thought, how I miss you.

These thoughts got her up and dressed and headed over to the diner to see if anyone had seen—what did she say her name was—Molly.

And there she was, right in the booth where Edith had left her. Looking more disheveled than ever. But with a big plate of blueberry pancakes in front of her, devouring them.

Edith gave her a long appraisal, then approached. "Molly?"

Molly jolted alert and stuttered out a good morning, and Edith sat down, facing the seat where she usually sat. Everyone in town knew she liked to face the door, but Molly had taken her seat.

"How did you find Neil's Harbour?" Edith asked.

"Never got there. I stayed here," she said.

"But there's no place to stay here."

"I know."

"But my dear, where did you sleep?"

Molly shrugged. "I found a little cove down by the water but far enough up from shore to be dry. When I was a kid, my family used to go camping. So . . ."

"My, you are a brave one," Edith said. "Must have been very cold."

For the first time, Molly smiled. "It was," she admitted. "But I'm almost warm now after a couple cups of hot coffee."

Edith noticed Molly's hands, wrapped around the coffee mug, were bright red.

As the bell tinkled, Edith looked up to see Muriel's daughter struggling to push the door open. The frightfully skinny girl lifted her hand in a quick wave as she sailed by their booth.

"That's Chrissie," she said to Molly. "A student at our school. One of the bright ones."

"Oh," Molly said.

"Her mom's Muriel, the waitress," Edith went on, "and if the wind had been blowing any harder, I might have had to get up and help her open the door." She lowered her voice and added, "That girl needs to eat more."

At the counter, Chrissie handed a card to her mother, who pulled a pen from her apron and signed it. Then the girl danced back by and was gone.

Once again, leveling her eyes back on Molly, Edith said, "You never really said what brought you here."

"I know," said Molly. "It's kind of hard to say."

"Marital problems?"

Molly shrugged and looked pained. "You could say that."

There was so much sincerity in the way Molly spoke, or maybe it was the way her lip quivered that reached into Edith and touched her.

"Look, I have this small cottage just above my house which Doc built. That's what everybody here called my husband. Anyway, it's empty . . . and if you need a place, you could stay there a few days."

Cookie's jaw dropped. "Really? That would be great."

Edith nodded, taking in the depth of her relief.

"How much?" she stuttered.

"It's not the money," Edith said. "I'd just like someone to be up there."

Molly looked up.

"And if it works out for both of us and you decide you want to stay around awhile, you could help me with some housekeeping, maybe a little shopping now and then, in exchange for the place."

"I could pay *something*," Molly said.

"We can talk about that later," said Edith, "but first, let's go up and I'll show you the place."

Chapter 3

Chrissie got home from school and flung herself at an angle on her bed. Homework? No, let that wait until later. Her life was so boring, yet she didn't want to do a thing but lay here and watch the shadows of the blinds on the wall. Slats and spaces. Slats and spaces. The sound of water sloshing the shore, down across the road from their house. Maybe she'd get up and go out and watch the waves from the swing on the porch, but then she heard the flap of the front door and her mother calling, "I'm home."

Who cares, Chrissie thought, but she was glad it wasn't another night with her father in charge of dinner while her mother worked a twelve-hour shift at the diner. "I'm *not* home," she called out, too weakly to be heard. If her mother thought she was doing nothing but lying there vacantly, she'd find a job for her and, despite how bored she was, Chrissie did not want her vacant musing interrupted. Well, maybe she did, but not for some ordinary chore like setting the table. She wanted to be jolted by something exciting, something she couldn't even see the outlines of in her imagination.

Pretty soon the door flapped closed again and Chrissie could tell by the footsteps that her father was home. She heard the fridge door, the pop of a beer can, then her mother telling him to call in her brother Kelly from shooting hoops in the driveway. Then the call for her, and she got up slowly, moving robotically, her version of a Michael Jackson slouch across the floor, heel, toe, her foot slapping.

Her mother served from the stove, giving each of them a pork chop, a scoop of applesauce, a baked potato, and a spoonful of string beans heated from a can and told them to dig in.

Her mother's saying *dig in* came across to Chrissie as if she were asking her to dig a grave. She split her baked potato down the middle, buried a small pat of butter deep within it, then pinched it back together. The thing looked huge, like some kind of cruise liner, and she expected her mother would try any minute now to make her eat the whole thing. And this would start the back and forth with her stomach, which, just after her twelfth birthday, had turned against food, taking on a mind of its own to rebel against eating. She hated feeling stuffed or even full. Though she had little idea about who it was residing under her skin, she liked being able to see her bones. Being able to pinch herself and not be pinching through fat.

"Chrissie, *eat*," said her mother, and Chrissie looked at her with her big blue eyes as if she'd just awoken from a nap.

Her mother stared back, not looking away until Chrissie picked up her knife and fork and began to cut her pork chop.

For some reason, having a stare down with her mother reminded Chrissie of going to the diner that morning, to get her mother to sign her report card.

"Mom, who was that lady with Mrs. Biddle this morning?" she asked.

"Who do you mean?"

"Sitting in Mrs. Biddle's booth with her. She looked kind of dirty. Had on a blue-green jacket and hair sticking up like she hadn't combed it."

Her mother nodded. "Oh, yeah, I know who you mean, but last night was the first time I ever saw her. Stayed even after Mrs. Biddle left, right up until closing." She shrugged. "I've no idea who she was or where she came from. She didn't really eat dinner, just apple pie, and then a corn muffin, same as Mrs. Biddle. But she seemed starving by the time she came back this morning."

Chrissie's father finished chewing and raised his bushy eyebrows. "Humph," he said. "Somebody must know. I'll ask around. Meanwhile, keep your distance." He fixed Chrissie with his eyes and declared, "We're lucky to live in a place where everybody knows everybody. No need for strangers."

Lucky, except for we're bored to death, and if we had a few strangers, it might pick things up, Chrissie thought.

A moment of silence went by before her mother raised her fork and gestured to Chrissie to start eating again.

Chrissie pushed her beans around, took a spoonful of applesauce and managed to swallow, then offered her brother half her pork chop. He stabbed the piece she cut off eagerly, in spite of her mother's evil eye.

"Protein, Chrissie, you need it. I want you to eat the rest of that pork chop, and your potato, too."

"We'll see," Chrissie said, mounding up her applesauce and taking another spoonful. She could get that down. At least, if she upchucked later, it wouldn't come out in chunks, nor would it make her feel impure, like hard food did.

There was the sound of forks scraping up beans and then, suddenly, her father boomed, "You heard your mother, 'Eat, goddamn it!' his fist coming down hard enough to bounce the table, causing Chrissie to nearly jump out of her chair.

"Okay," she said in a quiet voice. "I'm trying."

———

The next night was frozen pizza and a salad her mom had prepared before dawn at the same time she had slapped together lunch sandwiches for each of them, before scooting off for a twelve-hour shift.

Their father held up his beer glass to toast Chrissie and Kelly, saying, "Cheers," after he doled out the pizza. He instructed Chrissie to get the salad from the fridge and the three of them commenced to eat in silence.

Chrissie forked her pizza. It seemed like leather, its cheese thick and sticky. She missed her mother, in spite of her regularly doled out reminders to eat. Her father seemed not to notice whether she ate or not unless her mother brought it up, and then he would try to bully her into it.

But tonight he was quiet, until finally, he pointed a rolled-up piece of pizza at her and said, "You know that woman you were asking your mother about last night?"

She nodded, an odd thrill of excitement running through her. *The stranger in their midst.*

"Stay away from her, you hear?"

"Of course, I hear you," Chrissie said, "but why? Who is she?"

"No one knows. But she don't come from here and looks like she's up staying at Biddle's for a while, but she's not related to her nor to anyone else in the area, so just you keep your distance, both of you." He looked back and forth between her and Kelly, who shrugged those football player shoulders he was trying to build up by lifting weights every day.

"Why? Did Mom see her again?" Chrissie asked.

"We'll find out tonight when she gets home. But right now, I'm talking to *you*," and he pointed the pizza again.

Chrissie adopted Kelly's posture and imitated his shrug, then looked back at her nearly full plate. She managed a couple of bites of salad, picking out the cucumber as something that seemed edible and slipped her slice of pizza to her brother when her father wasn't looking.

Their father suspected just about everyone of everything. He didn't trust anyone. How boring. Her mother always said the opposite—might as well give people the benefit of the doubt.

"She might just be a tourist, don't you think?" Chrissie asked him.

"Do you?" he shot back.

"She didn't really look like a tourist."

"Well then, there's your answer," and he chugged back his second glass of beer.

"Anyway, don't most of the tourists come in July and August?"

"They do," he said, "goddamn them."

"Come on, Dad, what've you got against tourists, they don't hurt you," Kelly interjected.

"They clog up the roads I drive to put your food on this here table. Can't make up their minds which way they want to turn." He held up his fork and gestured toward Kelly. "Then, like fools, they pitch their tents out there in the wilderness and get their heads eaten off by coyotes. You heard that story, didn't you?"

Indeed, all of Cape Breton had been talking about the fool girl who slept outside her tent and nearly got her head bitten off by a coyote.

"Then it's our fault we didn't warn 'em or should have better control of our coyotes and bears," her father went on. "And whose taxpayer money pays our wildlife people to be out there hunting the coyotes who rightfully belong there, eh?"

"Mom likes 'em," put in Chrissie, hoping to balance things out.

"The coyotes?" he said, chuckling.

"No, you know, the tourists. The ones that give her real good tips."

"Yeah, well, maybe you don't realize she's always glad when the season's over, too, 'cause they wear her down."

Chrissie retreated further into herself, knowing this could go on forever if she didn't give her father the final word.

Kelly asked to be excused to do his homework.

"Me, too," Chrissie echoed, keeping her back to her dad as she dumped the rest of her salad in the trash and made a dash for her room. She'd watch for the woman and decide for herself. And she wasn't at all sorry the tourist season would be starting soon.

Chapter 4

Mrs. Biddle and Cookie climbed the steep, stone steps to the white frame cottage, Mrs. Biddle pointing out the house with the red door below, where she lived, her arm sweeping out toward the cliffs, which cascaded down to the glistening sea. Giving the cottage door a swift kick to spring it open, she led Cookie directly to the large picture window to look out at the spectacular view. After that, she assumed a practical, matter of fact manner, opening every closet and cabinet to reveal the sheets and pillowcases, the dishes and table linens, pots and pans. She pushed open the windows, stating the place clearly needed airing and dusting, and showed Cookie where the firewood was stacked and how to open the draft, in case, after the bungalow was fully aired, she'd need to make a fire. The wind was up and Mrs. Biddle said it might be chilly later.

And then, mercifully, miraculously, she said she had to be off to work soon and left her alone.

Cookie stood watching Mrs. Biddle bob down the stone stairs until she was out of sight, then scanned the wide expanse of the Atlantic. She wrapped her arms around herself and shook her head. She was a quiet person who had lived a quiet life, never going more than a hundred miles from home. Up until yesterday, that was. Until . . . oh my God . . .

She sat down and rested her head against the couch and shut her eyes, and in one second, without wanting to be there, she was back in Bearsville. Had she really done what she thought she had done? Was Warren gone? She wrapped her arms around herself again, trying to believe everything happening was real. Both that *it* was and *she* was.

She'd been so concentrated on making her way to Seal Cove—a place she knew only from seeing it on a map and liking how it sounded—that how her life might go on beyond getting there had been a total blank. And then this woman, nearly the age her mother would have been were she still alive, seeing her clutch her head, had offered her an aspirin, and for some unknown, maybe unknowable reason, had come back this morning to bring her to her home.

The first miracle had been her getting as far as Montreal, and then Nova Scotia, and now being here, where, except for the near-yelp accompanying those scenes she couldn't stop replaying in her head, she was surrounded by the quiet of this tidy space, and if she looked out, water, for as far as she could see.

She sat in stunned silence, then drifted off, only to be woken by that strange name being issued by Mrs. Biddle at the front door calling out, "Molly, I'm leaving you a few supplies to get you started." By the time Cookie recognized her new name and got to the door, there was a can of drip coffee and some coffee filters as well as a tuna fish sandwich on the top step, and Mrs. Biddle was gone.

Why was this woman being so good to her? Was she calling someone to inquire about her, suspecting she was a runaway? Or, was she just being kind? Was it possible this place was so isolated that people were more generous with each other?

By afternoon, she wandered around the cottage, opening and closing all the drawers and cabinets Mrs. Biddle had introduced her to, trying to imagine a day when she might grow comfortable enough to use the items behind or inside of them. She took a look at herself in the bathroom mirror. Still the wide-eyed stare of bafflement. And the hopeless hair standing straight up as if it had received a shock. Her eyes refused to stick with what she was seeing in the mirror but skipped to the seashell frame it was mounted in, and she reached up and gently fingered the shells, trying to imagine the organisms that might once have lived in them.

Mrs. Biddle had instructed her to make up the bed, apologizing for not having time to do it herself because she had to get to work, but Cookie didn't want to dirty the sheets. What if they came for her in the middle of the night? Might she get Mrs. Biddle in trouble for harboring her? That would be like throwing her to the wolves the way Annie had always done to her.

She didn't deserve a thing. Yet her stomach growled, and with the tuna fish sandwich seeming to stare at her, she went to the kitchen table and ate the first half of it. Then she brought the throw from one of the twin beds to the living room couch, draped it over her, and fell into a deep sleep for the entire afternoon.

For supper, she ate the other half of the tuna sandwich, and with the throw still around her shoulders, sat out on the bench in front of the window. The day seemed to go on forever, like time was stretching to make her remember where she had come from, the journey replaying over and over—the high reeds she had pushed through, the surprise when the Bilco door had opened, the squishy thing that had creeped her out, the mist on the lake in the morning, her eyes paying attention as if she was suddenly alert to every atom bouncing in the universe at the same time as she was filled with horror at what she had done.

Were they even in the same time zone here? She was not sure. Nine-thirty; the sun would have set in Bearsville. She went back in and saw by the kitchen clock that it was an hour later. Half past ten, and still not dark.

She stood by the window and watched as the sun finally went down. The great globe turned a brilliant orange before it sank, and the sky streaked the clouds red. Such beauty; she was awed, yet it didn't feel right for her to be. Still, she didn't turn away from the window until dark fully crept in.

Then she went to the couch and sat in the black of the night, trying to feel out who she was. What she saw was a dark hole inside her, misshapen like a giant amoeba. It seemed like that should be frightening to see, but she didn't feel fear or anything else. What do you feel, she asked herself over and over, but no one seemed to answer; she could only watch numbly from afar.

She remembered a time from her childhood, when they'd been hurling crabapples off of green sticks, competing for who could throw the farthest down the hill that ranged before them. Mean Annie had teased her in front of their friends, and suddenly Cookie had turned away from the hill, aimed her apple directly at Annie, and hurled her stick as hard as she could, her apple catching Annie squarely in her right eye. It had been hard to believe it was her who had thrown the small apple with perfect aim. Also, how good it had felt. Even though she suffered for days after as Annie's black eye turned from purple to gold to yellow, and without letting it be known she had provoked Cookie, Annie told anyone who would listen how Cookie had done this.

In the morning, she woke up shivering under Mrs. Biddle's throw, the throw not quite heavy enough to keep her warm. She had slept as if drugged and was shocked to see so much light all around her. And to hear the waves breaking against the shore below, sound traveling up to reach and console her. Why was she alive if Warren was not? She had so cruelly plunged the long, sharp knife into him, the mean Warren, but what about the good Warren, the Warren who had always pulled her in dearly to kiss the top of her head? How could she have done what she'd done to him? And now tolerate being surrounded by so much light?

She got up and cracked a window and the wind blew through like a whistle, while round puffy clouds moved past and the sun streamed down in long streaks. She stood there a long time staring at the sea, unsure what to do next.

It was Saturday, she realized a little later, when she saw Mrs. Biddle ascending the stairs. Mrs. Biddle had a short list of groceries and told Cookie to get her own groceries first, and if she wasn't too overloaded, to pick up the few items on her list.

"Oh, I can get mine another time," Cookie said, to which Mrs. Biddle replied brusquely, "No, you need to take care of yourself first, the cupboards up here are bare, in case you haven't noticed."

She proposed, too, that she'd like to pay Cookie a modest weekly sum so she'd feel free to ask a few extra jobs of her. She also asked if Cookie needed any money changed and offered to do it for her at the bank, and Cookie handed over a couple hundred in twenties, relieved to know she'd get back some Canadian dollars.

Before Cookie headed down to the Co-op, which Mrs. Biddle had said was the only place to shop, she made another attempt with the scissors to style her hair. In spite of evening it up a bit, she couldn't get rid of the blunt look. It was so short she didn't really need a hairbrush, but she put one on her list anyway.

She made it to the last aisle of the Co-op before a middle-aged fellow with a craggy, acne-scarred face patently stared, a wide knuckle pressed up against his mouth as he studied her. Another guy came along and knocked him on the shoulder, saying, "Hey, Logan, what's up?"

The man named Logan said something Cookie couldn't hear, and when that guy, too, looked her over, she skittered around to the checkout, without Mrs. Biddle's butter the two men had been standing in front of. She'd have to lie and pretend she'd forgotten the butter, in spite of Mrs. Biddle's careful list, written in highly readable cursive.

Cookie tortured herself the rest of the afternoon, with the notion that the man named Logan was onto her, then thinking maybe she was just being paranoid because of her guilt. The cottage was on the highest point around, and she couldn't stop using the picture window as a lookout, as if it would make a difference if she saw who was coming to get her before they got there, even though she had no plans to run. She'd already pictured herself holding out her hands to be handcuffed by the Mounties and going without resistance.

When she'd delivered the groceries, Mrs. Biddle had suggested she come back later, whenever it was convenient, to do some dusting. She'd said she'd be out, but her door would be open, so Cookie went down to have something to do to escape fretting about the man. Mrs. Biddle had an airy, well-organized and comfortable home, but she was a collector. Every shelf held an arrangement: fancy tea cups and saucers, miniature Scotty dogs, a collection of stone turtles, tiny hooked rugs mounted on tiny easels. Most of the objects hardly needed dusting; still, Cookie lifted and dusted each one carefully, hoping to express her gratitude for being taken in.

When no one came to get her that night or the next day or the next, Cookie began to relax a little. And as the days dropped into weeks and months, there were times the dark misshapen hole seemed to shrink and even disappear for short periods. Just sitting and gazing at the sea, hearing the lap of the water against the boats down at the docks, watching the sea-blue waves move in and the undertow pull out, walking the cliffs and the beaches, and taking in the scruffy windblown plants that survived the buffeting wind by growing at an angle, all began to heal her. She felt herself growing at an angle with them. Unable to grow straight up because she had always to be leaning away from whom she had been. Since no one knew her, it seemed as if she'd hardly existed as Cookie in her previous life, but was springing forth anew as Molly, and Molly lived as the day came and went, appreciating what was right before her.

There were still many ways she could not be a part of life. She could not go back to Woodstock or contact her friend Nita or even her sister. She could not renew her driver's license, nor open a bank account, use a credit card or a computer. Anything of this sort these days and you could be tracked down immediately. Not that Mrs. Biddle or anyone had a hookup to the Internet up there on the hill. They went to the library in Ingonish when they wanted to look things up on the computer.

One day she'd taken the bus to Ingonish to see if she might use the computer herself, thinking she'd try to find out for sure Warren was dead.

"I'll need your ID," said the librarian, "to issue you a card. Then, you'll use that card and its number to get on the Internet."

Cookie mumbled, "Oh, sorry, forgot to bring my wallet," turned beet red and exited the library as fast as her feet would move without running.

So access to the computer became one more thing she had to do without.

But she took great satisfaction in learning to recognize simple things like when she was hungry and when she was full by getting quiet enough to feel her own impulses. She saw that even before she'd married him, she'd given over to Warren's thoughts and feelings and ridden in the undertow of them. And going back even further, she remembered times she and Annie had frozen together, listening when their father came home drunk and her mother managed to haul him up the stairs to their bedroom across the hall, and he'd heave into a wastebasket, first whatever he had in his stomach, and then the dry heaves. And either Annie would jump in Cookie's bed or she would go to Annie's and they'd curl up cold and nervous, clutching each other as they listened. They'd think it was over and go almost to sleep, then he'd let out a wail and they'd come to full alert again.

Though somewhere along the line Annie had learned to go somewhere else and ceased coming to Cookie's bed and pretended not to hear their father's heaving or even Cookie's whimpers, leaving Cookie curled up alone.

Chapter 5

The CB radio crackled in the distance. Despite the static, Warren heard his name. It was Davy from the Rescue Squad, trying to rouse him to answer. Maybe Cookie had called them then. He coughed and blood came out his nose.

"I'm hurt, Davy," he called out, but his voice made such a thin, wavy line, there was no way Davy could hear it.

Christ, I'm bleeding out, he thought. Compression. He reached for the throw rug and tried to press it into his chest, but he had no strength. Maybe if he laid the weight of his body on it. He struggled to move prone and wailed as a bolt of pain stabbed clear through to his back. His head felt like it was rolling away from him, making him dreamy.

He found himself praying. "God help me!" But why should God help him? He remembered sitting in a pew at church as a boy, trying to keep his legs from swinging wildly, the Ten Commandments hanging on a scroll at the side of the altar. "Thou Shalt Not Kill. Thou Shalt Not Covet Thy Neighbor's Wife." He hadn't been able to make out "covet" and some of the other words in the commandments, so "Thou Shalt Not Kill" had been one of his favorites.

He remembered times he'd threatened Cookie, saying, "Do what I tell you to do or I'll fucking kill you." But the commandment said, "Thou Shalt Not Kill," not "Thou Shalt Not *Threaten* to Kill." How could Cookie go for killing him? She knew, under his gruff, he was a good guy who just went wild when he drank too much, his pants hanging ready over the back of the chair to be thrown on when the CB radio announced he was needed in the middle of the night.

Cookie, what the fuck? How could you do this? He couldn't remember what he'd done to bring out her anger . . . Oh, yes, it was coming back. He'd bent her over the kitchen counter, thinking he'd have a go at her. Yeah, stupid. She hated him even finger fucking her precious ass. Crazy. He knew that, yet it turned him on to do exactly what she didn't want.

Early on, she'd fought him when he got ornery. Pushed back. One night she'd even bitten his hand. "Christ's sake, that's dangerous!" he'd bellowed, grabbing it away from her and shaking it before he'd hauled off and walloped her up the side of her head, and she'd spun around with eyes afire, but then the light had gone out of them and she'd slid down the wall. After that, when he went after her, she'd just roll herself into a ball, riling him with her disappearing act. But now he could see she hadn't disappeared at all; she'd been lying in wait. And here *he* was, the fool, dying.

He was lightheaded, a sure sign he was losing it. His past seemed to be scattered about like a deck of cards randomly spread out on a table. He remembered his father stripping the belt from his pants, pulling him into the back kitchen, where his mama had a line strung with laundry drying stiff in winter. A pair of long johns looking like a pair of live legs hanging. He'd stick his eyes to that pair of legs while his father whacked his backside, raising welts as Warren stifled sobs.

Then, without warning, everything softened inside him and the father with the belt was replaced by the father who taught him to drive stick shift, coaxing him to calm his jumpy leg, and suddenly his whole life seemed to rearrange into some sort of order, as if the deck of cards had been gathered up, each one slotting into place with a clack of finality.

And then the black of the blackest night came over him.

Warren felt someone turn him over, then they were ripping off his shirt. Fingers probed the vein in his forearm and someone inserted an IV. Next, there was motion underneath him and a siren ringing in his ears.

Then Davy asking, "Who the hell did this to you, Warren?"

"Did what?"

"Goddamn stabbed you in the chest."

"Oh." Warren suddenly remembered Cookie, the hot look in her eyes, the way she had whirled around with the knife and held to her fury. He remembered the door slamming shut as the blood spurted out of him like a pulsing faucet.

"Oh," he said again, unable to talk, his head swirling like he was about to faint as Davy's brow came down in a frown and he went back to starting up the IV drip, placing the oxygen cannula in Warren's nose.

A state trooper and a Woodstock police deputy were waiting for Warren at the Benedictine ER. What did *they* want? He only wanted to drop into a deep slumber and would have, if not for the strong lights and the woman doc he recognized from times he'd brought people in to the ER, who now pummeled him with questions, in between barking out orders to the nurses.

"Blood," he heard, but he didn't know if she was talking about *his* blood soaked into the throw rug (he was surprised to discover his hand was no longer holding it pressed to his chest) or did the doc mean she was ordering a transfusion?

"A," he said, and she leaned over and asked him to repeat what he had said.

"Type 'A' blood," he whispered hoarsely.

She nodded. "Already checked it."

She asked him when had he last eaten.

"Missed dinner. Out drinking. Maybe a few pretzels," he added after a pause.

"What time?"

Jesus, who knew. "Five on," he said, remembering Cookie had

eaten without him. No idea even what time it was now.

"Am I gonna make it?" he asked the doctor.

"Maybe. No guarantees yet. You're going to surgery, see what's perforated. You've lost a lot of blood."

She was blunt and terse, in spite of her attractive face, surrounded by a halo of curls.

"You married?" she asked.

He nodded and his smart-ass self came out with, "You?"

"Where's your wife?" she asked, ignoring him.

He strained to think. Damn her, he should put them onto her and see her up in the state pen, but if he let her get away, he could go after her himself later, assuming he made it.

"She was out visiting a friend," he finally said weakly, the doctor leaning close to hear.

"Name?"

"Nita."

"Nita Wagner?"

He shook his head no. "Nita's the friend. My wife is Cookie."

She asked but he didn't know Nita's last name. Should have. She'd been Cookie's maid of honor at their wedding.

"Where's she live?"

"Bearsville Flats. Yerry Hill Road."

She looked at the monitor and barked out something about his blood pressure. "Losing" was the only word he got. He was losing something. Pressure or oxygen saturation or something important like that. "Help," he wanted to say but couldn't speak, only opened his eyes wide and tried to ask that way.

He fell into a dark hole, fading rapidly away from the curly headed doctor, couldn't pick his hand up though he had the impulse to wave. When he came to briefly, he was surrounded by figures in green scrubs, the OR lights making a kind of bright Heaven above him, the anesthesiologist telling him to count backward starting at ten. He only got to eight.

Warren woke up in the recovery room feeling someone pinching his arm, hard. He heard a loud whisper, "My boy, my poor boy, wake up. It's your mama." She was tiny, but she was up on her toes, leaning in, and even before he opened his eyes, he sensed she was halfway over the bedrails, about to get in bed with him.

"Ouch, Mama, you're gonna make black and blue on my arm," he said, his voice weak when he finally found it.

"Black and blue? Look what that bitch did! My God, we could be going to your funeral."

"Wait, Ma," he whispered. "Hold on."

She stopped screeching but kept on shaking her head.

"Calm down, please," he said, taking her small hand and squeezing it. "We don't need you having a stroke."

They were surrounded by IV poles and monitors, clicking and flashing their numbers.

"God help us," she said, her mouth and eyes puckered with worry.

"It's okay, Ma, I'm gonna live."

"It was that wife of yours, wasn't it? That's what I always thought. Looking all sweet and innocent. Too nicey-nicey."

"Ma, wait," he said again.

"She's on the run! It's all over the news. They haven't found her yet, but they will. They better."

"No, Ma, it was downright nasty, but it's not that simple. But you gotta just let me heal now."

She was shaking her head. "Cookie'll have to pay for this," she said, "but, my boy, you're right, you got to get well first. I'll bring you some good food."

"No, Ma. I can't eat," he said, casting his eyes sideways to the IV.

She groaned. "How can you get well on that?"

He brought his hand to the huge bandage over his chest. "Better than chewing," he said.

"Oh my boy, you could be dead."

For a second, his mama lit a flare of anger in him, and if he hadn't been tied flat with tubes, he'd have roared up and out of bed, ready to go after Cookie. But he only lay motionless, flat as a flat tire. He'd have to concentrate on mending for now, then figure out what to do about her.

He dropped off to sleep and the next time he woke up the state troopers were at his bedside. He kept his eyes closed to pretend he was not yet awake, only groggy as he was, he was hardly pretending. And he wasn't ready to talk yet because, sealed inside his groggy state, he had such a strange feeling. Almost as if he had died and was being reborn. As if, when he'd dropped down into that dark hole, he had come apart and been put back, newly arranged.

But just after they transferred him from recovery to the ICU, they sent up a detective he'd met before. Marvin—a giant of a guy, 6'5", with hard-packed shoulders. He'd come to the rescue squad to give a talk about how they should handle a call if they suspected it would become a crime scene. A good, jocular speaker he was. Got his points across and made you remember them.

"Your wife's nowhere to be found," Marvin started.

"That so."

"I need you to tell me exactly what happened," he said in his deep voice.

Warren closed his eyes. "For now, let's just say I did this to myself," he said quietly.

He opened his eyes to Marvin shaking his head. "We can't do that, Warren. Her prints are on the weapon. She's the prime suspect. There's a warrant out for her with a charge of attempted murder. Domestic scrape or whatever—we need to know what happened."

"Okay, okay, give me a minute," Warren said. He saw Cookie again, the fury burning in her eyes. What the fuck was he thinking? Why should he try to protect her?

Marvin shifted his weight and Warren sensed his patience was wearing. "So," he said, "I came home drunk. Nothing unusual."

"And where was your wife?"

"She'd been waiting dinner for me, but then she'd gone ahead and eaten. I moved up behind her to put my arms around her, thinking I wanted to screw her, even though God knows if I'd have gotten it up in my state. I was pretty woozy."

"And then . . ." Marvin said.

"She whirled around with the knife in her hand and told me to get away, and I backed off a couple of steps, but as I went to grab the knife, I tripped and fell right onto it instead."

"I see," Marvin said slowly. "And she ran off and left you there to bleed out."

"I guess so," Warren said. "She must'a gotten scared. Lord knows I've accused her of enough stuff that she'd think I'd use this against her."

"You're telling me this was an accident."

"In a way."

"Not so easy to stab yourself clear through to the backbone this way. I've never seen it done before."

"Is that where it stopped?" Warren asked.

"Seems so."

"I was drunk. Pretty much out of my mind."

Marvin was holding the bedrail. He rattled it a bit, maybe because Warren had closed his eyes again. "Was your marriage in trouble?"

Warren shook his head no. "Cookie's a great wife, always has been."

"She think the same of you?"

"Didn't like when I laid one on, that's all. Can't blame her."

"How often did you do that?"

"Oh, maybe once or twice a week."

"She ever leave you, ask for a separation?"

Warren said no, remembering the one time she had. He'd bounced her around and told her he wouldn't hear of it. "Till death do us part," he'd reminded her, laughing as she looked off in the distance the way a wild animal does when it's caught in a trap.

Then the nurse came to spare him further questioning, telling the detective he had to leave because the doctor was making rounds.

When the doc came, it wasn't the woman who'd taken care of him in the ER. This one was small, male, nerdy. "The knife just barely missed your airway," he said. "Went clear through your stomach and stopped when it came up against your spine. You're in for a long recovery. So far doing well but there's still the chance of a bleed and you won't be eating solid food for quite a while," he went on, matter-of-factly.

"I want you to make an effort to breathe as deeply as you can," he said, looking at one of the monitors.

"Where's the doctor with the curls, the one who took care of me when I got here? I'd like to thank her."

"Dr. Kohler. The ER doc?"

"I guess so."

"I'll tell her," he said, scratching a note on the paper on his clipboard.

He kept his word, too, because she came by later in the day—afternoon or evening, Warren couldn't be certain, as time seemed blended, both lost and at times stretched to such lengths that the large clock eyeing him from the far wall seemed to have its hands stuck in place.

"Well, I'm glad to see you made it," she said.

"Thanks to you," he said.

She shrugged. "Just doing my job."

"But you didn't let me fade out," he said, "and I wanted to thank you for that."

"The best standard of care," she said, "nothing preferential, it's what I try to give everyone." She added, "Though I did hear you're one of those guys who bring in the folks who keep my nights from getting boring."

"Think that bought me a little more time?"

"I'd say, more like, if you were a cat, you'd have only eight lives left now."

"So I'd better be careful who I associate with."

"Right," she said, and as she turned toward the door, "and how you treat your wife."

He struggled to spring up from the partially inclined bed. "How the fuck do you know how I treat my wife?" he screeched, his rage suddenly getting the better of him.

An alarm went off to his left, one of the monitors delivering an awful assault to his ears. And the ER doc turned back to stop the noise and reset the monitor with a few clicks.

"Better get yourself under control," she said coolly, "or you're liable to bust that wound open."

Didn't she realize he was the one who'd been stabbed, the victim? Damn women. "Humph," he snorted but kept his mouth shut.

They searched several counties, as well as the area of North Carolina where her sister lived, but Cookie was long gone. Warren was just beginning to grasp this when, five days after his operation, the discharge planner/social worker came to his bedside with a smile, asking if there was anyone to take care of him at home.

Damn it, there should be, he thought but did not say. I've been married eighteen years and don't know a thing about making beds or cooking. Times Cookie got sick or had some reason not to be there, he'd always ordered a pizza and run into town to pick it up. "Nope," he said, dashing her smile, wondering why she was even asking if she had read his chart. Or did it not say who had taken a nearly deadly crack at him?

"My ma's a spry ninety. She lives nearby, but she can't drive."

"Okay," she said. She told him as soon as they got him on solid foods, he'd be ready for discharge. Maybe two days more, maybe three, and she'd arrange a nurse who'd teach him to change the dressing and a home-health aide three times a week, to help him with washing up—no showers until the healing was complete, she emphasized—but the aide would prepare a couple of meals, make his bed, and sweep up. Only the bedroom and bathroom, she made clear. He could not use the aide to clean the whole house.

He nodded.

"One more thing," she declared firmly. "No drinking! The doctor already told you your liver's damaged and you're taking meds that are going to tax it further."

Warren nodded again, trying to pass himself off as someone

who didn't care about what she was saying, even though her instructions put him into a kind of shock. Holy shit, a good clean glass of scotch was the one thing he'd anticipated as his reward for surviving all this! Go home alone and not drink? Not likely.

But over the next couple of days, he had a whole lot of time to think and kept hearing her admonition repeat: One more thing, no drinking! Shifting side to side between those stiff white hospital sheets, at times shaking because the urge for a drink seemed like a lion inside him about to jump the cage of the hospital bed, he started thinking maybe he should be grateful they had managed to detox him. Of course, he was on a lot of pain meds. That helped. And then the nerdy doctor came by and said rather frankly, as he palpated Warren's abdomen, "Your liver's distended." He raised his eyebrows. "Wouldn't it be a shame to survive this, only to succumb to cirrhosis?"

What could Warren do but nod his agreement? They were talking life and death. Still, when the doc went on to warn him he was probably going to need some help to keep from drinking as he weaned off the pain pills, Warren only shrugged. He didn't know what kind of help the man was talking about and couldn't wrap his mind around how to ask before this snarky little doctor was already out the door.

Well, at least Cookie had left the place spotless, he noted with satisfaction two days later, when they let Davy pick him up and deposit him home. Cookie had always been a bit persnickety about having everything in its place and wiped clean. No dust bunnies, even on the ceilings.

Where the hell was she? He searched for evidence that she had come back to get some of her things but couldn't find any. Her parents were both dead, but would she have run to her sister? Not likely; she was not a big fan of her sister. Besides, Marvin had told him they had contacted Annie.

Davy brought in a few groceries to get him started: milk, cereal, bread, bananas, ground meat, and potatoes. Told him the other guys on the emergency squad would stop by to see what he needed day by day. He couldn't yet stand up straight but as long as he hunched, he could walk around the house, and the doctor had told him to keep increasing his activity as he felt able. He picked his way, slowly shuffling from the couch in the TV room, to the kitchen, to the bathroom, and back, in a state of collapse, to the couch again.

Each day, he wandered about searching for traces of Cookie. Damn her. He didn't want to miss her but he did. Grabbing a handful of the clothes still hanging in her closet, he buried his nose in them. He studied their wedding picture where it stood on the nicely polished table opposite the couch. She was everywhere and yet, she had abandoned him completely. She wasn't calling or writing to let him know where she was. All the time he thought he'd had her cowed—for Christ's sake, she'd practically roll up into a ball whenever he lifted a hand—she'd merely been deluding him. Who knew she'd only been storing up for the plunge? "The little bitch," his mother harped every time she called him. He still resisted his wife being called that, but maybe his mother was right.

The day he'd come home from the hospital, he told Davy to empty out his liquor cabinet and just take the stuff home and enjoy it. He'd found a bottle left behind and poured it down the toilet. A week later, he pounded on the table with regret, trying to pound out his compulsion to have a drink. He wasn't allowed to drive yet, but if you could get a pizza delivered, why couldn't he get a bottle of vodka?

He returned to the couch where he spent most of his time mindlessly watching TV and snoozing, bringing his hand up to his heart to cover that scar that snaked down his chest. Damn, whenever he stopped being angry, he missed her. He didn't know how he could have survived because, tough as he might look on the outside, there was not that much to him. But him and Cookie together, she had made him strong. He pictured a pear cut in half. Two halves that made a whole. He could see it in their wedding picture, not only how she had adored him, but how he had adored her. A full head taller, he'd held her up against him and often kissed the top of her head. She was not a great beauty, but he'd seen a side of her not everyone might see. A patient, sustaining power, which held up against his fly-off-the-handle self. And now it was like he was all the weight on one side of a scale with nothing to balance it.

————————

He was not yet completely off the pain meds later in the week when Jeff, one of the guys from the squad, brought a six-pack of Michelob. Pulling it from the grocery bag, Warren's hands started to tremble even before he set it on the counter and sat down to stare at it, tasting it in his throat and imagining its tickle as it went down. His dad had taught him to drink beer as a boy, to take a deep gulp and swallow wide and enjoy the hell out of it.

Jeff was nearly out the door when Warren yelled, "Whoa," signaling with this index finger for him to come back.

"What you need, man?" Jeff asked.

Warren took as deep a breath as his wound permitted, blew it out through pursed lips. "Could you use a few beers?" he said.

"Never turned one down," Jeff said, raising his eyebrows as if he suspected he was being set up.

"Take 'em," Warren said curtly.

"No, man, they're yours. I brought them for you."

Warren shook his head. "You don't get it," he said.

Jeff looked at him closely.

"Everything I ever did that got me into trouble, I did under the influence. And I never thought I could get out from under it. So they did me a favor in the hospital when I couldn't get anyone to put a shot of whiskey into my IV." He chuckled. "But now I been home, what, going on two weeks, and I'm still winnowing down the pain pills but I ain't had a drink since that bad night that put me where I am."

Jeff shifted his weight from one foot to the other. "Okay, man, whatever," he said. "I was just trying to help you out."

"Okay, so help me out then, take 'em."

"Take what? The beers? You don't want 'em for when the guys stop by?"

"Jeff," Warren said, sliding his eyes toward the table where the six-pack stood. "I'm not a saint. If you leave them here, they're gone by eight p.m., and I'm gone with them."

As soon as Jeff went out the door with them, Warren slammed down his fist hard on the table as the urge rose up in his gut. The taste, the feel of a beer. The way it would dull these gnarly feelings and release him. He wanted a beer like he'd wanted ice cold water after a day out haying in the field with his father back when he was ten. A scratch in his throat, a deep burn waiting to be soothed.

He let out a loud moan, though there was no one to hear him, then charged the kitchen door, hoping it might not be too late to retrieve those beers. But Jeff's truck was nowhere to be seen. He shut his eyes and pressed his head into the doorframe. Pressed hard. Bit into his lip. But when he picked his head back up, he was glad he hadn't caught Jeff.

C'mon man, don't give up. You can start over, he told himself.

———————

One morning a couple of weeks later, after sleeping through the night there on the couch with only the light throw over him, he woke up feeling like a bear coming out of hibernation, with an urgent desire to go after Cookie. He got up, fixed some oatmeal, disgusted with how it came out lumpy. He didn't know how Cookie always managed to make it smooth.

"Goddammit, Cookie, you're still my wife and you should be here," he said out loud in the shower. He shaved and put on clean clothes and looked himself over in the mirror. He was still a bit bent over in favor of protecting his wound, and when he tried to pull his shoulders back and take on a military posture, he could feel the pull of where the knife had gone in, enough to remind him he was one lucky man, or one unlucky one, depending upon how you looked at it.

He got in his truck, checked to make sure his pistol was still where it should be in the glove box, and headed north. Cookie had always liked nature, especially mountains and water. They'd gone to Lake George for their honeymoon and taken a canoe out into the wetlands, silently tacking through the reeds and seeing a dozen great blue herons. Cookie had loved it, and he had a hunch it was a place she might choose, were she deciding to start a new life.

He got to Lake George at lunchtime, put change in a meter, and went into one of the restaurants. He took a table by the window overlooking the lake and saw the lawn stretched down to it was overrun with tourists. They were everywhere—on the sidewalks and filling up the restaurant, too. Late July, high tourist season. He had been here with Cookie in early June that time nearly twenty years ago and there had been a whole different feel to it. Quiet enough for the two of them to make it into their own special world.

In the restaurant, he quickly sized up all the waitresses, vaguely hopeful he might find Cookie among them. She'd waitressed her last year in high school at what was then Huey's, the closest thing they had to a diner in Woodstock, now an oddly mixed Chinese and Japanese restaurant. He watched the swinging door to the kitchen until he was sure he had seen each waitress come through. Then hunger grumbled in his gut and he took up the menu and ordered more food than he'd eaten at one time since the injury, because he was still supposed to be on a diet that didn't tax his stomach.

He paid for the meal, digesting uncomfortably, as he sauntered down the sidewalk after his lunch, his eyes sweeping each woman he passed as well as glancing into each storefront. He looked and looked, his chest wound aching.

Finally, he went down by the water and just sat, watching the tiny whitecaps, breathing a bit deeper because the air was clear and cool. He remembered times Cookie had suggested they do this on a Sunday afternoon, and he had only harrumphed and said, "Give me a break, I've been working like a dog all week." All he wanted to do was break out a six-pack and watch a football game and have her hand deliver his supper to the couch.

"Damn you, Cookie," he whispered, sorry he hadn't listened to her requests, yet with a fury rising in his gut. He got up and skit a few flat stones into the water, but he couldn't even do that without provoking a sharp pain in his chest.

That day of looking for her was only the beginning. He became tortured by the question of where she was and was sorry if he had contributed to letting her get away. Should he forget to obsess on this even for a day, his mother called every suppertime to remind him.

"She has a legal obligation to be your wife, doesn't she? Otherwise, divorce you and let you start anew." She'd take a breath, then add, "The little bitch. Did I tell you I never cared for her? So sly. She looked at me with those small eyes. Cat eyes!"

"Ma," he'd try to stop her. "Let's talk about something else."

"Yes, let's."

"What'd you have for supper? You eating well?" And that would remind him all over again that he'd had to stand over the stove and fry himself a hamburger.

He'd wake up in the middle of the night, feeling across the bed for her and want to holler, "Cookie, where the hell are you?" but then his anger would dissipate and he'd end up whimpering. How the hell could she abandon him like this?

In the light of day, he'd think more rationally, sometimes wondering what *she* might be thinking of *him*. But he realized she probably thought he was dead, so if she did think of him, it would be in a grave. He thought of the big detective hovering over his hospital bed. Why hadn't he put him onto her right away? If she were up in the pen, he could go visit and torture her whenever he felt like it.

He hadn't told any of this to his rescue squad buddies, but one day Davy stopped in to ask when they might count on him getting back onto the squad schedule. He hadn't considered it, had even let his contracting business go dormant once Rocky, his first-class carpenter, had finished the main project they'd been working on. He was collecting some disability insurance and had reached a bit into his and Cookie's savings, but he was going to lose Rocky if he didn't start up again soon, and he hated to think of how that would affect his business. He saw from their statements Cookie had not dipped into their bank accounts, except for the first morning. What could she possibly be living on? It was almost as if she was the one who had died, not him.

"One of these days, you're going to have to get off your duff," Davy said.

Warren just nodded. "But which day?"

"Better sooner than later."

"I know, but I don't feel up to it."

"Chest still hurting?" Davy asked. "Or is it depression?"

"A bit of both, I guess."

Davy gave him a push on the shoulder. "Big life changes."

"You said it," Warren agreed, nodding.

"You never know when they're going to come."

They sat in silence at either end of the couch, the sun's rays slicing through the picture window. It was going to get too hot in the room if Warren didn't soon get up and let the blinds down. But he didn't get up, he just sat there with his head hanging forward, and then without warning, his head was in his hands and he was sobbing and Davy's arm was around his back and Davy was saying, "Hey, man, it's okay, go on and let it out. You'll be all right."

When he pulled himself back together, he started talking and couldn't stop, "Davy, of course Cookie did it and I still can't believe she did, but what you don't know is why I can't really say it wasn't my own fault." He shook his head. "Not only that night, but a lot of nights, I took a swipe at Cookie. And not just a light jab, man, I was always drunk when I did it, but the next day she'd look like all she wanted to do was hole up in some corner to heal, the way a wounded animal does. Bad. Man, it was bad. And I didn't even remember doing it, but she swore I had, and there was no one else here." He turned up his hands. "I don't know what I thought I was doing. I wasn't thinking, that's for sure. My daddy always beat me. *For nothing.* I guess I was trying to get back at him."

Davy had moved back a little but his eyes had not left Warren.

"I didn't stop there, either," Warren went on. "I pushed sex on her. Really, I did whatever I wanted, even when she didn't want it. I treated her like my fucking sow." He dropped his head into his hands again. "I'm a sorry human being, Davy, if I am one at all."

Davy's look was impassive and Warren couldn't tell if he was repulsed or what. "Maybe that's why I didn't tell them right away that it was her. But now I miss her so bad I want to look for her."

There was a long pause while he waited for Davy to speak. "What?" Warren asked him. "Are you shocked?"

"No, man. I wondered sometimes. I saw that Cookie looked a little beat up a couple of times."

Warren picked his head up. "I'm tellin' you I was bad."

"So what do you want to find her for?"

"To let her know I'm not drinking anymore, at least, and that I can see why she lost it."

Davy seemed to relax a bit. "Yeah, man, that would probably do you both some good."

"There were a couple of times I felt sure my light was out, and when I discovered I was still alive, I got this feeling like I'd been stamped here and wasn't supposed to leave. Such an odd feeling. I don't know what it means, really."

Warren started to shake again and his voice came out accompanied by a sob. "I wish I could tell Cookie it was wrong—what I did to her—but I don't have a clue where she made off to. "

"Canada," Davy said, sitting back and sweeping the hair off his forehead and up over his head.

Warren's eyes popped open wide. "You know that?"

"Only because when they put out the all-points bulletin the day after you were stabbed, they checked the bus station and someone named Wagner had bought a ticket to Montreal."

A few days later Warren was changing money at the border, then studying the map to see which bridge he'd need to take to cross the river into Montreal. *Ponte*, they called it.

At the Courtyard by Marriot he threw off his shoes and stretched out on one of the beds for a few minutes, clearing his head from the drive, and thinking of how the clerk had greeted him.

"*Bonjour, Monsieur*," she'd said before seeing the blank look in his eyes and changing over to English. Why the hell did these people need to speak French anyway, why not speak like the rest of the Canadians, keep things simpler for guys like him? He got up and went to look down on the avenue. It was a busy one all right, with a constant flow of traffic both directions, a steady stream of pedestrians on the sidewalk, as well. He felt like a fool. Cookie could be anywhere. What did he have to go on besides Davy saying she'd bought a ticket to Montreal?

"Well, get out there and start looking, fool or no fool," he said out loud.

He studied the map until he found the closest police station, constabulary, they called it, and headed there on foot.

There was a protective kind of feeling at the constabulary, maybe because it was an old building with high ceilings, marble pillars along the sides. Reminded him of how banks had been when he was a boy, their marble floors and counters making you feel your money was being well-tended.

The officer at the desk was courteous but not helpful. He, too, spoke French until he saw Warren's eyes darting around searching for help.

"I'm looking for someone, and I can tell you the exact date she would have arrived here," said Warren, "the date she ran away. I know she came to the bus station."

"Is there a warrant for her arrest?" the man asked.

Warren shook his head no. "I only want to find her."

The man shrugged. "Sorry, I can't help you."

"Why not?" Warren asked. "She's my wife."

"She has the right to privacy."

"Even from her husband?"

"Even from her husband," he said with a tone of dismissal, maybe even suspicion.

"She stabbed me," Warren said, his legs fixed in a stubborn stance, his hands fixed on the button of his shirt, as if he was about to open it up and show his scar.

"Is there a warrant for her arrest?" the officer repeated, this time raising his bushy eyebrows.

"No, I don't want her arrested; I just want to find her."

The man only looked askance, as if to say, "A likely story, bloke, and you want me to help you go after her?" He pointed toward the door, as if to imply he had used up his words. Maybe he would have conversed further in French if Warren had been able to speak it, but he was done with English.

Warren walked a long way, glancing up at each woman he passed like he had in Lake George. There were plenty of solid-looking women like Cookie, not too tall, a bit blocky at the hips, but they had something different about them. A way of wearing a scarf flung about their necks, belts made of coins or other metals, some sort of fashion consciousness that put them into a realm beyond Cookie.

Back in his room, he made a cup of coffee in the machine. He read the room service menu, then the drinks menu, and all of a sudden got knocked back with an intense desire for a whiskey. He could go down to the bar, maybe find someone to ease his loneliness, maybe even find a woman out on her own and bring her back to his room.

There was a mini-bar in his room. Now *that* he hadn't anticipated. Seagram's in a tiny bottle, cold beers in the small fridge. Maybe that's why Davy had offered to come up here with him, since Warren had admitted how scared he was he'd take up drinking again.

He slammed the door to the mini fridge and lay back on the bed. What the hell *was* he doing here? It was another one of those things Cookie had sometimes suggested they do, go to Montreal and see the old World's Fair site, which she claimed had been turned into a garden. Maybe he'd go see it in the morning. But why would he want to see a garden without her? She knew the names of all the flowers, planted tulips and daffodils every year and kept track of what survived the winter. Their yard and gardens were sure to go to hell without her.

He put his shoes back on and examined himself in the mirror. Big circles under his eyes. His hair was almost fully gray, these past six weeks had certainly speeded up the process. How the hell did hair know when you were under stress? But he'd seen it with the younger presidents, like Clinton. He'd watched him turn gray while under the threat of impeachment. All for a feel of that babe. Damn fool. Well, who was he to criticize? Wasn't it his pecker that had gotten him stabbed? Not entirely, but combined with times he'd slapped her around.

Still, holy cow, she'd tried to kill him!

He walked down Sherbrooke, looking for a restaurant that appealed to him. He started to loosen up a bit, proud of himself for getting past his temptation to stop in at the hotel bar. Maybe he'd gone a half mile, when he saw a woman walking a block ahead of him the same height as Cookie. Same slightly wide buttocks. Arms a little disproportionately long for her legs, swinging beside her. No purse, she had a backpack perched tightly on her back instead. Her hair was brown and bobbed up and down as she walked. He had to restrain himself from calling out her name as he sped up and got closer. She turned up a side street and he turned up behind her. He caught a bit of her profile as she turned and it seemed all the more to confirm that she might be Cookie.

She started up a hill. The sidewalk was wide enough that he could have caught up and passed her, but he held back, wanting to see how far she was going. Had she turned off because she thought she was being followed, or was this the street she lived on? She picked up speed and he felt a pull in his chest as he strained to keep up with her. Then she abruptly turned to climb up the stairs to a brownstone, pulling keys from her pocket.

His hand went out as if to reach her and his mouth opened as if to call out to her, but then she turned around and held a cell phone in her hand, pointing it almost like a gun as she yelled at him.

"Who the hell do you think you are? Get away from me this instant or I'm calling the police."

She had a flat nose, cheekbones much wider apart than Cookie's. He stopped short. She was not anything like Cookie, except for the fury in her eyes that showed how angry she was.

"I'm so sorry," he said, "I didn't mean to frighten you. I'm just looking for my wife." The words tumbled out of him, inadequate, and he took a few steps backward to let her know he was not after her and held up his hand to make a feeble wave as she stuck to a firm stance and reduced him to a worm with her eyes.

He did not make it past the hotel watering hole the second time. He was steered as if by a magnet right up to the shiny wood of the curved bar that drew him, where he signaled the bartender to come to him without delay, threw back a double whiskey and chased it with a beer. Oh, man, did that open up his mind and his gut. He felt as if he'd come home to some kind of a heaven where everything was going to be all right. What the hell had sent him chasing around after that fucking wife of his? All he needed was this feeling of heat in his gut, a wide-open blast of oxygen entering his brain and his hands tingling with the energy he had clamped down for days. "Another," he called out to the bartender. Hell, if the guy wanted him to, he'd be willing to learn how to say it in French.

He woke up with a huge head, surrounded by white curtains, bells and whistles, and clicks firing off at his side. Holy shit, this had to be a nightmare! But a petite nurse passed by the end of his bed, cheerfully saying *bonjour* to the man in the next bed. In return, the man rained down one hell of a sentence in French. Warren didn't understand a word of it, and trying to make it out only worsened his headache. What the hell was *he* doing here?

He raised his hand to call the nurse as she passed back by, and when she signaled him she'd be right back, he closed his eyes and tried to remember the night before. All he could see was that woman, aiming her cell phone at him like a gun. His mind was a jumble, his memory a blank. He had no idea what else he had done. He pushed halfway up to sitting, with his elbows. Ouch. Raising his head only made the headache speak louder. That nurse better come back soon or he was going to jump out of bed and get going, Johnny gown or not. He stretched to reach the cupboard door to the bedside table to see if his clothes were in there but was thrown back to the center of the bed when a huge stab of pain pierced his abdomen. What the fuck? He grabbed his belly. Remembered the doctor in the Kingston hospital pushing it one way, then another, saying, "Your liver's so enlarged it's coming out to meet me." But shouldn't it be all better now that he'd been off the booze so long? Well, including his time in the hospital, at least a month.

The doctor entered, the nurse tailing him and introducing them. Dr. LaBarre, who asked Warren how he was feeling without even a hint of a French accent.

"Like shit," Warren replied, holding his head as if it were about to shatter into pieces.

"I'm not surprised," said the doctor. "But I hope you understand what a lucky man you are."

Really? Stabbed once, now in a hospital for the second time. Was this guy playing him? "You'll have to clue me in."

"Do you know where you were last night?"

"That's where you've got me," said Warren. "I've lost some time."

"Fortunately, a good bartender knew a bad situation when he saw one and called the rescue squad immediately when you lost consciousness."

Warren shook his head, having a hard time believing that. "I only stopped in at the hotel bar for a couple of drinks."

"Right, but what else had you taken earlier? OxyContin and other pain meds?"

Warren reddened with embarrassment. "How'd you know that?"

"Your bloodwork."

"Oh."

The doctor leaned in to examine him and Warren stayed still until he jumped at the same stab he'd felt when he'd stretched to look for his clothes. "Tender," the doctor said, more a statement than a question. "Liver's badly inflamed."

"Man, oh man," Warren said. "I've been off the booze for over a month trying to calm that thing down."

"But the big belt you gave it last night poisoned you. A lot of bartenders would have given you some time to come around, in which case, you well might not have made it," Dr. LaBarre said.

"Holy shit," Warren declared, then asked the doctor to excuse his language.

The doctor tapped his big scar, then went on in a formal tone. "I've been in touch with your doctor in the States."

"How'd you get to him?"

"Our authorities here contacted the authorities there."

Warren restrained himself from saying "holy shit" again and massaged his skull instead. "Can you give me some aspirin?" he asked.

The doctor shook his head. "Nothing other than the medication you're already on. You'll have to sweat this out. You're detoxing from both the alcohol and the pills."

"Well, if that's all it is, I'd just as soon go home and do that."

"Absolutely not," the doctor said. "You need to understand this is life threatening. We'll watch you for at least another twenty-four hours; then, if you have someone to accompany you, they can take you home."

Warren forced himself to keep his mouth shut as the doctor pulled the sheet back up over his belly and told him to get some rest, they'd discuss this further the next morning.

Once he was alone again, it hit him. At death's door and he hadn't even been aware enough to know it. Suddenly his shell cracked and his tough-guy humor seemed to have gone down the corridor with the doctor. More than just his head ached. His chest ached, his belly where the doctor had pressed. He was one sick motherfucker and he wasn't going to be able to take another drink to numb himself.

He pulled the sheet up over his head, turned on his side away from his neighbor, and a sob escaped him. He tried to choke the next one down, but it came out despite him, and he began to shake and cry like he had not done since he was a small boy. Well, maybe once or twice when he'd been in Cookie's arms, telling her about his father. His chest heaved, his heart pained. He had lost Cookie. There was no sense trying to find her because he hadn't known how to treat her in the first place. He was out of control, always had been. Now, without even knowing it, he had nearly offed himself. Tears poured out of him like he couldn't believe.

Then, suddenly spent, a moment of peace came over him, and someone seemed to speak in a no-nonsense voice from inside him. Get some help! is what he heard. Holy cow, he thought, spooked, but his headache went down a notch, and he breathed easier as he got that newly put-together feeling again, like he'd had when he'd woken up from surgery.

Part II

June 2008

Chapter 6

"C'mon up to Mac's, Molly, and let me buy you a beer when we finish here." The invitation slipped out of Butch's mouth as he fastened the boat to the dock.

Cookie unwrapped the coil of rope and threw it up to him before she shrugged and gave him a quiet, "Okay."

Back on the boat, Butch set up to unload their lobster catch as Harvey, the weighman, rolled over his cart and nodded a silent greeting first to Butch, then to Cookie, before beginning to load their catch on his scale.

"Not a bad day," he grumbled.

"Not at all," Butch replied. "And no rain even on the horizon."

"Right, almost odd," added the wiry, white-bearded Harvey.

When they were finished, Butch tilted his head toward the street and he and Molly walked up the hill together. At the top, he stopped to turn back and gaze at the sea. He'd often seen Molly do this and been drawn to her because of it. Regardless of how familiar the view was, she also seemed to appreciate that she'd landed here in Cape Breton, a place where the sea was large enough to swallow all, where its roughness thrilled, yet its bay held a great, gentle stillness whenever the wind died.

Butch pushed through the double doors with Molly behind him and chose a booth. The light was dim and the place empty except for a couple of guys on barstools and Mac, the bartender-proprietor. Butch sidled up to the bar and asked for two beers but didn't make talk with Mac or the others, as he was suddenly self-conscious about bringing in a woman, even if she was the woman who was his right-hand worker, and a good, hard worker at that. He was aware of how small this town was, and what a curiosity she'd been when she'd arrived a few years back, head shorn to nearly a crew cut and dressed in a manly way, yet with a frightened little girl look on her face.

"Cheers," he said, returning to their table and raising his mug to Molly's, and they each belted back a long swig.

Butch played with the coasters on the table, stacking, then unstacking them, his eyes flickering across Molly for a second here and there, then returning to the thick wooden slab of table between them.

"Good day out there today," he said, gesturing with the mug again.

"Yeah," she said. "Nice when you can get really good and warm," and she rubbed over her heart as if there was a cold spot inside her always yearning to heat up.

They sat in silence another moment. There was a question he had held back from asking these two lobster seasons she'd been working with him, but now was as good a time as any to ask. He was feeling something for her, maybe more than he should, and he needed to know. "So, what brought you to these cold waters?" he inquired.

Her face seemed to darken as if they were outside and a cloud had passed across the sun. She hesitated. "I ran away from my husband," she said quietly. Her eyes darted from side to side. Slowly she added, "Before he could throw me around anymore."

Butch nodded. "I figured it was something like that."

"What about you?" she asked.

"A long story," he answered. "My mother moved our whole family to Canada in 1968 when my brother and I were about to get drafted for the Vietnam War. She'd raised us to be pacifists, so we were pretty strongly against the war. Still, she was the gutsy one.

We probably would have been drafted if not for her."

"Oh dear," Molly murmured, thinking about Jake, her classmate who had come back in a box, the memorial his parents had kept in their front yard, his high school picture fading through the years.

Butch stacked and unstacked a few Budweiser coasters in front of him. "I never felt I belonged in the US after that," he finally said.

"Wasn't there a time when one of our presidents—maybe Jimmy Carter—issued an amnesty for guys who had gone to Canada?"

"Right," Butch nodded. "My brother Ian went back then. I did think about it, but I already had my fishing boat, and the way of life here settles into you and makes you wonder—is there really any better place to live?"

"Less rain elsewhere," she offered, "and not so cold either."

"True, but hey, we just bought a couple of days of sun. Don't challenge it."

Molly chuckled, and Butch realized he was no longer looking at the table more than he was looking at her. It felt good to be talking about where he'd come from and remember his mother packing them up, telling them convictions were worth nothing unless you stood up for them and her sons were going to be warriors for peace, not war, and she was going to be damned proud of them. It also felt good to be sitting across from a woman who had a bit of mirth in her blue eyes. He'd always been aware of the color of Molly's eyes, just not the mirth. Her face was broad with high cheekbones, smooth skin tanned enough to draw out the crow's feet showing at the corners of her eyes. He had a yen to touch her face. And that temptation made him push his back hard against the wood of the booth, remembering Janet, the one woman who had gotten to his heart, and how he had failed with her.

"How is it living up on the hill above Mrs. Biddle?" he asked.

"It's cozy, except for when the wind blows strong enough to buffet the cottage, and if it weren't tucked up so tight against the cliff, it feels like it might take flight."

"I bet," said Butch. "It's solid enough, though. I helped old Brownie lug some huge timbers up that hill, back when Dr. Biddle decided to erect it there."

"You did?"

"I did, indeed."

"What was he like, Dr. Biddle?"

"Oh, he was a tough and determined little man. Bent on getting that view for them. That's what he always wanted—to see as far as he could see. And he figured he'd use the house below for his office, after he and Mrs. Biddle moved up to the cottage. Only she would never go. She refused to move from the main house and made him keep his office right where it was, down on the Cabot Trail." Butch chuckled. "Stubborn woman."

"What happened to him?" asked Molly, her eyes brightly curious.

"He had a bad heart attack right up there in his solitary refuge, and no one was with him to call for help. It would have been a big deal to run a phone line up there. This was before we had the cell phone towers. He used to stay up there a lot. Evidently, it became a two-house marriage."

"Did she find him?"

"Sure did." Butch narrowed his eyes, taking on the look of a detective but a playful one. "She went looking for him when he didn't show up for breakfast, but he was a stiff already, right there in the bed."

Molly shook her head and put up her hand like a stop sign, saying, "Yeah, I knew that, but I guess I deliberately forgot it."

"Right," Butch agreed. "Morbid subject."

"It's just . . . I suppose that's the same bed I've been sleeping in for just about four years now."

"Yeah, sorry, I hadn't thought about that. Let me get you another beer on that one," Butch said, and off he went to Mac.

When he came back, he raised his glass to her again but didn't know what else to talk about. She'd looked hurt when she'd talked about how she'd gotten here, so he didn't want to ask any more about where she'd come from. He was used to silence; that was nothing to him. He had lived alone for many years and cultivated the art of making conversation in his own head, or with Jimbo, his half huskie, half shepherd, (under the table at his feet right at the moment), who knew just about everything he knew. But now he felt obligated. After all, he was the one who had invited her for a drink; he ought to keep her entertained. Maybe this was why he kept to himself so much, because now, under obligation, he felt trapped and a bit resentful for her making him feel awkward.

Just as he felt he had come up against a dam, Molly gracefully broke the silence. "When was it you lugged those timbers up the hill? That must have been some job."

"Right, sure was. But I was, what, no more than twenty-five and fit. Still, it was a steep incline." He told her how Doc had built those stone stairs into the cliff himself, with a little help from Brownie. And ascending them was the only way of carrying construction materials up to the site, until they built a hoist with a pulley to lift some of the supplies up. "Doc could have been an engineer," he said. "He designed that hoist himself."

Molly was smiling. "I've been wondering the whole time I've been here how that cottage got built. It looks like it got dropped in place by a helicopter. Which makes it really special, but I'm glad I'm not a sleepwalker. You could tumble right off the cliff and land down on the Cabot Trail."

"No way. But you can see why everyone, especially Mrs. Biddle, tried hard to talk Doc out of it."

Molly bobbed her head. "Lucky for me they didn't succeed," she said, and Butch agreed. Indeed, Molly had the best view on this whole coast.

"How awesome the view is shocks me every day," she said. "I thought eventually I'd tire of watching the sunset, but every night its different. More clouds, fewer clouds, pure open sky, overcast, foggy."

"I know," he agreed. "Even from my place it's like that, which is why I sit out most nights with Jimbo."

The next day he worried they'd be different on the boat, but she acted as if nothing had changed between them. They had another good catch and the sun shone all day and she went up the hill ahead of him at the end of the afternoon, saying, "See you tomorrow," as usual. And when he stopped in for a beer, with the diplomacy of a small-town bartender, Mac didn't remark upon the fact that aging bachelor Butch had been in with a woman the after-noon before. On Saturday, he invited her again. And then, what the heck, they went on down to the diner for supper.

He hadn't been lonely before he'd started up with this, but now it crept up on him. He wanted more company. He thought back to Janet in a way he hadn't in years. The delight of waking up to the smell of her cooking bacon. He cooked it himself, but it never smelled the same as when someone else cooked it for you. Her long torso, he remembered that, too. How he'd loved to run his hands up and down her thighs. Why had he been reluctant to marry her when that was what she wanted?

He'd felt they were just fine, living separate but with Janet stay-ing over most weekends and, for the moment, he hadn't wanted more. She wanted children, and he thought he might grow into wanting them, too, but he didn't want them right then. It wasn't about loving her; he had definitely loved her, and yet when she said, "Why not prove it then, by us getting married?" he'd bucked, pushing her away. Until the day she told him she was leaving. She'd already bought her ticket to Vancouver, where her sister was, and given him all the chances she was going to give. She'd cried and said she'd always love him, but she wanted to have a family and didn't know if he'd ever be able to have one.

Not able? he'd thought. It's not that I'm not able. Just don't want to move so fast right now. He'd said this to himself and then out loud to her, but she'd only dried her tears and taken his hands and wished him luck. And then she was gone.

When he and Molly came out from the diner, they stood a moment looking out across the still ocean, not at each other. It was light yet, but the sun was heading toward the horizon and a chill wind was coming up. As Molly tightened the scarf around her neck, he inclined his head toward Mrs. Biddle's hill and asked, "Shall I see you home?"

"No, I'm fine," said Molly, that independent spirit he liked firmly planted behind her words.

"All right then," he said, adjusting his cap.

"Thanks for the supper," she said, her tone a bit softer.

That's when he took her hand and squeezed it, and she squeezed back for just a second before she dropped it, saying goodnight and turning away to begin her walk home.

"Oh, Jimbo, what am I getting myself into?" he said out under the stars, lying atop the stone wall at the end of his patio, the dog nuzzled into his side. "Why am I suddenly thinking of more, when it's *more* that always gets you into trouble?" He ruffled Jimbo's fur. "You tell me what to do," and Jimbo came out with a low guttural moan.

"You think so, Jimbo?" he said. "But she works for me and just happens to be the best shipmate I've had in years, and I don't want to spoil that." He thought of how he'd first taken note of her hanging around the dock when he unloaded. She'd said she'd been up cleaning for Mrs. Biddle and had come down to get some fresh air. And he'd felt a freshness about her. Blue eyes that had a curiosity in them, not the dullness that many of the local women seemed to have.

Milt Granger had been working for him then. Milt, who had to be told what to do every moment, else he went off into some sort of a trance. Butch believed he had ruined his mind and motivation with too giant a daily dose of pot. So the day Milt didn't show and Butch couldn't find anyone in town to be his second, he didn't go out. But when he went down to the dock later that afternoon at unloading time to see if he could find someone to hire, there was Molly, out for her stroll. And when he complained about Milt as a no show, she asked him if he'd consider her for the job. She didn't know a thing about boats or lobster fishing, she admitted straight out, but she was a fast learner and didn't mind hard work. She didn't think Mrs. Biddle would care; she only really needed one day a week to clean for her, and the rest of the time she suspected Mrs. Biddle was manufacturing extra work for her just so she could feel she was earning her keep.

His first reaction had been to laugh. A woman on his boat? But she'd propped one foot on a docking post and stood still, looking very firm and he'd thought she might be one of those women, like his sister, whom he hadn't seen in a couple of years but who might show up with her girlfriend on her arm any day now. A real *girlfriend*. Her current one, whom she'd been with a number of years now, downright appealed to him and seemed like someone who might fit with a man, unlike Lil, who'd been a tomboy from birth and played rough with him and Ian and would clobber him if she thought he was not hiring this woman because she was a woman. She'd clobber him even harder if she knew he was permitting the thought, "Might she be a dyke?" to run through his mind.

Two weeks more and the lobster season would be over—it only went from May 15 to July 15 now because the waters were too fished out. The season, even for other fish, would be over in a few days. Since he couldn't afford to miss another day, he asked if she had any idea what this job entailed. "We leave home four or four-thirty, take oil gear on at the wharf, and head off for the nets. The idea is to haul the nets first thing in the morning before the wind picks up. The nets get picked clean for bait. Then we head out to my traps, one person gaffs the buoy, puts it through the derrick block, and the traps come up in ten to fifteen seconds."

Her lips pursed in concentration. He could tell she didn't understand what he was talking about, but she hadn't stopped listening.

"Used to be the traps were hauled in by hand," he went on. "That meant maybe for one season hauling up to 12,000 pounds, but now we have the hydraulic. Once the trap is on the washboard, its door is opened and the lobsters are taken out." He told her how one crew baited the trap with mackerel or herring and looked at the sounder to make sure they were on good bottom while the other crew gauged the lobster to determine if it was large enough to keep and good for canner or market. "Once the traps are done, we head back to the wharf, unload, and wash down the boat," he concluded.

She nodded.

"Time back varies. Might be early afternoon, might be later."

Her eyes were on him, steady. "How do you know which traps are yours?" she asked.

"Buoy color and design. An old-fashioned system but it works."

She nodded again. "There'd be a lot to learn, but I'd be glad to try it."

He had offered her a chance that day a year ago June, and it was true she was a rapid learner and knew how to anticipate what he needed and didn't have any qualms about doing whatever it was, unlike Milt who he'd always had to wake up. She'd gotten seasick a couple of times, but then she'd learned to go with the swells and somehow got her belly to settle down. And they'd just gone rolling along—her always there waiting for him at 4:00 a.m. to go out for the bait, then working competently and steadily at unloading and setting the traps.

They hardly talked most days, but the quiet between them had been easy and time passed without a hitch. Until now, when something had awakened in him. He thought of the whales, which sometimes rode alongside the boat, popping up to create a waterspout on one side, then traversing to the other side and reappearing a few minutes later. Playful. He suddenly had the urge to be playful like that.

The sun went down and he went inside and lay gazing up through the skylight he'd installed in his slanted cottage ceiling and watched the stars multiply the longer he looked and the darker it got. His heart quickened as he remembered Molly's hand squeezing back, and he looked on in wonder as the light of the stars spanned a great arc above him.

Sundays, they didn't fish. When he woke up, he was almost sorry it was Sunday because he wasn't likely to see her. He cooked some eggs and bacon and shared them with Jimbo, who fully appreciated the generosity of his mood. When the church bells rang out, he wondered if Molly was there. It was a simple Presbyterian Church, not overly religious. He'd been a couple of times with Janet, who went because she liked the singing. He considered taking a walk down to the village just as church was getting out, in case he might catch a glimpse of her but decided against it, because he couldn't see her going there. Mrs. Biddle went to the Catholic Church up on North Hill, but he couldn't see Molly going there, either. She was an independent; that's what he liked about her.

All day he lay about, reading, walking around and musing, throwing the stick for Jimbo, but unlike past Sundays during lobster season, when he would bask in the free day's rest, he couldn't settle down. Light poured in through the window to make a cone of lively, dancing dust mites, and he felt as if he had been activated like them; cells bounced around inside of him, all from a drink at the bar and supper at the diner, and small as it was as a signal, her squeezing his hand back kept popping up in his mind and giving him a charge much larger than what it might be worth—a jolt really.

He made it until suppertime, then combed his hair in front of the mirror, wetting and trying to tamp down the cowlick that always made him look unfinished. He went down the hill, figuring he'd have his meal again at the diner, but before he got halfway there, as he hit the bend where he could see his dock, he spotted a figure at the dock's edge. He strained to make out if it was a person but was too far away to tell; it was almost like a floater in his eye, one of those gray spots that keep coming every time you look to a certain angle. Yet he knew it was Molly even before he could see her outlines, and the jolt went through him again as he quickened his step.

He slowed to a saunter as he came up onto the dock. She turned around from gazing onto the sea and smiled and said sure when he asked if he might sit down beside her.

"What do you do Sundays?" he asked her.

"Clean Mrs. Biddle's house," she replied. "But I finish by early afternoon and then I have some time to myself."

"Right," he said, realizing he had forgotten that his giving her a job had not absolved her of this other obligation.

"You don't really get a day off," he commented.

"I don't mind," she said. "I like to keep busy."

He caught a glimpse of that frightened look again, a tightness around her mouth and a worried frown on her forehead. He bumped his shoulder into hers, saying, "You could always ask your boss for a day off, you know."

"Yeah?" she said.

"Well, if the season weren't so short. Back when I started, we'd go on fishing right up until frosty weather set in. The crab season we had after lobster season went on for at least six weeks, and then there was some cod fishing."

"What happened to that?"

"Fished out by big boats from other countries. Canada only had a two-mile shore protection so we got taken advantage of, and now they have to restrict what's left of the catch."

"Well, at least we know there'll be plenty of days off ahead," she said.

"Right," he said, agreeing that how to keep busy all those days when the boat was up in dry dock could be more of a challenge than the workdays.

They were silent a while, listening to the lapping of the water against the dock posts, feeling the late-afternoon sun, which came at a slant against her right side.

He got that desire again to touch her, but it had been so long since he'd touched a woman he no longer remembered how to tell if she'd want him to. And there was the risk of ruining everything if he did reach out and she rejected his advance. Why did it always have to be the man to make the first move? His sister would say, "No, that's sexist, and furthermore, not so."

Janet had been the one to lean her head onto his shoulder when they were sitting out one night together. He tried to suggest this mentally to Molly, leaning a bit closer to her shoulder, close enough that he felt those mysterious vibes like iron filings going toward a magnet. Were they his or hers? Or were they coming from them both? So darn hard to tell. He thought they were mutual. But couldn't be sure. Finally, he just let them draw him that last couple of inches until he was against her shoulder and put his arm around her, and she moved in against the side of his chest and locked in as if he were the magnet. They avoided looking at each other, just continued to watch the sea. He was holding down his breathing and thought she might be, too, and then she did look over at him and he met her eyes and held them, saw the mirth again as well as possibly fear, and a studying of him, as if she were seeing him for the first time and trying to comprehend just exactly who he was.

And then he took her chin, lifted it a fraction and kissed her. A soft kiss, it sealed them together, but not with any effort. It was as if they each knew how much intensity to hold back, and did.

The thought flew by him, someone might easily see them, but his desire was such he was not going to let this matter unless it mattered enough to her. She rested her head back against his shoulder and let out a deep sigh, and he inhaled the sweet scent of her hair and then kissed her again and again, and between a couple of the kisses, he suggested they take a walk up to his place, would she care to, and she murmured yes and they stood, practically as a unit, and parted enough to walk up the hill, holding hands and bumping into each other's sides as they went.

Later, he remembered he had not had any supper and found out she hadn't either, so he popped some frozen tortellini in a pot and melted butter over it and sprinkled some parmesan cheese, and they sat at his square old-fashioned slab of wood table and greedily consumed the make-shift meal.

He had tossed her a fresh T-shirt when she'd still been lying in his bed, the sheet pulled up to her chin, and she wore that now like a short dress, her legs crossed, one foot swinging under the edge of the table as she stabbed another tortellini with her fork and swabbed the buttery sauce from her plate and plucked it into her mouth. He watched her chew and then swallow.

"What?" she asked as he followed her every move. "What is it?"

"Nothing," he said. "I just like to look at you, especially your mouth." Her mouth was small, her lips well defined, something like a rose. Whereas her stance was strong and steady, her mouth was vulnerable. Her lips might even be a bit swollen now, for they'd kissed long and hard before venturing into removing their clothes and falling length to length together.

He'd watched as he'd entered her. Seen a moment when she'd drawn in her breath and then stopped breathing and a shadow of fear had crossed over her face again, but only for a flash, before she'd tilted her head back, her chin pointing toward the ceiling, and gone somewhere deep inside where she looked to be in ecstasy, and he'd come back to himself, to the drive that pushed him into her and to the warmth surrounding him.

Chapter 7

When Butch had taken Cookie on as his shipmate, her life had grown even more full. Although they only went out until mid-summer, he went on paying her a few months longer in the fall into winter, while they repaired the nets and set the boat in order. He'd wanted to put her on the books so she'd qualify for unemployment when the boat was out of water, but she'd asked him only to pay her outright for the weeks she was working and told him the rest of the time she'd get by fine.

He'd arched up one eyebrow as if he thought she was a little cuckoo, but said, "Suit yourself," and let her be.

She'd never expected to have a desire for sex after what had happened with Warren, but the lapping of the ocean at the shoreline, the constancy of it, made her want to touch herself and test her dormancy. And she had discovered desire was still there, though shamefully, it often came with thoughts of Warren. Memories of nights he'd carried on with her. Especially when he was pushing against her will. She would feel as if she had been reduced to nothing and hated that feeling, yet when her body would succumb to another orgasm, she'd be torn between letting it pleasure her and the idea she'd betray herself if she took the pleasure. This was what came up now when she would manipulate herself. Her body would go all warm with desire, then nothing seemed to take her further until she would think back on Warren getting rough, lifting her with his strong arms and moving her around and taking her whatever way he wanted to, and that would bring her to a climax, but then she'd feel what? Satisfied but not really there with herself.

But now, with Butch, this was something else. She had begun falling for him when the lobster season started up again, and they'd been meeting each morning at 4:00 a.m., sleep still in her voice and in his eyes, his smile growing wider as the sun rose over the water. Her secretly approving his smooth, wiry body as he'd leap to the stern or lean over to pull out the knot and release the boat to putter out of the harbor. She'd been careful, though, not to let him see her admiring him.

Even though Butch was not one bit like Warren, she didn't want to chance being with a man again. She saw how Mrs. Biddle lived; yes, she was a widow and had only been living like this for a couple of years, but she had a life unto itself and appeared quite satisfied, and Cookie felt such a life would serve her just fine, as well.

But how could she have stopped herself, once they had shared their first kiss? What a man Butch was. Smart, hard-working but not out to get anyone. He seemed to flow with life, smiling his slightly crooked smile, crinkling up his just a hint of Asian-looking eyes. A gentleman and a scholar, her mother would have said. Well, in a way he *was* a scholar because he liked to read and to muse. Why were people this way or that? She thought he had gone to college, but she wasn't sure; nor why, if he had, he'd ended up a fisherman. Most men in these parts took up fishing because it was the only thing they knew.

He'd been gentle with her from the start, patiently teaching her how to bring up the traps and judge a lobster. The opposite of Warren, Butch's voice would stay modulated, even if they were beating it back to shore with a storm pushing in behind them. And he'd never laid a hand on her unless it was to show her how to tie a special knot to secure the boat. Until this afternoon. Until he'd sat beside her on the dock and they'd both let the water lull them until they were leaning up against each other, and then . . .

She couldn't quite believe how much warmth she had down

below where Butch had only hours ago been with her. Gently. Carefully. Caringly. He had brought her along to a peak that had shaken her like a ripe seed in a seedpod, and then the waves had traveled out, lighting up pathways to her fingers and down to her toes, and she had been awed by the power of it, scared for just one moment before she became defenseless. Wide open in a way she'd never intended to be. Aware of Butch and yet completely unto herself. Clear and clean, no violence; this was true lovemaking. She felt cradled in some kind of light.

Butch had wanted her to stay the night, but she'd said, no, she had to go home; she wasn't sure why. Was she afraid Mrs. Biddle would note her absence? But with his usual ease Butch had not tried to keep her; he'd agreed she should do whatever she needed to. She missed him already, but awareness grew in her the way light came up at dawn until she knew why she'd needed to be alone—so she could sit here in the middle of her couch and hug herself the same way she'd done the first day she arrived.

Chapter 8

It was the deep of winter, a fire crackled in the woodstove, and Butch was once again amazed at the good fortune that had befallen him. It had been six months now, but life with Molly still felt new. Each time they made love, it seemed a life-giving experience. "I can't get enough of you," he said, kissing his fingertips and bringing them to her lips.

He'd been building a list of things he needed to make a trip to the supply store in Halifax worthwhile—boat stuff, windshield wipers for his truck, new waders, and the idea had popped up that maybe while he was there he could look in a couple of fancy jewelry stores for a ring. At least, if he didn't take her with him. Though it would be hard not to. She'd seen too little of Nova Scotia, and it would be an opportunity to show her they had a big city where people were more up-to-date with the rest of the world.

Not that he had asked that all important question yet, but he was determined not to make the same mistake he'd made with Janet, acting as if his bachelor's freedom was too precious to be interfered with. He'd been alone so many years, people didn't think he wanted to be any other way, but what they failed to understand was how, since he'd found Molly, he'd gone from being a jolly fellow content to lay around talking to Jimbo, who always wildly agreed with him, to becoming a man who knew he'd been missing something all along.

"What are you smiling at?" Molly asked, as they lay facing each other.

"You," he said. "How you landed in such a tiny town as Seal Cove, and I got lucky. What were the odds of that?"

She smiled back. "My luck, too. How is it you escaped getting nabbed by one of the women here all these years?"

"Some kind of intuition that I was waiting for you."

She shook her head as if she didn't believe him.

"Some of it was that I didn't mind a bachelor's life. And then, when you live in a place like this, the years roll by and all of a sudden you've moved into your fifties and haven't grown up yet."

She pinched his small roll of belly fat and said, "Here's the only place that shows you've grown up."

He pinched off more of it, saying, "Right, this here's grown like gangbusters since we've been cooking all these meals together, and that's not all you do to whet my appetite."

The thought of food roused him to get up and put on the pasta water and she donned one of his large T-shirts the same way she had the first Sunday they'd come together and, as the two of them savored the ravioli he'd dressed up with some frozen peas and olive oil and parmesan cheese, he smiled his broadest smile, which came out of the warm, almost holy feeling he had in his heart. And she smiled back.

Then, because they were in that glow, he leaned across the corner of the table, took both of her hands in his and cleared his throat. "Molly, I want . . ." He drew in a breath. There was no non-awkward way to say this. "What the heck, I wish I was better at words . . ." He plunged onward. "Will you marry me?"

The smile fell off her face, her breath caught, and while she didn't let go of his hands, she drew back, her eyes opening wide, as if she'd never considered he might think of such a thing. "But, but . . ." she uttered.

"But what?" he asked, his eyes not leaving her face, his eagerness losing intensity as he sensed her retreat.

"I don't think . . ." she stammered. "I'm not . . . not able." Her face had blanched white.

"Not sure you want me?" he said softly.

"No, no, it's not that," she said, shaking her head vigorously.

He waited. Then what? he wanted to ask but didn't, his heart sinking to a new low. His gaze moved to the window, where there was nothing to be seen but the late afternoon darkness that went with the season.

She squeezed his hand, saying, "It's not you, Butch, not about loving you. I do . . . so much." She shook her head again. "It's just that . . . I should never have let this get started. I don't deserve you."

"Why on earth not?" he asked, suddenly filled with adrenalin and with the sensation of a lead weight residing in his chest.

"I'm so sorry," she said. "I can't tell you more." She continued shaking her head as tears traversed her cheeks, and he reached out to take her in his arms and wipe them away. Only he no longer quite knew whom he was holding.

The following Saturday night, as they resumed their lovemaking for the first time in a week, just as he brought her to the crest of an orgasm, her face turned bright red and she gasped for breath. He lifted his head from its cradle between her legs and called out, "Molly, what is it? What's the matter?"

She groaned and tossed her head back and forth like a person in delirium.

He took her in his arms, stroked her and muttered for her to cry, because whatever she was holding inside seemed to be crushing her. But she only continued to breathe with a catch in her breath and a small heave of her chest.

As he held her, he couldn't stop telling himself he'd been too blind. He didn't know enough about her, like why she had come here and from where. He countered by telling himself he knew the important things: what a great worker she was; how she could sit with him for hours in a comfortable silence, at other times be playful; how that little wrinkle under her eye flexed until it was almost like a wink when she was worried.

She'd told him she'd come here to escape a husband who knocked her around. He'd just assumed she was getting a divorce, maybe already had one. If she hadn't, they could work on that.

But why was she so reluctant to tell him where she had grown up, even? Her parents were both dead and, far as he knew, she had no siblings. She'd spoken only of one good friend, Nita, with whom she'd lost touch. Said she'd lived in New Paltz, a college town in Upstate New York, where there was lots of drinking on the streets on a Saturday night, which she didn't care for, but she had liked the nearby mountains. Why hadn't she kept up with Nita? Who knew? He didn't really have a best friend himself. Had once had a couple of good buddies he'd shared stories with every afternoon after the boat was rinsed down, but one of them had gotten married and hatched a slew of kids fast, and the other, Jeremy, ended up in a head-on crash on his motorcycle, coming back across the Cabot Trail from Pleasant Bay and was now living out his time in the head trauma center down in Halifax.

Molly pried out from his embrace, and with her eyes skirting away, told him again it was not him; she had not ended her marriage properly.

"No divorce?" he asked.

She shook her head emphatically.

"You think he's out looking for you?"

A tremor passed her lips, then she closed her eyes.

"I'm sorry." She swallowed hard. "Can't say."

"Christ! What could it be?"

"Please," she said. "Leave it."

He'd taken her again in his arms and cupped her face and her ear had been on his heart and she seemed to be holding her breath until she let out a small whimper, and when he asked again, "What's the matter," she said, "Nothing. Only I can hear your heartbeat. Lub dub, lub dub, it's there so strongly right under my ear."

"Well, isn't that a good thing?"

"It is."

"You make it sound like the kiss of death."

"No," she said. "Don't say that. Only hold me."

Chapter 9

Ominous, gray clouds socked in solidly over the horizon the day Mrs. Biddle saw Chrissie in her office for the first time.

The girl was down to a point of nearly vanishing, evidently less than eighty pounds, and her mother was desperate to get her to eat. When Mrs. Glenn, her English teacher, said the girl was super smart, wrote the best papers but wouldn't speak in class, and asked Mrs. Biddle as the guidance counselor if she might intervene and find a way to encourage her, Muriel needed no convincing to give parental consent.

The girl sat on her hands, her knobby knees showing through her slim jeans, her eyes too deep in their sockets.

"How are you today?" Mrs. Biddle asked, and Chrissie gave an almost imperceptible shake of her head.

"What would you like to talk about?" she tried again, and this time, the girl brought up a hand and held it across her mouth as if to silence herself.

Mrs. Biddle faltered. Why should utter silence strip her of her authority? But her intuition for asking the right question, her aura that usually put people at ease, was gone. Was she losing it? Because this made her really uncomfortable. She should be able to sit out a few minutes of anxious silence.

She took a deep breath and set her mind on what she might say to break the logjam. She suspected Chrissie didn't get a lot of attention at home. Her mother worked such long hours at the diner. Nice woman, but when Mrs. Biddle had counseled the son with learning disabilities, she'd found her not particularly understanding about his acting out. At home, she imagined Chrissie would be the easy one to skirt over. Ironic that Muriel was in the business of serving food, and her daughter was refusing to eat.

Well, the least she could do was to remain calm, sit quietly, and make the girl know she was being seen and heard. She held to her eyes like an owl gazing upon her from a forest and determined to keep this up for the full forty-minute period, if that was what Chrissie desired.

Mrs. Biddle studied the girl, now sixteen, strong cheek bones, mild eyes, a sweetness in her mouth, blonde locks held back tightly in a ponytail. When Chrissie realized Mrs. Biddle was looking at her, she looked away, seeming to comb the room for its details: the university degree on the wall behind Mrs. Biddle's desk, the bookcase with its neatly arranged books, the vase atop it with its arrangement of Mrs. Biddle's blue hydrangeas dried to a brittle mauve.

Chrissie swung one of her feet, tipping a toe to touch the floor repeatedly, as if that touch was all she needed to ground her. Her eyes fluttered down into her lap, and Mrs. Biddle got the feeling she wanted to be invisible. She'd seen other kids like this, good readers who wanted to be inside a book instead of outside it. Chrissie stirred, moving off her hands, but looking as if she didn't know what to do with them. She put them in her lap, one on top of the other, squeezed one with the other, then bent forward as if guarding her stomach. Was she hungry?

"What's the feeling?" Mrs. Biddle asked.

Chrissie looked as if caught and shook her head no, she was not having any feeling, but Mrs. Biddle did not look away. Finally, Chrissie shrugged and folded her arms across her stomach. "Lump in my stomach," she said.

"Ahh," said Mrs. Biddle.

Chrissie's stomach growled loudly.

"Did you have breakfast this morning?"

Chrissie nodded. "Oatmeal."

"It's not hunger then?"

Chrissie shook her head no.

Mrs. Biddle wasn't at all sure she believed that. "Your teachers are concerned about you."

Chrissie dropped her head to her chest and her shoulders folded forward, as if she wanted to disappear. Don't talk about me, she looked like she wanted to say. Don't care about me. Tears came to the girl's eyes.

"It's okay to cry," Mrs. Biddle said softly, handing Chrissie a tissue from the box on the table beside her chair.

Chrissie wrapped the tissue around her index finger and wiped the tears from the corners of her eyes. She stuck her bottom lip out in a pout.

"I don't mind a little lip, either," Mrs. Biddle said with a smile.

Chrissie held her fingers against her mouth, as if to still the quivering lip, her hands looking overly large because the bones of her forearms showed through so strongly.

"Troubles at home?" Mrs. Biddle ventured.

Chrissie shrugged.

"You know that anything you say here will be kept confidential. It does not go outside this room."

"What about my parents?"

When Mrs. Biddle shook her head strongly, Chrissie went on. "My teachers?"

"No. They speak to me about students they feel might need a chance to talk, but I don't go back and report to them."

"Oh," said Chrissie.

"Do you get along with your father?" Mrs. Biddle asked.

Chrissie shrugged. "Guess so."

"Does he spend time with you?"

"Sometimes," Chrissie said. "Sometimes when he gets home from work, he sits me and my brother down at the kitchen table and pours us each a juice glass of beer. He says, 'Cheers,' and we all raise our glasses and take a sip."

"You enjoy these moments?" asked Mrs. Biddle.

Chrissie nodded. "I guess. He's been doing that ever since I was a little girl."

"Are there other things you do together?"

Chrissie shook her head. "Not really. The rest of the time he's either gone to work or sitting with the newspaper in front of him in the big recliner."

"Does your mother join you, when you sit at the table with him?"

"Oh, no, if she's home she tells him he shouldn't give us kids beer, but she doesn't stop him, 'cause she'd rather he stay home than go down to the legion bar."

"Why's that?"

"'Cause once he's gone there, it's hard to get him home. She goes down and begs him, sometimes she even takes me with her because she says I'm his favorite, and we pull at him and pull at him, trying to drag him off the stool, but he becomes dead weight, so heavy it's like trying to move a tractor, so we end up just leaving him there."

"That must be hard," said Mrs. Biddle.

Chrissie shrugged.

"I mean, when you have to go down to the bar and try to bring him home."

The girl shrugged again. "What's so hard about it?" she asked.

"Well, it must be hard to try to move someone who's as heavy as a tractor, and maybe it's not that easy to concentrate in school when you've been up late worrying about your parents."

"I don't really worry about them." She shook her head. "They're just my parents."

"Do they get along?" Mrs. Biddle asked.

Chrissie pursed her lips and frowned. "They argue," she said. "Mostly they never agree on anything."

Having gotten Chrissie to break the silence, Mrs. Biddle decided to wait to broach the eating problem the next time. "Well," she said, instead, "you seem to have a way of handling this, but would you mind coming to talk to me, maybe every other Tuesday, instead of study hall? I think it might be good for both of us."

Chrissie raised her eyebrows and seemed to weigh the sacrifice of remaining invisible with the prospect of having someone's full attention showered on her.

"Okay," she said, before getting up and slinging her backpack up over her shoulder, her collarbone protruding abnormally. At the door, she turned back and paused, her eyes finding Mrs. Biddle's for a second as she asked, "Why would it be good for you?"

Edith was taken aback, not at all fast on her feet the way she expected of herself, but managed to stutter out, "Well . . . well, because I'd like to get to know you."

As Chrissie slunk down the hall, Edith thought of Molly. The two of them had such a lost quality about them, a shyness that overshadowed their smarts. She felt sure they had a lot in common.

Chapter 10

After the night of Molly listening to his heart, Butch thought they were okay until a few days passed without her getting in touch. Molly had one of those cell phones on which she bought minutes as she needed them instead of having an account, and she hardly ever turned it on.

He rarely went up to her cottage, because it seemed a sacrosanct place to her. Even some nights when he walked her home, he'd leave her at the bottom of the stairs, then wait until she reached the top and waved to him, signaling she was home. Oh, he'd been up there to see the place, of course, even had a few meals she'd fixed there and seen how she glowed within its confines, keeping the bed made with a yellow and white quilt neatly covering it, the dishes washed up, a blue vase of wild flowers arranged on her small table, changing to dried flowers for winter. He'd seen how she feasted her eyes on the simple but attractive aesthetic of the place, all the furniture oriented toward the windows looking out to the sea, lending the main room a deep calm.

Now, day four since he had heard from her, he thought of going up there but passed down Centre Street first, gazing into each of the shop windows, hoping to spot Molly running errands for Mrs. Biddle, as she often did in the late afternoon. Before his proposal, on days when they weren't working together, Molly almost always called, and the last thing Butch wanted was to let this *thing*—whatever it was she couldn't tell him—destroy their connection. She wasn't any ordinary woman; she was special, even if he couldn't say exactly why. He could only say the person she added up to *in toto* had gotten past some barrier and touched him where he didn't know he could be touched, melting whatever had held him back from pursuing another woman since Janet had taken off for Vancouver years ago. Whatever was keeping Molly from explaining herself, he didn't need to know. He didn't need to marry her; they could go back to before the proposal. Spending their days together on the boat in summer, going to the tavern, nodding to Mac, the owner, who by now recognized them as a unit when they stopped for beers, and come Saturday evening, going down to the Lobster Shack or cooking some fish for Molly at his place, or sometimes, her bringing supplies over to stir up a nice soup in his kitchen, and then, oh Lordy, the way they enjoyed each other. The way he liked to kiss her and experience her kissing back. Jimbo would make a sort of musical moan to let them know he thought he was privy to their kisses, even after they'd throw him off the bed. *Especially* after they'd thrown him off the bed.

Molly was delicate. He enjoyed that about her. In spite of the solid stance he'd counted on when he'd hired her as a boat hand, in bed she became a fair and delicate woman.

As Butch approached the far end of Centre Street, almost as if he'd called her, Mrs. Biddle happened along. He smiled a warm hello.

She shook his hand firmly and asked how it was going.

"Can't complain."

"Yes, you can," she replied. "Especially to me."

Was the woman reading his mind? "You suspect me of having a complaint?" he asked, teasing in his voice.

"I do," she said. "There's a bit of a cloud written across your forehead."

Caught out by her knowing he was not okay, Butch looked away. Mrs. Biddle reminded him of his sister—she was franker than frank, when most people were only interested in saying, "How are you? Fine," as a way of greeting you.

Still, she numbered among Butch's favorite residents of Seal Cove. She had an eye on the town, not because she was of those women who sat at a neighbor's kitchen table drinking coffee and eating slivers of coffee cake, airing each morning's gossip, but because of being the guidance counselor. He'd watched her hand-pick the kids who were both smart and seasoned enough to leave their provincial town to go to college and get spit out into the world. And, often enough, she picked them right. Unfortunately, her strong sixth sense led to her being considered a busybody by some. But not Butch. He believed her ability to see inside people a whole lot better than most was a valuable asset.

Like, when Molly had arrived in Seal Cove, Mrs. Biddle had immediately seen this newcomer was someone she might safely take in. It was as if she was able to see around a corner, while the rest of the town was still saying, "Who's that new woman with the whacked-off hair, who wears jeans too big for her and goes around looking as if she just came face-to-face with a moose? What the hell's she doing here?"

"I'm about to go in the diner for a corn muffin and a coffee, if you'd like to join me," said Mrs. Biddle.

Butch tilted his head one way, then the other, but said, "Okay, sounds good," and they went back up Centre Street together.

"Where's Molly this afternoon?" she asked as soon as they gave their orders.

He shrugged. "I was about to ask you."

Mrs. Biddle only drew her mouth tightly closed.

"I figured she might be doing you an errand."

Mrs. Biddle shook her head.

"You need anything done around the house? You know I can always come up and help you out with repairs," he said, deliberately changing the subject.

"Thanks, but no. Not that there isn't always something going wrong in a house," she added. "But Molly's a big help."

"I'm sure she is." This brought him to wonder just how much Molly talked to Mrs. Biddle, and did she know that Molly had turned down his proposal.

Mrs. Biddle stirred a spoonful of sugar in her coffee, holding her hazel eyes directly upon him, as if she were seeing the dark cloud cross his forehead again.

He sipped coffee and his cup clattered in the saucer when he put it back down. What was the big deal, making him feel like a schoolboy? She wasn't *his* guidance counselor. Finally, he drew in a deep breath and asked what he wanted to know. "How was it you came to meet Molly when she first arrived here?"

As Mrs. Biddle quartered and buttered her corn muffin, taking her time to answer, Butch felt the sinkhole on the booth seat beneath him, hollowed out by the rear ends of the regulars like Mrs. Biddle, some of whom frequented this place more than once a day.

"I was sitting right where I'm sitting now when I noticed this forlorn-looking young woman holding her head as if it was about to split apart, so I offered her an aspirin." She went on, telling him how she'd beckoned her over, and then seen she wasn't as young as she'd originally thought. "She was nervous, almost shaky, but I met her eyes. Years of settling down misbehaving kids has taught me how to assure people I'm not going to bite, if they'll just sit down. Though, just yesterday, I had a session with a young girl that made me wonder if my talent was drying up."

Butch hadn't expected it to be so easy to get Mrs. Biddle to talk. Her reputation was for knowing everything but also for keeping it to herself.

"When I asked Molly what brought her here, she told me she'd seen a magazine ad with waves crashing against the cliffs, the forests rising up a dark green, and how the coast line looked so rough, like the land was fighting to be here against the huge sea, and that picture had stuck in her mind and made her want to see Cape Breton."

"Yeah," Butch said, "she's definitely drawn to the water."

"She asked if I had always lived here, so I told her about Doc, how he worried this place would be too provincial for me, but he was wrong. I was homesick the early years, but he'd take me every spring back to Montreal—making sure I kept up my French—and gradually I became someone who might be considered a Cape Bretonian.

"Of course, I had to tell her Doc was dead nearly two years. She seemed so shocked she went pale. I sent her over to Neil's Harbour to the B&B because she didn't have a place to stay. But the next morning, when I found out she'd slept all night between some rocks down at the shore, I offered her Doc's cottage."

Butch drew in a quick breath. My God, Molly had been through more than he had even imagined.

"I sure am glad she stayed," he said after a long silence.

"Yes," she said. "I wasn't sure you were ever going to run up against someone to bring you outside of yourself."

He was sure she was thinking of him losing Janet to his bachelor foolishness, and would have taken her remark as a criticism, had she not said it as if she was merely yielding to his nature. And she was right about that.

"I hope nothing's gone wrong between you two," she added, her gaze steady.

He looked down into his empty coffee cup, then out the window. The sea was roughing up a bit. It would be choppy tomorrow. Not that it mattered. Boat was up in dry dock. He wasn't sure how much time passed as he contemplated the weather.

"I hear from Janet every Christmas," Mrs. Biddle said, breaking the silence. "She's got three growing girls on her hands."

"I know," he said. "I get those same Christmas pictures." He shrank a bit, thinking Mrs. Biddle was bringing up Janet because she thought he was about to lose Molly the same way.

Another silence and then Mrs. Biddle came right out with it. "So where is that Molly?"

Butch sat more upright. "What do you mean? Don't you think she's back up on the hill by now?"

"I don't know, because when I looked, it seemed like she had taken some of her things from the cottage. That's why I was looking for her in town before I ran into you."

"What?" A shiver of fear ran through him. "I asked her to marry me over a week ago. She said she couldn't, but she wouldn't explain why. And she's been rattled ever since," he blurted out, dropping all pretense of holding anything back.

Mrs. Biddle signaled for the check, took out some money, and snapped her purse shut. "Let's go find her," she said.

They did a quick scan of the town, going through the Co-op grocery and then Butch went in the bar to make sure Mac hadn't seen her. They went down to the water, in case she had gone to the wharf, and although there was no one in sight, he called out her name while Mrs. Biddle stood quietly, arms folded across her chest, as the wind blew in a stiff breeze.

He became more alarmed by the moment. My God! Would she leave town of her own accord? Or might that husband have come after her? Maybe she was walking out on the cliffs, trying to straighten out things in her head. But then why would she take some of her things from Mrs. Biddle's cottage?

"She could be up at your place," Mrs. Biddle suggested. "Why don't you go back and check there, and I'll check the cottage again, and then you call me."

"Will do," he said, and silently they ascended the hill up past the diner and parted at the split in the road.

Jimbo was hungry and followed Butch around as he called out for Molly and peeked around corners, foolishly hoping she'd be there, despite knowing something was wrong. He quickly filled Jimbo's bowl, then called Mrs. Biddle to learn she had also found nothing.

"I'm going out in the truck," Butch said, "To the cliffs down toward Neil's Harbour."

"Take your phone," she reminded him. "Call me if you find her."

"If I can get service, I will."

"I'll await your call," she said, in a voice that steadied him.

He parked and walked the cliffs, calling out and looking down the steep, jagged inclines, dreading she might be found there. The wind whistled in his ears and the dark was coming in like a curtain being slowly let down. The waves crashed, and these sounds that often soothed him now created a cacophony. Where was she? Had his asking her to marry him caused her to leave without even saying goodbye?

As he yelled out her name and it echoed off the cliff, he let out a sob. Christ, she had his heart, how could she go off and leave him?

He went back to the truck and started down the Cabot Trail. Fortunately, there was only this one perimeter road that went either farther out and then across to the other coast or else back west toward the mainland. Surely that was the direction she would have gone. The light was almost finished and the temperature was dipping. He peered out along the roadside, straining to see someone walking, and casting his eyes off into the short, scrappy woods that sided the road.

About two kilometers out, he thought he saw a figure on the right. He put on his brights, but it was only a homemade sign someone had put up adjacent to a mailbox. BLUEBERRIES, YOU PICK 'EM. You'd think they'd take it down after summer was past, he thought. Then, just as he had begun to despair that he'd ever find her, there she was, her old black backpack on her back and a gym bag slung over her shoulder, riding at her hip. Walking at a steady pace, not looking back, not putting out her thumb.

His heart was seized with a joyous charge of adrenalin. He pulled up and was about to honk when she looked around, saw him, and turned her hands up along with a shrug of her shoulders that said, "Okay, I've been caught and I don't know that I really wanted to get away." He hit the button to open the passenger window and gave her a big smile.

"Please," he said, "you look like you could use a lift. Get in."

She hiked herself up and in, throwing the small shoulder bag onto the floor and cradling the backpack in her lap as if it were a baby.

As soon as the door slammed shut, he cut the engine, turned to her, his eyes washing all over her face, looking for whether she wanted him, and he saw the small muscle twitching beneath her eye, which made her seem so vulnerable he couldn't hold back any longer but reached across and kissed her. She didn't stop him, but she didn't kiss him passionately either, the way she had the first time on the dock.

He called Mrs. Biddle as soon as they got back to his place, to tell her Molly was safely with him and would be staying the night and probably not coming back to the cottage until after their workday tomorrow.

"Thank God," she said, sighing in relief.

As soon as he hung up, squeezing her eyes shut, Molly said, "I know I need to explain."

"Yes, you do," he said, "but not tonight. Let's just fix some supper and go to bed." After a pause, he had another idea. "Or maybe just go to bed hungry."

Chapter 11

Edith Biddle went from school to the Ingonish library the next afternoon, determined to do the search she should have done when Molly first appeared. She took the computer farthest from the librarian's desk and strained to remember when exactly Molly had arrived. June, but early June because school was still in session, although the kids who helped with lobster season would have already skipped out. Was it five years ago or four? Upstate New York, Molly had said, but Butch had pinned it down to New Paltz, a college town. Edith googled for a local newspaper and found one—*The New Paltz Times*, a weekly. Fine. It wouldn't take much to look through the whole month of June for 2004 *and* 2005, if she needed to.

Dottie, the librarian, came along wheeling a cart of books she was shelving. "Hello there, Edith, nice to see you."

"Nice to see you, too. All's well?" she ended with an inflection, hoping to push the conversation to a point of termination.

"Janie'll soon be coming out to visit with Jason, my grandson. I'm sure she'd love to see you," said Dottie.

Edith nodded without looking away from the computer. "Indeed, I'll be happy to see her." A smart girl, Janie had been one of those Edith had encouraged to go to college. She'd become a writer and published her first novel, a romance set in Cape Breton, and now she had a baby. She'd have asked more about Janie if the library wasn't due to close in less than an hour, but now she made a small, dismissive wave to signal that she was here on urgent business. Which, indeed, she was.

Yet, once Dottie moved on with her cart, Edith found her fingers reluctant to press the proper keys. It was too simple to look into things these days, as if there was no such thing as privacy, and she objected to that. As it was, she knew too much about many of the townspeople because of having to delve into the secrets of their children. The children carried the disturbance, but so often they were only acting out because their parents were at each other, or were out of work and didn't know where to turn, or someone in the home was lying in a hospital bed in the middle of the dining room, dying of cancer. She was privy to enough of people's troubles to be happy to be left out when it came to Molly's silences. It was a pleasure just to share a quiet hello in the morning when they crossed paths, or to sit together a few minutes outside in the evening if the weather was good, taking in the mood of the ocean as the clouds puffed past or strung themselves across the sky, the varying shades of pink stunning them as the sun went down.

The first morning she'd brought Molly to the cottage, she'd meant only to offer it to her for a few days, maybe a couple of weeks. She'd sensed through and through the woman was running from something that had her scared witless. But she'd also sensed she was no one to be frightened of.

And she'd been right. Molly was a gentle soul. She kept the place immaculate and kept Edith from being so afraid that going up to Martin's cottage would set off a morose pining for her loss. Which is why she had kept Molly on, and she didn't want that to change.

But yesterday, when she and Butch had split up to search for Molly and she'd gone to the cottage to see if she might find a clue as to where Molly had gone, in the bedroom she'd stopped in front of a small exquisitely-carved wooden box Martin had brought home from one of his trips, and something had compelled her to turn the catch and flip open the lid. What had she found there but a long ponytail held together with one simple rubber band, curled up into a bun. She'd jumped back, unnerved, remembering the blunt haircut Molly had arrived with.

She should have asked more of her then. Pushed to find out what sort of trouble she was in. Well, better late . . . as they say.

The librarian rolled the rattling cart past her again and squeezed behind the desk to check out a book for a young girl. Looking up, Edith realized immediately that the girl was Chrissie, who was wiggling her bony fingers in a quirky wave. Edith waved back, then returned to the computer. Just do it, she prompted herself and punched the search key for the first week of June 2004. She could at least determine what sort of a newspaper this *New Paltz Times* was.

It was a real local rag, listing cultural and community events. The front page carried a story about the push for construction of a new town garage with solar panels on its roof, and a story about the new, very young mayor, twenty-five. How had he gotten elected, even in a college town? Who had married several gay couples and become a magnet for proponents of gay marriage, even though he claimed he himself was not gay. Hmm. Here in Seal Cove they had a couple of women who lived together, and there was a household of two men over in Neil's Harbour whom no one seemed to mind, but did they need to marry? Or did that make things more complicated than they needed to be? Still, she admired the young mayor for taking a position and standing up for others. Not enough young people thinking for themselves these days.

She quickly scanned the rest of the paper, looking for someone who resembled Molly, even searched for the name Molly, but nothing came up. Relieved, she breathed deeply and realized she'd been holding her breath. What had she thought she was going to find? That sweet woman . . . What could she be guilty of?

Still, no sooner had she shut down the site, it occurred to her that of course Molly had likely changed her name. But she didn't go back to look again. Enough for one day, she decided.

She searched for a good book instead, and when she went to check out an Agatha Christie she had never read, there was a picture of a good-sized baby with a robust smile propped in a frame on Dottie's desk. Her grandson Jason, must be, thought Edith, as she noted Janie's DNA in the shape of his mouth and the bright eyes.

"Tell Janie to bring Jason up to meet me when she's here," she said as Dottie stamped her book and handed it back.

Later that evening, when Edith went to the window and saw light emanating from the cottage, her heart skipped lighter. She hadn't blamed Butch for not wanting to let Molly out of his sight the night before, but seeing the cottage dark had created a darkness in her. She still had a gray feeling about Molly not being willing to marry Butch. Plus, there was the rolled-up ponytail she had found in the box. But at least Molly was back.

Edith Biddle had been married and a full partner for most of her life, standing devotedly at Martin's side. People thought they were quirky, especially after he built the cottage and went up there to live, while she stayed in the house below, but that was just what happened after thirty-five years of marriage. You didn't always have to be tuned to the Discovery Channel. You already knew each other quite well, and if you wanted some time to yourself, so what. She liked her privacy as much as he liked his. It was only tragic he hadn't been down below with her the night he had the heart attack, but she'd promised herself not to go over and over that track. There wouldn't have been another doctor to call within seventy-five kilometers, even if she'd been right at his side, but she might have been able to do something like what she'd seen him do to Timothy McMahon when he'd pressed his chest and blown air into him and brought him back to life. Although when Timothy was a bit daft after that, Martin speculated he'd lost a few brain cells before the air got into him. And Martin would have hated living on, had he lost even a smidgeon of his brainpower. So maybe it wasn't so bad he had gone that way.

Of course, there had been times she'd wondered what life would be like without him, but she'd been thinking age seventy-five or eighty, not sixty. She'd speculated. Would she return to Montreal, where her sister still lived but where she now felt very much a stranger? Or would she live out her time in Seal Cove?

She had enough years in the school system that she could have retired and gone back to Quebec straight away when Martin died, but she stayed on because her job was an anchor and she felt untethered in every other way. Too light. As if a swift wind might blow her off the cliff. She'd been afraid to go up and revisit the cottage for a long time after he passed, and if she tried to pinpoint why, it had to do with this lightness.

She took off her navy-blue corduroy blazer and hung it in her closet, dangled her slacks from their bottoms and shook them to reestablish their creases and folded them over a hanger. Then she donned a pair of well-worn sweat pants and a flannel shirt, and shuffled into her fur-lined slippers. She often thought she might as well put on her pajamas. Why have to change into them later since she was not going anywhere and no one was coming to see her? But if Martin were still here, he'd have come down to spend at least a part of the evening with her and certainly would have thrown a fit had he caught her going straight to her pajamas like a depressed person.

In the kitchen she cracked a couple of eggs to make an omelet with some local goat cheese and popped a piece of bread in the toaster. She ate her omelet with contentment, knowing Molly was up above. The night before she hadn't been able to stay seated but had paced and paced until Butch called to say he'd found her. He hadn't said why she'd taken off, only that he'd found her on the road and wasn't going to let her out of his sight, so she'd be staying the night with him. Edith wanted to know more but was not going to chafe about it. She was happy enough just to know Molly was back.

After she ate, she took her plate and cutlery to the sink and went to the kitchen window seat, where she could see up to the lights of the cottage. The moonlight struck the bench Martin had so carefully crafted, glinting off the smooth sandstone, and she remembered the night she had sat up there longer than usual with Molly, sharing one of the secrets she'd never told another soul on this island. She hadn't meant to; she'd only meant to ask Molly if she'd ever had children.

"No," Molly said, "I don't have any," drawing each word out so that Edith detected a sadness, before Molly turned it around on her, saying, "You?"

And it popped right out of her. "I never had any, either. Martin and I thought we would have at least two, but we tried for a while, and it didn't happen."

Molly looked away as she so often did and Edith interpreted this as shyness, but when she turned back, it seemed as if she was waiting for Edith to go on.

"It would have made for a very different life if I had gotten pregnant," Edith said, trying to iron out the wistful tone that had made its way into her voice. "I suspect I compensated with the children I counseled at school. Some of my favorites, especially when they were having a tough time at home, seemed as if they became my kids."

Molly nodded. "My seventh-grade gym teacher was like that. She seemed to really care about me and what was going on at home. I was pretty good in track. That's why she liked me—she wanted me to win the broad jump in intramurals, and then later in the county—but it meant a lot that she really seemed to see me."

Edith was hoping Molly would go on to say what it was the teacher brought out about her, but she only said, "Schools could use more people like you."

There was a moment of silence and then she added, "I'm sorry you couldn't have your own children, though. You'd have been a good mom."

"Likewise," Edith returned. "Did you want them badly?"

"At the time, I guess I did," Molly said. She told Edith she always assumed she'd grow up, get married, and have kids. She shifted her weight on the bench then and seemed to cast her concentration on the sea, as if deciding she had said too much already.

Edith asked if she'd ever considered adopting or inseminating.

"That wasn't in the cards," was all Molly said.

Edith went on to tell her she'd had the testing but nothing

showed up. The next thing would have been to test Martin for his sperm count, but he resisted. "I might have pushed him harder," she said. "I often regretted that I didn't. I don't think he would have gone against me on something as important as that, but time went by and then it seemed a sore subject to open up, and next thing I knew I was getting too old to bear children anyway."

Edith, too, now concentrated on the sea, the great expanse of it, and the smallness of the two of them looking at it from above. But the relief of speaking out drove her on. "I felt it again as I went into menopause, though, that my body was finishing up with that purpose, and I went through a melancholy not quite like any mood I ever had before, as if it was hooked right up to my organs and they were weeping. That went on for maybe six months, but then it passed and left me alone."

"That's good," Molly said, contributing nothing further.

Now, lying back far enough against the pillows in the window seat so she could see the stars, Edith wondered whether Martin had lost a certain proclivity for sex when he'd been forced to speculate his sperm either didn't travel well, or there weren't enough of them, or they swam away from the egg instead of toward it. As a doctor, he would know it would be pure ignorance to correlate these possibilities with sexual prowess. But she wondered if he might have felt something like what she'd felt with menopause—the knowledge he was not going to be procreating taking away his energy.

Martin had courted her before they married in the most respectable way. He hadn't pushed for sex like the other fellows she had dated. And she liked that about him. He was serious about where he was headed. He would take her out to a movie and kiss her goodnight at the door, sometimes staying there in the shadows with her for a considerable time, the two of them pressing the heat of their bodies together, before he'd pull back, kiss her nose playfully, and say, "I'd better go, lots of studying to do for tomorrow."

In medical school then, he was convinced he was not up to par and would be found out as a fraud if he didn't study enough. She was sure this was an illusion, he was as smart as any of them, but she saw that he put a great deal of pressure on himself because of this feeling.

Anyway, sex had waned after a few years of marriage, and at first she hadn't minded, as she hadn't always felt inclined, at least not until he got her warmed up. But he'd been a good, considerate lover, staying with building her up to a pitch, and she couldn't say she hadn't enjoyed that. And those times she had felt as if her body had shattered, as if she were a star that had split into a million pieces in the universe, some of them falling to earth and some of them floating away into the galaxies, she'd carried those times forward in her memory for as long as she could hold them.

But after they'd stopped making love on a regular basis, she'd started being shy again, modest, like she'd been as a girl. And in later years, self-conscious about the places where her body was sagging. Like if she was over him and saw her stomach falling forward, its tautness gone, she didn't like her body anymore. She had never thought of herself as a beauty but had once had a good, if stocky, shape, and Martin had admired it, and secretly, she had, too.

She wondered if Martin had ever looked elsewhere for sex. He attended his medical school class reunions annually, usually without her, and two or three times a year he'd go to conferences or courses to stay up-to-date on new developments. And sometimes he returned with what she perceived to be a gleam in his eye. Was it possible he had visited a prostitute? The medical conferences were always more heavily attended by men than women, so she couldn't imagine he'd found a woman to have casual sex with, but what about another man? Before she'd married Martin, her sister had once asked her if she thought there was any chance he was gay.

"Why do you ask?" she'd said, covering the shock that was jarring her like an earthquake.

"I don't know. Just a certain way he carries himself."

"Well, he's very sure he wants us to get married," she said with conviction, but she'd been left with her sister's comment popping up in her mind for many years to come.

She missed Martin every day still, his handsome features, his dexterous hands with their long, delicate fingers, his warm voice telling her of his day. She missed how he ate so carefully, maintaining good manners always, touching his napkin to his lips when he was finished. Those lips that had nightly kissed her gently on the mouth before he gave her a little wave as he stepped out to climb the very stairs he had carved into the side of the cliff, leading up to the cottage. She had felt the loss of him at the very center of her core.

Still did now, but not so achingly, because most of the time Molly was up there watching over her. Thank God Butch had found her. Though she must not forget, in spite of her relief, to continue her search at the library.

Chapter 12

Cookie slept fitfully and woke to Butch's eyes upon her. The longing in his gaze reached into her but, at the same time, confused her. Did he want her to wake up and explain what she'd been doing walking out there? Or did he just want her?

He touched her nose and kissed her forehead, like a wayward child's. They got up, ate breakfast, and entered the day as if it were any day, spreading out nets, repairing them, talking about the fishing back in June, remembering times when they'd seen the seals that had likely created these good-sized holes in the nets. Yet, she was heavily aware it was not any day as she waded through it, studying him aslant, dreading the moment he'd ask her to explain more clearly why she couldn't marry him.

She was glad when he suggested they finish early and resume their work the next morning, and she gathered up her things to go back to her cottage.

"Let me give you a lift," he said as she hoisted her bags onto her shoulders.

"No, thanks." She shook her head. "I need the walk."

"Carrying all that weight?"

"I guess I carried it a bit further yesterday," she said, then instantly regretted her words, realizing she had given him an opening.

"Indeed, you did," he said soberly, but he didn't ask for more.

She didn't get off that easy with Mrs. Biddle, who came out with a wave and a smile as Molly was about to pass her patio, and while she didn't let on that she knew Molly had been missing or ask for an explanation, she stopped her cold, saying she had a small special request.

"Chrissie, the girl who's been dropping pounds week by week until she looks freakishly thin . . . I'm at a bit of a loss with her."

Cookie watched and waited as Mrs. Biddle interlocked her fingers in a prayer position. Mrs. Biddle's confidence, which usually ran high, seemed at a low. She cleared her throat, said, "I'd like to bring her up to meet you and see if you can give her some encouragement. I have a hunch you can help her. Just a hunch, but it would be a great service if you'd at least give it a try."

Cookie's hands started to tingle. "Me?" she said with a catch in her throat.

"She doesn't seem to feel she's worthy of being seen, or maybe someone has undermined her sense of entitlement. Regardless, she needs a boost, and the situation is becoming critical."

Critical? Small, special request? Cookie's brain jumped to alert.

"What do you mean by critical?" she asked, her breathlessness from walking up the hill compounded by the fright this special request was bringing on.

Mrs. Biddle opened her hands and turned them up, as if to emphasize her dire need of help. "I'm afraid. Some anorexic girls become so firm in their resolve to stop eating, they can actually die."

Why her? How could she possibly help? Cookie wondered.

"What would I be able to do?" she squeaked out through her tightening throat.

"You're a calming presence, and like I said, it's just a hunch . . ."

What about the father? she wanted to ask, but how could she tell Mrs. Biddle he was the one person in Seal Cove she most dreaded running into because he still slid his eyes sideways when he saw her, with a look that said, "Bad egg, go back where you came from. I know there's something wrong with you." Just about everyone else in town, if they did have suspicions, didn't announce them. Oh, these were rugged, nonsmiling people; some of them actually *liked* it when the weather got colder in winter! Still, his scowl couldn't be attributed to that.

"Is this too much to ask?" Mrs. Biddle's eyes narrowed the way they had that first night in the diner.

Cookie owed her everything. How could anything be too much to ask?

"I'll try," she said at last. "I don't know what I can say to her, but I'll try." And then she escaped to her cottage as rapidly as she could.

In the middle of the night, she woke with her throat so constricted she felt as if she had breathed in the feathery contents of a milkweed pod. She made her way into the kitchen and took a sip of water, hoping to wash away the awful choking feeling. Leaning in over the sink, she coughed and coughed but still managed to gasp only tiny bits of air. Her hands went numb and there was a strange ringing in her ears.

Heart attack! Was that what she was having? Like Doc? She threw cold water on her face and took another sip of water. That seemed to help, so she did it again. Her heart fluttered. Was this what it did in a heart attack? No, it squeezed and gave you chest pain. Hers wasn't chest pain so much as *chest panic*. Maybe this was asthma. Although she had never had asthma. In fact, as a girl she'd been proud of her ability to hold her breath longer than any of the other kids.

No, this was not a heart attack or asthma; this was the result of being in a trap. How could she help that poor girl? What if Chrissie's father found out that she, the evil Molly, was with his daughter? And what was going to become of her and Butch once she told him what she had done?

She went to her couch that looked onto the sea. The silver moon was three quarters full, and she could see far in the distance, making out the docks where Butch's boat was moored in summer, and then on out to the great beyond, where they went every day during lobster season.

By now her breathing had deepened and the feeling of fuzzy stuff in her throat had disappeared. Still, she was afraid to go back to bed, afraid sleep might bring on another attack. Was it possible to have an attack and not wake up? She wondered had Doc woken up in time to realize he was dying. You always heard. So-and-so died in his sleep. But was that just because no one saw him die?

She sighed deeply. Butch had asked her to marry him. Under other circumstances she would be celebrating, but instead his proposal seemed to ruin what they'd had these past six months. She'd imagined they'd made a silent agreement to stay in the moment. She'd never thought he might want to make a future with her. She closed her eyes, remembering the Sunday he'd come down and sat with her on the dock, inching closer and closer, and she'd thought, I shouldn't, but how can I not, as he leaned in to kiss her.

Now everything was a lie except that she loved him, and he loved her like she'd never been loved before, but he didn't really know who she was, and how could she tell him without destroying everything? Her crime had to be paid for. Yes, she had paid every day for many days with her nightmares, her four years of loneliness, and before that, she had paid in advance with all the times Warren had abused her, but these past months it was as if she had ceased paying for her crime, and now she was back to paying in spades.

She wondered about Nita. And her sister. What must they have felt when she disappeared without a word, leaving her husband stabbed and dying on the kitchen floor. To this day, she was not sure Warren had died from the wounds she inflicted, except that if he hadn't, he'd have found her, and she'd likely be dead by now.

She ran her hand through her hair and felt the dampness left from her full-blown panic attack. It wasn't just the idea of taking on Mrs. Biddle's request with the father lurking in the background; it was the trap of having to hide who she was from Butch, walking gingerly to avoid a misstep. She'd suffered that walk with Warren almost from the start, and it almost drove her crazier than the actual beatings and forced sex. The deception to keep him from being provoked started when they were only maybe a year married, the day her old high school classmate Lenny came to do some remodeling of their bathroom.

She'd simply offered Lenny a cup of coffee and sat with him at the kitchen table while they spoke a few minutes about some of the others kids they had known. "Do you know what happened to Monty?" he asked her. "He went to Vietnam and didn't come back."

"Oh yeah, I heard about that. So sad," she said.

"What about that Betsy who smelled bad, who used to sit between me and you in English because the teacher made us sit in alphabetical order?"

"Oh, yeah, I'd forgotten all about her odor."

"Wasn't easy to forget," he said, holding his nose and squinching up his mouth the way he used to as a boy.

"No," she said, laughing at the face he made just the way she always had at school, a refreshing breeze flowing in through the screen door from the patio as she remembered how much she had always liked Lenny.

Then, with good manners, Lenny had taken his empty cup and deposited it in the sink and gone to pack up his tools.

But when Warren came home for lunch and saw the cup she had not yet put in the dishwasher, he wanted to know who had been there. "No one," she said. "Just when Lenny finished putting the new sink cabinet in the bathroom, I gave him a cup of coffee."

That was all it took for Warren to become convinced she'd been ready to take Lenny to bed with her, or wanted to, or was thinking of maybe doing that in the future. God forbid, he came home and found Lenny doing anything but carpentry, he would pick her up and throw her into the wall, and then throw Lenny out the window. He was rigid with anger as he made these threats and by the time he finished, she was shaking with fear and begging him to calm down. Telling him she loved him and had no interest in another man, but had just liked Lenny as a person in high school, and please, she hadn't meant to cause any trouble.

But her mentioning liking Lenny, had set him off all over again. "See, you're contradicting yourself. You say you don't like anyone but me, but then you admit you like him."

"But not *that way*," she objected.

"Woman to man or man to woman, *like is like*, anyway you put it," he lay down as the final word.

She didn't think so, but seeing Warren steam like that, she thought of Lenny so carefully putting down his cup in the sink and rather wished she were with someone like him, which made her start to question herself. Was Warren right? Had she been flirting with Lenny when she'd laughed at him holding his nose?

It went on from there. If she stayed home from work (at Warren's request) to supervise someone coming to fix something or clean the furnace or deliver a load of mushroom manure for her garden, Warren would suddenly find time to pop home for lunch, but she knew it was really to check up on her.

"Just making sure everything is A-Okay," he'd say.

"If you'd have let me know you were coming, I'd have made you some lunch."

"You already did," he'd say, "and I ate it onsite an hour ago."

He'd put his arm around her neck in a hammerlock then and squeeze it just a little too tight, lean over, kiss her on the top of the head and whisper, "Be good," before releasing her.

Why hadn't she left him way back then? He'd trapped her with shame. Filled her with doubt about how trustworthy she was.

She remembered one afternoon she lost track of time, out swimming at the Big Deep with Nita. It was nothing but a big bend in the river that had hollowed out, and on a hot day, lots of people stopped by there for a swim. Not a lot of space to swim, but you could hang out on a rock, dangling your feet in the cold water, or you could get all the way in and just float around, trying to stay in the places where the cold springs kept the water cooler. It wasn't like a public pool where you could look up and see the time on a big clock, and her watch was up on the bank where they'd left their stuff on a towel, and she and Nita got to talking, Nita telling her about a talk she'd gone to at the monastery the day before, how the monk said, "Everyone has a dark side," and she'd said to Nita, "Really. What do you think mine is?"

"You're too nice," Nita said. And before she could ask how being too nice could be dark, Nita went on, "and it lets people walk all over you."

That's when she noticed her fingers were turning into prunes, heaved herself out of the water, and discovered it was already past five.

She rushed home as fast as possible, but Warren had been waiting half an hour, drinking cold beers on their front steps, working up a seething sweat.

"Man works hard all day to bring home the bread," he said, "and no wife to greet him. Where is she?" He raised his eyes to glare at her. "Out gallivanting somewhere."

"Sorry," she mumbled.

"Where?" he asked, raising his voice a notch. "Where were you?"

"I got off work at three and met Nita in Woodstock, and we went to the Big Deep for a swim."

"Were there guys there?" he demanded.

"I guess so, a few. It was hot, so there were a lot of people, but I was just hanging out in the water with Nita."

He only gave an exaggerated nod of his head, as if to indicate he was imagining exactly what happened. And she'd skipped past him, saying she'd have dinner ready in a few minutes, calculating what she had in the freezer that would be fastest. But when he came in as she was putting a cubed steak on a plate for him, he twisted her arm up behind her back and leaned over, pretending to take a bite out of her neck and whispered, "I'm a mason, for Christ's sake. If you want to swim, I'll build you a goddamn swimming pool. But I don't want you swimming over there with just anyone in the creek."

He was pretty drunk; she saw him sway as he made it to the table while she rubbed her shoulder, thinking he didn't know how to judge his own strength.

She asked her mother shortly after that if this strong-arming sort of stuff was to be expected in a marriage.

"He makes good money," her mother said, barely looking up from the peas she was shelling, "and, long as he holds his temper when it comes to dealing with his clients, he's bound to take out his upsets on you."

"But I work, too," Cookie countered.

"And make a lot less money."

"Doesn't mean I'm not on my feet all day, in front of those hot baking ovens or else out front, trying to be friendly to the customers."

Her mother merely nodded. Then, after a moment of contemplation, she shocked Cookie with, "Why don't you get yourself pregnant and start having a family?"

"Are you kidding me?" Cookie said. "Warren doesn't want kids, at least not now." And she thought but did not say, *What's to keep him from beating up on the kids, too?*

"Just skip a few days of your birth control."

"Mom!" Cookie covered her mouth with her hand. "I'd be scared to death what Warren would do if he found out I'd gotten pregnant that way."

"Once the child arrives, he'll be thrilled," said her mother, but Cookie did not cotton to the idea, which seemed off the mark. Cookie knew her mother had taken her own abuse; maybe she just wanted everyone else to have a taste of it.

It was her sister, Annie, who had clued her differently the summer she bounced in, all glowing, and sat Cookie down and said, "So can you see I'm happy?" and went on to explain, "I'm in love . . ." And before Cookie could get out, "Who is he?" Annie added, ". . . with a woman."

"Wow, well, I'm so happy for you," Cookie said, doing her best to disguise her shock.

The woman's name was Denise and she was a police detective who worked with domestic abuse and sex crime victims. Annie seemed so proud of the work her girlfriend was doing, educating the police force as well as the public about things like battering. She went into it loudly and clearly right in front of Warren at dinner when she visited, announcing attitudes like "blame the victim" had to stop. The phrase rang up an alarm in Cookie, sending a charge right out her limbs. It made her wonder if Annie even remembered how, often when they were kids and should both have gotten in trouble, she handed Cookie over to their father when it came time to get whacked.

The first time Warren actually beat her, it had been over an offense no greater than her coming home late from the swimming hole. They had gone to place a gravestone on his father's grave. Cookie's mother came along to show her respects for Warren's father, and after standing around in the cemetery with the preacher saying a few words, Warren asked her mother to drop Cookie off at home, so he could stop and have a few beers with some of the fellows he worked with at the emergency squad.

Cookie's father had died not long before so, feeling a bit rocky about going home alone, she asked her mother to drop her off at Nita's instead, knowing Nita could drive her the rest of the way later. And that's exactly what had happened. Only Warren had gotten soused so quickly that one of his buddies had driven him home. Putting him there already when she arrived.

When she went to put away her coat, he came at her. Though he was barely able to stay on his feet, he stalked her into the corner of their bedroom and smacked her across the face, even while she was apologizing for being late.

"Sorry," he said, "I'll make you sorry," and he pressed that spot just under her breastbone and ground his thumb into her, making a black-and-blue mark that stayed for weeks. Then he pulled her, lurching, to the bed, and they bounced down on it, and he yanked off her waist button and fumbled to pull down her pants.

She was still clutching both hands to her chest where it felt like he had put a hole in her. He managed to stand halfway up to drop his pants to his knees, fell back down on top of her, spread her legs and pushed into her, muttering, "Sorry, sorry, you'll be sorry." Raking away at what seemed like her nothing of a body.

She'd slept in the guest room that night after nursing herself in the bathroom, holding a cold washrag to her face, examining his thumbprint on her chest and feeling the soreness of his invasion down below. She remembered holding onto the edge of the bed, trying to stop the thoughts of escape that raced round and round in her head. Where would she go? What would he do without her? How would she cover up the purple marks on her face to go to work in the morning?

But morning came and Warren acted truly stumped about who had given her that big shiner. "I know I have a hangover," he said, "but I wasn't *that* drunk."

"You were," was all she said, sullen but firm. "You certainly were."

And hard as she tried to make her face look right with makeup, (and she would later become very good at it), she called in sick for the next two days, so that everyone wouldn't be asking who slugged her.

Butch was a life-giver, not a life-taker. He did not trap a mouse, except in a Havaheart. Whatever she had done to deceive him was because she didn't want him to know what she was capable of. And yet, there was no way they could go on without her telling him, and she so dreaded doing that, fearing it would be the end of them.

The sea churned out there in the distance, and she thought about the day she had been seasick on the journey here. Maybe she should have jumped overboard and been done with it. But she'd clutched so strongly at life. The hours and days after she'd escaped Bearsville, she'd not known what she was doing but had pushed on to get to somewhere she might have a chance to just plain live. She'd been held down so long under Warren's hand, which she'd come to think of as a dark cloud looming over her. Shading her. Keeping her in a sort of hibernation. Oh, she got outside, she planted her garden every year, thank God, because that had been the place where she could feel some life as the plants she tended grew robust. Sometimes they turned moldy and wilted, and she identified with them then, too. Mostly, she grew quiet, but not in a harmonious way, because she was guarded, all hush-hush. She kept to herself and didn't let anyone know *what* she was feeling, like a tea kettle on a burner turned down low enough it let out a whine instead of blowing its whistle. She was all the time breathing around this constriction, which she could now see had been rage, the rage which had made her execute the act she still found nearly impossible to believe she had carried out against Warren, who weighed almost double her weight. Warren, who had many times bloodied her nose or chopped his fist into the middle of her back or held her up against the wall with one hand while he undid his pants with the other, his eyes mad with whatever notion he had concocted about how bad she was and why she deserved this.

Her breath got short and ragged again and, remembering him that way, she was not sorry she had done it. She was only sorry about how it had made her leave everyone she had ever known behind. Despite the darkness still hanging over her, she'd do anything not to lose the life she had now.

Chapter 13

Early in the morning, she chugged up Butch's walkway, looking a bit worn but waving to him as she got closer, then turning up her face for his light kiss.

Jimbo had already charged out to meet her, jumping with exuberance.

"Looks like it's going to be a nice day," Butch said.

"Umm," she agreed, casting her eyes out on the ocean, which was still coming fully to light from the sunrise.

Butch took up the other end of the net she'd been trying to straighten out and shook it so that the knotted area came free. She couldn't help but notice what she always noticed, how his eyes crinkled up at the first hint of a smile, like a signal that he was first and always driven by a friendly impulse. "Okay," he said, "we've got it."

"Wow, look at the size of that hole," she said, shaking her head. "Are you sure this net's worth saving?"

"Why not?" He shrugged. "The way I figure it, we have all day, and just about everything's worth saving." He stepped deeper into the room. "Let's lay it out in front of the woodstove."

Now with the net on the floor, the hole in its center looked about the size of a large seal. Seals were usually the culprits, eating through to steal the fish caught in the net. Their lazy way of fishing.

Still, she adored their slick movements and the way they teased and played when she and Butch were out on the boat.

She lifted one jagged edge and tugged to position the hole closed, smoothing out the tuck in the net. Then she stood to reach for one of the large needles, and backed into Butch, who turned her and grasped both her hands and gave them a little squeeze.

She thought he would ask her then, "What in the world is up with you, running away like an adolescent just because a man who's crazy about you asked you to marry him?" But he only said, "Shall we thread the needles then?" and she murmured a grateful, "Yes."

While she threaded the giant needles, Butch put more wood in and stoked up the woodstove. Then they sat on either side of the hole and worked quietly together, with the sort of comfort they'd established long before they'd begun their extracurricular activities, and Cookie felt her breathing grow deeper, and it seemed as if the warm, dry air coming off the stove was able to set her upright after the hard, nearly sleepless night she'd had.

It wasn't until they'd finished and folded the net like a bedspread, stretching it from the four corners first, then halving it, then coming together in the middle to half the length of it, she began to grow nervous again. But Butch only folded his hands over hers as they still held the net and lowered his voice to say how glad he was to have found her out on the road. "Please don't ever scare me like that again, can you promise?"

"I'm sorry," she said. "So sorry." Then added, "It wasn't about you at all." She let go of her grasp on the net, handing it over to him.

"What, then? What *was* it about?" He squinted and those crinkles appeared at the corners of his eyes again, lightening what otherwise might have been a dark look.

She shook her head, No, can't tell.

"Let's have a coffee," Butch said, neatly folding the net a couple more times to lay it at his feet, a squared bundle.

He went to pour the coffee but before he could, she called him to sit beside her at the table, which he did, scraping the chair back, then leaning forward, his hands on his knees, his long legs angled out toward her.

"I didn't want to ever have to tell this to anyone," she started, her eyes fully focused on him, an intense blue green, something like the color the sea had come to be with the full light of morning. She stopped, breathed deeply, closed her eyes for a moment, then opened them again. "I . . . it may be hard for you to believe this. I'm, by nature, a gentle soul, but . . ." she hesitated.

The world seemed to stop still. Butch thought it could be anything. He wished she wouldn't go forward, maybe go backward, maybe start the morning over again and he wouldn't ask her why she had been running away. They could go out that night—it was supposed to be a night of shooting stars—and lay on the stone wall with Jimbo butting up against them to keep them warm and watch those fast beams flying across the sky. But it was too late. A thing had started to unravel and it was too late to wrap it up and pretend it was just a ball of thread. He thought all these things yet did not take his eyes off her.

Finally, she sighed and told him what she had done. She was shaking by the time she finished, her voice wavering, as if she were speaking underwater.

Butch, mouth open and eyes wide, got up and walked away, trying to take in what Molly had said. Holy mackerel, where had she gotten the guts to do that? His Molly, his quiet Molly.

He shook his head, looked to the water for answers but found none. Then his eyes landed on Molly bent forward over the table, and he realized he had left her in horrendous pain.

"What must it have taken to do that!" he said, sitting back down beside her.

"It didn't take anything," she uttered. "I just couldn't stop myself. As if it wasn't really me, but it was."

"I'm so sorry," he said, moving closer to take her by the shoulders and nurse her face with the compassion that now flooded his own. "I only mean what a lot of shit you must have taken to bring you to that point."

She shook her head. "I did, but that doesn't absolve me."

"In my eyes, it does," said Butch.

She let out a deep breath, her head down on her arms as they stretched forward on the table. He laid his hand on the center of her back and waited. He wanted to ask how she had gotten away, if someone might still be looking for her, as he felt the delicacy of her wing under his hand and thought how lonely it must have been all this time for her without anyone knowing. He felt her breath come and go, life going on now, in spite of his knowing, and neither of them able to perceive just how this would change things.

"I love you," he whispered, leaning over her back so that his lips came close to her ear.

She shook her head again, just small motions this time, as if saying she could not accept his love.

They stayed that way, the two of them stretched over the table, until finally she broke and sobbed, her tears flowing steadily, and she let him hold her, his arms trying to tell her he did not care a damn for what she had done, he only wanted to care for her.

Eventually, when she stopped crying and sat back up, he suggested she must be hungry, that *he* sure was, and would she mind if he fixed them some breakfast. And she sniffed and wiped her eyes and said she didn't know how she could possibly be hungry but in fact she was starving.

Over sausage and eggs she asked him if he needed to know more and he held up his hand and said, "No, enough for one day. Let's just digest what we've got, along with our breakfast, for now."

She saw the questions running around in his mind. He must be wondering if he should expect a marshall to show up any moment, looking for her.

"I'm amazed that I'm sitting here with you," she said. "You're a good man."

"Don't be," he said. "You've brought a lot of sun into my life."

"And now maybe trouble," she said.

"We'll see about that," he said, getting up to pour them another coffee, which they drank in near silence, watching what they could see of the turbulent sea.

Chapter 14

Edith Biddle had slept well, knowing Molly was back up above, which was why she'd been up early enough to see Molly make her way down the steep stone stairs with a flashlight just before dawn. Assuming she was going back over to Butch's, did that mean things were more or less back to normal? She'd intercepted Molly yesterday to ask if she could bring Chrissie to meet her but not dared ask anything more.

Edith went back to bed for a short while before she'd need to get up and dress for school. She loved waking up slowly, had learned to appreciate doing so back when Martin started spending nights up in the cottage. Before that she'd not been aware that her natural rhythms were modified by being tuned in to his. Always waking to think about how she'd best get up to prepare his breakfast instead of lolling about with her dreams. Do this, do that, was the impulse that seemed to drive her, but this drowsy napping was delicious.

As she peeked through the curtains an hour later, the sun was starting to redden the sky. She got up and put on water for coffee, then began the ritual of preparing her oatmeal, stirring it intermittently while she dressed.

She donned long underwear, yearning for an early spring so she could leave off this layer, then pulled on a pair of herringbone slacks, a blouse, and a colorful, handwoven sweater, given to her by the mother of Daryl, one of her favorite pupils. A pistol of a boy, Daryl's obstreperous behavior had challenged every teacher until ninth grade, when she had discovered his talent for acting and provoked the English teacher, Mr. Peter Blake, to give him a chance to audition for the school play. When Daryl won the role of supporting actor, he suddenly became brilliant at memorizing his lines. He showed up whenever he was supposed to, shared his skills with the other actors, and no longer had a spare moment to act up or create trouble.

"But how did you guess he had this talent?" his mother had asked Mrs. Biddle, thrilled at the change in him.

"I was impressed with his gift for imitating his teachers or any-one he wanted to mock," Mrs. Biddle replied. "He has a great facility for leaping right into others."

"Indeed," his mother agreed, "but I didn't encourage it. I was afraid it'd get him into trouble for being disrespectful."

"Yes, it well might have," said Mrs. Biddle.

"But you put his talent to good use, and he's so much more satisfied with himself now," Daryl's mother said warmly. "I thank you for that."

Edith knew she was good at what she did, but it was especially nice when a parent recognized it. But Muriel's girl, she wasn't so sure she had the resources to handle. She was seeing her for the second time today, and if she were honest with herself, she dreaded it. Every time she thought about how empty the poor girl's stomach must be, she felt desperate. Well, at least she had men-tioned her to Molly, and while Molly had frozen for a second, she hadn't said no. But now how was she going to convince the girl she should meet Molly?

"How are you?" asked Mrs. Biddle a couple of hours later, as the girl sat hunched sideways on her chair, curled into her bony self.

Chrissie gave a barely perceptible shrug.

"I see," said Mrs. Biddle, though she didn't see where to go next. Chrissie not willing to look at her ignited a stubborn vein in her, anger even. She was used to being highly attended to, not ignored. "Look," she said at last. "We have this time to talk . . . so let's talk."

Chrissie shrugged again.

Mrs. Biddle spoke softly. "I'd like to know what's going on with you. Then maybe I can help."

Chrissie's eyes darted her way a moment, then returned to the wall, leaving Mrs. Biddle's words to fall flat.

The girl looked both haunted and hungry. Mrs. Biddle wished she had a cookie to offer, but no, she'd done some reading about anorexia, and that would be a textbook no-no. She squashed down her feeling of inadequacy and marched on, saying, "Chrissie, everyone is very concerned about you. Your parents, your teachers, *me.* The longer you go on eating so little, the more you are endangering your health. Your bones . . . Did you know this can affect your bones later in life?"

Chrissie muttered something.

"What? What's that?" asked Mrs. Biddle, leaning forward.

"Who cares?" Chrissie said a bit louder.

"We all do," said Mrs. Biddle. "Can you tell me something about how you're feeling?"

Chrissie shook her head.

So they sat in silence, time passing slowly as the wall clock ticked away. When only five minutes were left in the session, Mrs. Biddle went straight for it, interrupting the quiet to tell Chrissie there was someone she wanted her to meet.

Chrissie's hooded eyes rotated around to meet hers. "Who?"

"A woman I think you might like. She's from the States. Molly's her name. She lives up above me in Doc's cottage."

Chrissie's mouth dropped open and her eyebrows went up. "Really?"

"Really. Do you know her?"

"*I* don't, but my father thinks she's some kind of evil witch."

"He does?" Mrs. Biddle faked a smile to cover her alarm. She'd forgotten about Chrissie's father, Logan. Molly, who rarely expressed curiosity about the people of Seal Cove, had asked about Logan way back when she'd first arrived, leading Edith to wonder if the two of them had had a hostile encounter.

Chrissie closed her mouth tightly and nodded.

"Quite the contrary, she's a gentle, lovely woman," said Mrs. Biddle. "Maybe a bit lonely. I think the two of you might hit it off and be good company for each other."

Suddenly the more lively Chrissie, the one who'd described, in her first session, how she'd try to fetch her father off a barstool, was back. "You better not tell my dad, is all I know," she said, her eyes coming to rest on Mrs. Biddle with humor.

The bell rang to signal end of period, and Chrissie grabbed her stack of books that seemed too large for her wan arms and headed out the door, leaving Edith to speculate.

It had been almost too easy. Maybe Chrissie's enthusiasm had less to do with Molly and more to do with defying her father, and inadvertently, she had handed her a way to do that.

———

It was a Saturday at the back end of winter. Cookie was working on a 1000-piece picture puzzle on a card table when Mrs. Biddle knocked on the door with Chrissie, a small shadow behind her. Cookie shook the girl's hand with the bones-too-loose feeling and again wondered what she, of all people, could possibly have to offer her.

"She's very quiet sometimes, but then so are you," Mrs. Biddle had said the other day, "so it might just be the two of you sitting together quietly, that would be okay."

Cookie brought a second chair to the table with the puzzle and indicated it as a place for Chrissie and, as soon as the girl sat down, regretted she hadn't put a pillow on the chair to cushion her bones, which seemed to stick out everywhere.

Mrs. Biddle said she'd return a little later and gave Cookie a nod of encouragement as she backed away, and Cookie went back to her place at the table. She'd gotten only as far as completing the rectangular frame of the puzzle and had reached a point of despair about getting anything to fit, to fill in the center.

Chrissie studied the pieces, then began to sort out and join some white pieces, and lo and behold, a boat emerged.

"Wow, that's good," Cookie said. "Even great. I've been stuck for a while."

Chrissie was now assembling a series of blue pieces, mumbling in a singsong voice, "blue . . . sky blue . . ." as she searched the scattered pieces.

"Here's a blue one," Cookie offered. "Can you use it?"

"Let's see," said Chrissie, holding it against her other blue pieces, wrinkling her nose when it didn't match, her eyes rising halfway up to look at Cookie, but then quickly diverting back to the table.

Cookie knew this feeling of not being able to look someone in the eye. In her, it came from secrets. Not wanting anyone to ask her about her bruises, *if* they could see them through her heavy makeup. Then, in Cape Breton, not wanting anyone to see her, period.

After they worked away at the puzzle for over an hour, Cookie declared she'd be right back and went to the kitchen to make a cup of tea. She came back with the tea and four Lorna Doones for each, which she set out on a TV table beside the card table. Chrissie never stopped studying the puzzle pieces but, like an automaton, reached for a cookie, dunked, then ate it and sipped from the cup, her eyes still concentrated on the puzzle, until she had imbibed all that had been allotted to her end of the TV table. Cookie hardly dared breathe. She didn't say a word, but marveled at how happy she felt to see the girl eat.

"I hope you'll come back and help me finish," she said, when Mrs. Biddle came shortly to take Chrissie home. "I don't see how I can possibly do it alone."

Chrissie shrugged. Again her eyes darted nearly up to meet Cookie's, but then strayed. "I don't know," she said. "If you really need help, I guess I can."

"I'd be happy to have your help," Cookie said. "I certainly need it."

"Tomorrow?" Chrissie asked, her voice shaky with doubt. "Tomorrow would be fine."

Part III

Chapter 15

Summer came around again and work took over. They had a good two months in terms of the lobster haul, ending July 15, and then went out to take their catch of crab and brought in all they were allowed in less than a week. After the fishing season, with no reason to leave the boat in the water, they'd brought it into dry dock. There was work to be done on the boat but nothing that couldn't wait, so might as well do something to help with the tourist season and save the other work to keep them busy in the fall. Cookie and Butch began volunteering at the North Highlands Museum in Cape North, where Butch could keep up the ironwork skills he didn't want to lose, and Cookie could create some structure in her life, now that she didn't have to be up and out by 4:00 a.m.

Chrissie had continued to visit Cookie on weekends through winter and spring and had begun to eat almost normally again. At least when she was away from home. So, when she learned that they were becoming volunteers, Mrs. Biddle engineered a plan to have Chrissie sign up for the same days and volunteer with them. Her father resisted, saying she should stay home in case someone called with a last-minute babysitting job. This was his excuse, but Cookie knew better. Whatever he *knew* about her, he *suspected* more. But Chrissie's mother, insisting the job experience, even unpaid, might help Chrissie get a job in the future, prevailed.

Cookie loved the museum. It had given her a way to learn about the quirky history of her new home in this far-off place. The video, made by the first doctor's wife, explained why the hospital was in the tiny hamlet of Neil's Harbour instead of the larger settlement of Ingonish. Because the good doctor had lived there! His was the first car in the community, a Jeep, which he took out on home visits. His wife, an amateur photographer, must have often gone with him. She shot pictures of all the big winter storms, with the tractors plowing the snow into enormous mounds. Her photos showed how the snow was so heavy a second tractor would get behind and push the first tractor until they were both stopped by the weight of the snow. Then the huge mound of snow would become the end of the road out of town, until the snow thawed in spring. When the road was blocked like that, the doctor resorted to visiting his patients with a horse and sleigh, crossing the iced-over coves and bays to get to the next town, often at risk of falling through.

Cookie's job at the museum was to open the doors, put out the donation basket, greet people, and answer their questions. If she didn't know the answers, she would send folks out back to Butch in the blacksmith shop, where he was fashioning fire irons, iron hooks and the like, for sale, to benefit the museum.

In fact, she was about to stride across the floor and ask the man in the tan jacket if he had any questions when she was suddenly riddled through and through as if struck with a bolt of lightning. My God, was that Denny, her cousin? She jumped back through the door and flattened herself against the wall, her heart crashing in her chest. It was Denny! It had to be! It couldn't be. She dared not peek around the door and look again, just quickly unlatched the cellar door and ran down the cellar stairs, where she pressed up against the cold stone wall, her arms across her chest as she struggled to get her breath back.

Denny! My God! She hadn't seen him since his mother's funeral maybe ten years ago. She'd gone with Annie, a rare excursion without Warren because he couldn't leave a large foundation pour he was in the middle of.

She crept closer to the high, cellar window. There was a white Kia in the parking lot, besides Butch's truck and her Honda. Must be Denny's. She tried to calm herself. He didn't really see me, she told herself. But is he staying around here? She leaned against the wall again and took a long, deep breath. The air smelled musty and damp and tangy with iron, from the bins full of old iron tools lined up on the wall opposite.

The smell brought back the night in the blue cottage cellar. What a state she had been in. The worst night of her life. She and Butch didn't talk about it. She didn't know how he managed to hold onto it so silently, but there had been no more talk of marriage. They had retreated to an earlier period before his bright idea of proposing and were staying in the moment. The way so much of her life had to be lived now.

Over these years, she had thought so much about her sister and about Nita, yet that next level of family had just fallen completely from her radar, and suddenly, thinking of Denny, she felt a huge void.

She and Denny had been close as children, when her family's vacations had consisted of visiting Denny's family in the Pocono's. Smack between her and Annie in age, Denny had preferred her to Annie, which had made her crazy about him. He had brown hair, cut like fuzz in a crew cut, deep brown eyes, and an impish smile with dimples. He'd gone to junior college, then became a lineman for the power company, and that was what he probably did still, traveling around the country when they had a natural disaster with a power outage, here, there or wherever.

Oh my God, Chrissie! Chrissie was probably in the main room right now, answering Denny's questions. Denny might be asking who she was and Chrissie would be looking for her.

Cookie tried to lower her shoulders from where they had risen with tension nearly to her ears. She looked back out to the parking lot again and the white Kia was driving away. Damn! She could only see the back of a man's head, a woman with long salt-and-pepper hair in the passenger's seat. She'd missed her chance to make sure it was Denny.

Lots of times in August people came up from the States. She knew that! But it was so remote here she hadn't thought someone she knew might show up. You are going to have to stay on guard for the rest of your life, she chided herself. Well, at least she wasn't going to be stuck in the cellar for hours, she thought, as she ascended the stairs. But *if* that were Denny, where would he be staying?

"You okay?" Chrissie asked a little later, when the screen door banged as a couple entered the museum and Cookie jumped.

If she thought she had gotten relaxed, she stood corrected, having nearly catapulted right out of her shoes. "No, no," she said, "I'm fine. I was just deep in thought."

"I do that all the time," said Chrissie. "I'm reading a book and my mother comes into my room, and I don't even hear her feet until she speaks, and I jump so hard my bed bounces."

"Excuse me, I have a question," the man said, holding up his index finger to point to something on the display board, and Cookie nodded to Chrissie to take his question. Chrissie had quickly learned most of what there was to know about the museum and of course knew more than Cookie would ever know about Cape North or Seal Cove or Ingonish, having grown up here. Cookie hung at the doorway, ready to dart back to the cellar door, which she had left ajar, in case Denny should return. If he'd gone for lunch, he might swing back by. Theoretically, they were open until three, and it was only one-thirty. She was getting that dizzy feeling again, first sign of a panic attack, pins and needles in her hands, her head spinning, and doubted she could make it until three.

She didn't make it much past two when Butch came into the main museum building to tell her that a guy had come out to the smithy's workshop a little while ago, asking about her.

"Asking what?"

"If you were from the States? If your name was Cookie Wagner?"

Cookie held her body rigid and her mouth tightly closed as Butch went on, telling her how he'd said, "No indeed," holding the poker poised in the air because he'd been so surprised at the idea the man would even think he might know her.

Chrissie was right there, listening, so Cookie just shrugged and said, "I must be somebody's double," trying for a chuckle that came out more like a clearing of her throat. Then she asked if they'd mind closing up shop a few minutes early, as she had some errands to do for Mrs. Biddle. Butch told her to go along and take his truck. He'd ride back in the car with their new young driver, Chrissie, if Chrissie didn't mind bringing him and closing up the museum.

"You up for that, Chrissie?" he asked. The girl beamed and her dimples showed. She was still thin but her cheeks were no longer just hollows.

"Course," she said. "There's not that much to it."

It would be good experience for her, Cookie rationalized, as she gathered her bag and hiked it on her shoulder, and Butch came forward to kiss her on the forehead, handing her his keys.

She left Butch's truck at his place and walked the quarter mile back to hers, hunched over, afraid to look and see who might be coming each time a car passed. Often no one passed her during this fifteen-minute walk, but today at least five cars went by. One even slowed. She didn't dare turn her head, just grew rigid and picked up her pace, but then it passed and she could breathe again, because it was not the white Kia. Finally, she reached the tag of a street that went up the hill to Edith's and climbed the stairs to her little, isolated cottage, which she thought of as her castle. She was so glad that she hadn't given it up to move in with Butch, as he'd once suggested she do. She stayed at his place more than here, but she treasured this private place to retreat to, where the secrets she lived with could remain more alive. Mostly they came to life in nightmares, but there was a kind of freedom in knowing where she came from, a connection which she lacked when with others who knew nothing of her past. Well, Butch knew some of it, which helped, but also strained them, as they kept what she'd revealed in a back drawer.

The name Cookie Wagner! When Butch had spoken it out loud a huge torrent of adrenalin had landed in the pit of her belly. How long since she had heard her name?

In the morning she feigned a stomach virus and called Butch to tell him she couldn't open the museum, he'd have to find someone else or stay inside himself because she didn't want Chrissie alone in the shop all day while he was out in the shed. "It's probably just a twenty-four-hour thing," she told him, not knowing what excuse she'd use the next day. It was only Thursday. She couldn't imagine going there again this week. Lots of rentals went Saturday to Saturday, so Denny might be staying in the area for a week. Of course, he might just have driven out from Halifax on a day trip. Who knew?

She didn't have a lot of food since she often ate at Butch's, but she had cans of soup and some staples like rice and pasta, so she'd be fine until the end of the week. She paced. In front of the long couch and the wide coffee table, there was plenty of length to the room. The sea usually calmed her but now she couldn't stop long enough to let that happen. She felt as if she were a prisoner and couldn't help thinking she might have been pacing a prison cell for these last five years and more. Would her cousin Denny want that? She hardly imagined he would, but people didn't necessarily *think*. People who were not in her shoes.

Butch showed up at suppertime, uninvited, bearing fat turkey sandwiches and coleslaw he'd picked up at the Co-op.

"How's the stomach?" he said, "Ready to try solid food?"

Cookie touched her middle. She was actually hungry. "I was going to have soup, but I guess I might try a bite of sandwich." He had already pulled down two plates from her open shelves. "Better skip the coleslaw, though," she added.

"You okay?" he asked, as he sat down with her at the table.

She didn't know what to say. She wished he weren't looking so closely.

"Chrissie go up to the museum with you?"

"Nope, we both took the day off and left the place closed. Decided it would be better to open tomorrow. More folks coming out on a Friday and we didn't know if you'd be up to it." He paused, then added, "Besides, Chrissie had to help her mother do some housecleaning today."

So he had been in touch with Chrissie. "Did you let her drive you home yesterday?" Cookie asked.

"Sure did. And for someone on a learner's permit, she's a good little driver. Didn't give me one scare." Cookie and Butch had taken up the cause of giving Chrissie driving lessons because Chrissie's mother didn't drive at all and her father, who drove a delivery truck for a living, refused to have anything to do with teaching her to drive. Mrs. Biddle was the one who'd come up with the idea, and it had been impossible for Cookie to reveal that her driver's license was expired, and she had no way to renew it.

Butch had fixed up his old blue Honda, sitting dormant for more than a year, so Cookie could drive it around the end of the island. He kept it registered in his name and said it was nothing for him to add in the insurance at the same time he paid for his truck insurance. She worried whenever she and Chrissie went out driving that a local cop might stop them.

Between nerves and the fact she had hardly eaten all day, she wolfed down half the sandwich before she realized Butch's eyes were upon her.

"Guess I was hungry, after all," she said, grinning sheepishly.

"Guess you were," he said, watching her closely.

"I'm sorry I flaked out on you."

"No problem," he said. "I was just wondering if that guy stopping by Wednesday upset you."

He was looking too closely for her to lie. Besides, what was the point? She sometimes forgot that he knew the worst about her.

"Yah," she said. "I got scared. That might have been my cousin."

"Oh, God. I was afraid it was something like that."

"He saw me, didn't he?"

"Seems like he did, but only for a second. Where'd you go?"

"Ducked into the cellar."

"Oh," Butch said, almost smiling, the crinkles at the corners of his eyes showing. "Good thinking."

"I'm afraid he might be around here for a week."

"Right," he said, his brow in a furrow. "He well might be. But if he is, I'm sure we can outsmart him. I already went looking for that white Kia at all the rental cottages and didn't find it. And I'll go again." Then he added, "And me and Chrissie will manage the

museum tomorrow. If he comes in, I'll pick up my poker again."
He faked sword-like jabs in the air.

Cookie smiled for the first time since Denny had appeared at
the museum. She grabbed Butch's hand to stop his sword jabbing,
held it to her face and said, "Thank you, my knight."

"Pleased to be of service," he said, cradling her head against
him. "Cookie Wagner."

"Shh," she said, shaken once again by hearing her name.

He held her tighter and said, "I hate to see you go through stuff
like this."

She broke and cried then, feeling trapped, with no way out of
hiding, short of going back and turning herself in.

But Butch kept them in the moment, telling her to go wash her
tears away and finish the other half of her sandwich and they'd go
out on the bench and watch the light change, and meantime he'd
make them a cup of coffee, and maybe after dark he'd challenge
her to a game of Scrabble.

She hoped he wouldn't be looking for sex then because, dis-
tressed as she was, she didn't think she could get aroused, but
then she remembered Butch was Butch and not Warren and never
pushed her against her will. In fact, he held back so much she
usually was the one to initiate their lovemaking, and the thought
brought a wave of feeling she almost didn't recognize—telling her
she was, through and through, a creature with a strong urge to
open up and connect.

"Please, God," she prayed again as she had been praying all
day. "Don't let Denny go back and tell anyone he saw me."

Chapter 16

Warren clinked water glasses with Melinda as they looked out over the Esopus Creek from the Catamount deck. The water rushed past and swirled in a whirlpool just beyond where they sat, then burst over a pile of rocks and moved downstream, leaving behind the fresh, clean odor of ozone.

Melinda held him in her gaze.

"Here's to . . ."

As he paused, she cradled her tiny belly in her hand and added "us."

He smiled and finished, "Yes, to the three of us."

It was the second anniversary of their meeting, and he was buoyed by his good fortune. He thought back to the evening in Ashokan, the meeting in a church hall where he'd never been before. He'd gone late. He'd been to plenty of other meetings where alcoholics shared what they were going through, but never this particular one, and when he'd entered the room, it had been dark except for a series of votive candles up and down the table. Disoriented, he finally made out an empty chair, sat, and his guard slipped away, as it tended to in these meetings.

He listened to the woman speaking, her voice wavering as she described her long struggle to leave her husband. She'd wanted him to come along on this journey with her after she'd gotten sober, realizing how many of their problems were related to their drinking. But he hadn't been interested. He'd taunted her, passing his glass of scotch under her nose to remind her what she was missing. And worse, the woman said her husband had been abusive. Warren's ears perked up. He wished she would say exactly what she meant. What ranked as abuse for a woman like her, he wanted to know. She seemed so strong-minded and capable, so 'in charge' as she told her story, even though her voice was weak. Cookie wasn't much of a drinker, but if she had been, is this the story she'd be telling?

It jarred to think he was an abuser, but he'd been told—first in rehab and then in special counseling—that his only chance of changing his default MO was to own it. The same way he'd had to admit he was powerless over alcohol. *That* he had known, instinctively. But Big Sam, the counselor, with his freaking bulging arm muscles filling his sleeves till it looked like they might split, had imprinted himself upon Warren when Warren asked, "What do you mean by default MO?"

"Your default MO is to batter," he answered gruffly. "Fear is not in your vocabulary. Before you let fear through, you're gonna do everything in your power to put it onto somebody else. Knock whatever they do, push 'em around, make *them* feel it instead of you." Sam's dark onyx eyes zeroed in on him. "You want to get better, then open your ears and shut your mouth."

A bit of a miracle perhaps, but for once, Warren had let someone tell him what to do.

He was glad for the dim light. It kept him from seeing this wisp of a woman clearly as she went on about her marriage vows. "What about in sickness and in health?" she said. "My husband was sick with alcoholism, but so was I, and I needed to help myself first. I couldn't afford to stay with him, drinking like he was."

When she finished speaking, it was the meeting's tradition to go around the table, with each person sharing. When it came to Warren, he looked directly at the woman through the dark and admitted he had once been a lot like her husband. He had done some horrendous things. But now, he hoped to make amends by changing whatever he had to, so he'd never be that guy again. He hung his head, not going into what Cookie had done to him or admitting he still hadn't found a way to forgive her. It had been all over the papers, so most people knew Cookie had stabbed him. But no one knew how badly he had treated her.

When the meeting was over and someone turned on the lights, there was a strange moment as this woman, Melinda, ceased being the figure squared off in her chair and came to life. He went over and shook her hand and thanked her for her honesty.

Then he went home and railed at Cookie. "Goddamn little bitch!" He hated when his mother called her this, yet sometimes he just wanted to find her and grab her by the throat and see her terror, as life ebbed away, as it had been draining out of him when she'd turned her back on him and run out the door.

The following week he returned to the meeting, and when the lights came on, asked Melinda out for coffee. Two weeks later, he took her out to dinner, then brought her back to his house and led her to his bed. With a candle on the dresser the only light besides the moonlight shining in the south windows, he held her small frame against him and ran his hand up along the prominent knobs of her spine. She was small and doll-like, which made him feel protective. Cookie had been taut with muscle and blocky, nearly his width, though much shorter. He breathed in the lemony smell of Melinda's hair and let out a contented sigh. He didn't want to rush anything. He was just so happy to be lying in bed with a woman he cared for, after two plus years of reaching over to an empty space.

Melinda ran her hand through his thick hair and then held the back of his neck. When he kissed her throat, he heard her breath catch. Gently, he began to unbutton her blouse and peel it back over her shoulder. Her breasts were small and tight; he reached behind and released her bra and caressed them, bringing her nipples to a rise. That's when she pulled up his polo shirt to help him take it off, and despite the near darkness of the room, her eyes landed and stayed there on his large scar, jagged at its center. It created a part down his middle where no hair grew. For a long time, the scar had been red and angry. but now, clean and white, it only looked tight, as if it were holding him together. As she ran her finger down it, he felt the warmth of her hand. "What?" she asked. "What happened?"

He didn't answer right away, only drew her in against him again, savoring the heat of their bodies, until the heat turned to anger coursing in his veins. Damn, he didn't want this to get ruined. He sat up, swung his legs to the floor and dropped his head into his hands.

"Tell me about it," she said quietly.

"Were you living around here in 2004?" he asked.

"I was still down in Jersey with my husband then."

"Otherwise, you would have known."

"Known what?" Her voice took on a note of alarm.

"That my wife stabbed me and left me for dead."

Her hand came up to her mouth and her eyes widened. "You're kidding." He shook his head slowly. "No kidding."

"Where is she?"

"Probably Canada. I tried to find her at first, but clearly she didn't want to be found. Especially by me. I treated her like shit when I went on my wild binges."

Melinda's eyes were still open wide.

"At first, I wanted to kill her, but when I stopped drinking, everything changed, and I thought it would be good if I let her know that."

"When did you stop?" She watched him intently, waiting for him to say more.

"You've heard of a 'near-death-experience'?" He let out a nervous laugh. "Well, that's what I had. Only once wasn't enough for me, so when I had just about thirty days sober, I ventured up to Montreal looking for her, but like I said, I went out drinking instead. On top of the pain meds I was still taking, I managed to poison myself." He squinted. "I got close enough to the edge that seemed like I was peering over it. And when I woke up, something inside of me seemed rearranged. Least it felt that way. Like, 'Hey, buddy, you survived again, must mean you're here for a reason. So maybe it's time to make something of yourself.'"

She looked away, and he felt her waver. She must be wondering if she was in the arms of someone like her husband.

He wanted to kiss her brow where a furrow had formed but held back. Words would be better if he were any good at them, but he wasn't. Finally, he just took her hand and pressed it full length against his scar. "Trust me," he said. "Please. I am not going to hurt you."

Tears welled in her eyes.

"It's scary, I know," he said.

"It is," she admitted, "especially because I'm not sure when to trust myself."

As the tears ran over her sharp cheek bones, he leaned forward to kiss them, and her angular frame softened and came back in close, and the mood moved from fear to exploration, and her breath caught again as he nuzzled her breasts and then felt the length of her, as he traveled down her front.

He was sweetly rewarded when she came to the motions of his hungry mouth, swirls of electric energy surrounding his head, filling him with greater desire than he could have imagined. Still, he took care to enter her gently, holding her delicate frame, wanting very much to let her know how much he cared.

Now they were celebrating their coming together as well as the life growing in her belly. Melinda didn't seem to mind that they couldn't marry. He had found out he would have to wait a number of years with Cookie not being found to declare his marriage over on the basis of abandonment.

What had bothered Melinda more was moving to the home he'd lived in with Cookie. She'd wanted them to get another place, but real estate was too high. More folks who had received big bonuses from Wall Street had bought second homes and sent the prices up, so he was happy to already have a home where the mortgage was nearly paid off. He'd talked her into trying it out and told her she could rearrange anything she wanted to if she'd move in. And she'd had some ingenious ideas. Like creating a new doorway to open the master bath into the second bedroom, so they could sleep there instead of the room where he'd always slept with

Cookie. He didn't mind at all, because he liked the mountain view they had from the second bedroom when the leaves came off the trees. And when the baby was born, the master bedroom could be split up into a smaller bedroom and a playroom.

"Katarina told me I was glowing today," said Melinda, solidly returning his wandering mind to where they sat at the restaurant. "I thought she was hinting that she was noticing my belly, so I admitted I was pregnant."

Katarina was Melinda's boss at the beauty salon where she cut hair.

Warren gave her a closer look. "I see that glow," he said. "I thought it was the light and maybe the water flowing downstream here, giving you a backdrop, but I guess it's just you."

Melinda turned to watch the water and they both listened to the flow. "It's no wonder if I'm glowing," she said. "I've waited a long time for this. And, coming up on forty the same time as I was getting a divorce, I almost gave up on the idea it could happen."

"That makes two of us," said Warren.

"C'mon, men don't stop making babies at forty," she said, running her hand down his forearm.

He shrugged. "No, but Cookie and me didn't have much luck at making babies together."

"Maybe it was all the drink," she said.

"Or maybe it was two years of my storing up sperm before I met you," he countered, chuckling. Somehow his shame at having a low sperm count, which had once had the power to drive him into a hurricane of fury, had dissolved.

"Whatever," she said, her hand holding her belly again. "Let's just hope we can keep this one going."

Even before they had gotten the test, she'd told him she'd miscarried the one other time she was pregnant, back in her early thirties. He reached now to cover her hand on her stomach. She still had the flattest belly he had ever seen and he found it hard to imagine how she was going to look when she began to fill out.

They finished the dinner, splitting a piece of berry pie, remarking how this served just fine for celebration, in place of wine or the after-dinner drink which once would have put them on the road in a precarious state of inebriation. Yet Warren couldn't say he didn't have a tickle of desire to belt one back as they approached the bar on the way out. He could almost feel it lighting up his belly, making it easier for him to relax with Melinda. "A delusion," his sponsor would say, but Warren wasn't sure.

Being with a woman still wasn't easy for him; he had a couple of devils to keep his eye on, and his confidence he could handle them frequently faltered. Certainly, getting sober hadn't taken away his temper. If anything, it had brought it out more, since his feelings were no longer anesthetized.

At first, it seemed as if he'd lost the protectiveness of skin, like he only had his chest, where the one thing he *could feel* was the thick scar where Cookie had stabbed him. On the booze, he'd been able to convince himself his skin was tough as leather, and the thing laying beneath it was rage, when someone crossed him, or *he thought* they had crossed him, a rage that would lead him to boil and make his head go blank.

One day in counseling Sam had asked, "What's it like when you go ballistic, Warren?"

He'd given Sam his impish look. "How would *I* know? I'm always in a blackout. Have to find out what I did the next day and trust no one's joshing me about it."

Sam narrowed his eyes, and Warren could tell he'd best stop trying to get over on him.

"Okay," said Sam, "so then what's it like the *moment before* you go into the blackout or the blank out or whatever it is?"

"Dark, like a curtain's coming down. And flashes of red, like maybe I'm on fire and I should be panicking, but at the same time, a huge wave of fatigue splashes over me, and I only want to close my eyes and sleep. Kind of like it felt when I was bleeding out and darkness was coming in. I cared . . . but then I didn't care. Things were falling into place and I was just falling . . ."

He leaned his head back against the tall chair where he sat across from Sam for their weekly private hour. Closed his eyes. His fist clenched and he jabbed at the air. "I don't know. That doesn't really describe it. I'm just kind of making up bull to get you off my back. It's more like, 'Goddammit, don't mess with me.'"

"Self-defense," said Sam.

"Damn right."

"Except no one is coming after you, *you*'re going after *them*."

"Right," Warren nodded, then added, "except when I was small and my daddy was coming after me."

Then it was Sam's turn to say, "Right."

"That's when I first saw that black curtain."

"How do you feel about your dad now?"

"He was a bastard when he whooped me, but otherwise . . . a pretty good guy."

"Why do you think he did it?"

"Frustration. He was too smart to be doing nothing but driving a truck, but he had a wife and a child to support. He was trapped."

"That's very generous of you."

Warren shrugged. "Well, maybe *his* daddy had beat him, and he was just following suit."

"Most likely," Sam agreed.

Now that Warren had skin, it was like living in an entirely different body. He could feel pulses he never knew he had. Wants and itches. Or sadness. He would look at his face in the mirror, shaving, and stare at how his eyes looked droopy. He didn't like looking like that. It made him mad. One time he thought he saw his father in the droop and that made him even madder.

His sponsor told him to just feel whatever came up. "Don't worry, it's nothing but a feeling." But that was damned scary. Tough him, the Warren who had passed himself off as fearless and believed in it, was afraid to feel sad.

He wished he could ask his father why he'd always been whacking him. Had he really been so bad?

"Maybe that's what's making you sad," his sponsor said. "Why not try to talk to him?"

"Because he's long since dead."

"Well, call him up," his sponsor suggested. "Call him up in your mind."

So one Sunday morning when Warren was lying around in bed too depressed to get up and make breakfast by himself, he shut his eyes and said, "Dad, what the hell? Why were you so tough on me?"

Then he waited and, goddamn, if a voice didn't come back at him. Was he making this up? He didn't believe in this kind of shit three quarters of Woodstockers believed in. Still, he listened. *You were too wild for your own good and your mama did nothing but spoil you. Oh, she whacked you with a wooden spoon now and then, but I believed if I didn't tame you some, you'd get yourself in trouble.*

Warren paused, breathed deep. He wasn't sure he believed that. "But, seems like you always hit me when something was bothering you."

Probably so, the answer came back. Then silence. He'd owned it but wasn't going to explain further. Warren spoke again, hoping not to lose the connection.

"I don't know if I can do this—not drinking and trying to live sober. *You* never had a shot at it, so why should *I?*"

And he heard back, clear as day. *Go for it, son, with my blessings.*

Man, his chest flew open and he wept like a baby. It was the gentlest touch he had ever gotten from his father, and after that, his skin started to grow back a little. Oh, he got waylaid into a fury and felt like throwing whatever was in reach, and did sometimes. He had his meltdowns.

Once he threw some dishes, and another time, when a couple he poured a foundation for out in Willow accused him of failing to insulate it on the outside before he filled it, he punched the door-frame hard enough to break one of the bones in his hand. But at least he hadn't beaten up anyone. And by the time he met Melinda and she gave him a chance, he knew he had two sides to him and had to watch himself, do like he was told by his friends in the pro-gram: call someone up and tell them what was going on whenever he was about to boil over. Let other people in and change just about everything he ever thought he knew about living—*that was all.*

He spent six months after rehab running up and down the thruway to Albany to participate in a special group therapy for batterers, where he was instructed to literally talk himself through his feelings. They wanted him to do stuff like sit with his "inner child"—whatever the hell that was—on his lap and rock him and tell him he'd be taken care of. He thought this was all bull, and yet, times when he was desperate enough, he stooped to doing it. He never knew exactly what happened, but the mood would pass. So, though he didn't advocate it, he no longer mocked it.

A couple of times when he'd started to get sarcastic or accusatory with Melinda, he actually called one of the guys from his group. Took the phone out in the yard and nervously hoped no one would answer, but when his buddy did answer, he took a deep breath and said, "Man, I don't want to drop my stuff on her," and his buddy told him he was doing exactly the right thing.

He kept his back to the bar as they paid the bill, Melinda suggesting they make this an anniversary tradition.

His heart flipped a little at hearing her talk about another year, and the on-the-edge-of-a-cliff thrill he'd once thought could only come from drinking passed through him.

In the Catamount parking lot, just as he opened the truck door for Melinda, he caught a flash in his peripheral vision of someone he swore he recognized. For a moment, he thought it was a hallucination, like a fish you see scoot by underwater, then you study the water farther downstream to see it again, but it's gone. But as he turned, he saw she was not gone. She walked toward him with another woman at her side. Her hair had turned gray and there were crow's feet at the corners of her eyes, but there was no mistaking Cookie's sister. She had the same tense, hard look to her. She'd always been a nonstop talker, which had made him stay away from the house as much as possible whenever she came to visit Cookie, but now she looked downright sour.

He looked away, in case she hadn't seen him.

"What's the matter?" Melinda asked.

He took a deep breath and said, "Someone I know, that I'd just as soon not see," before he shut the door.

He wondered if the other woman was a friend or her lover, for Cookie's sister had come out as a lesbian back in the eighties, when they'd all still been young. She'd insisted he call her and her girl-friend women, not girls or gals or ladies. He really didn't get the difference so, afraid of a misstep, he stopped calling them anything. Annie was tough, much tougher than Cookie, although Cookie had turned out tougher than he'd ever imagined she could be.

He walked around the front of the truck and had opened the driver's door when she called out.

"Warren! Just who I was hoping to find."

"Annie," he said, raising his eyebrows, "What are you doing up here?"

"Can't you guess?"

Warren shrugged. "Cookie has not been seen. She's made a complete disappearance. Surely, you know that."

"I wouldn't be so sure," she said.

Warren couldn't tell how much Melinda had heard but thought he saw her cringe. "Annie, this is Melinda," he said, inclining his head toward her. Then he added, "Look, I need to get Melinda home."

"That's fine, but I need to talk to you." Annie stood feet apart, her voice as firm as her stance.

"Now? Can we meet somewhere tomorrow?"

"I'm staying right here, at this lodge," Annie said. "How about breakfast, ten o'clock?"

What could he do but agree in order to get her away from Melinda, even though he was due to pour a foundation in the morn-ing and despite the weight of a deep dread descending upon him.

Chapter 17

Annie was there, waiting for him on the wide wooden porch when Warren arrived promptly at ten. Tall and wiry, wearing white shorts that showed off her tan legs, as if she had already run, showered and changed into a clean tank top and shorts. No wonder Cookie had called her an exercise junkie, saying Annie was convinced she would croak if she couldn't get her run in.

He didn't dislike her, only experienced being run over by her whenever she started to go on and on about something. He didn't want to yell, "Stop yacking!" but that was all he could think to say. Often, she rattled on about a tennis match she had played and how her knee had given out on her just as she was about to win, or her golf game, and what had been wrong with either the course or the weather.

But now, a couple of years since he'd last seen her, she looked, for a change, as if she had more on her mind than games.

"Let's go out back by the river," she said, and led them to the exact table where he had sat with Melinda the night before, but he guided her over to the next table and pulled out a chair for her, relieved she seemed to have gotten over being insulted by the old-fashioned gesture, the way she had been in the old days, always sneering at him, reminding him women were just as capable as men of pulling out a chair. Well, yes, but his mother, despite her crude self, had raised him to have some manners.

"How are you, Warren?" she asked, unrolling her napkin and placing it in her lap.

"I'm fine," he said, surprised she was even asking. "All healed, working hard, the boom's over here locally, but there's still some new construction, additions, that sort of thing." Why was he telling her all this when he wanted to cut straight to the point? But he held back, letting her set the agenda. After all, she had asked for this meeting. "What about you? Still in Durham?"

"I am," she said. "With a new partner, Diana, the woman you saw here last night. She's a basketball coach for the women's team at UNC." She studied the menu as she reported this. The waitress came and he ordered eggs and bacon while Annie ordered a fruit salad.

He started to relax a bit. Thank God she hardly seemed the same woman who'd stormed into his house just weeks after the stabbing, eyes narrow with accusation, voice sharp, asking, "What the hell did you do to my little sister to make her turn on you like that?" Then, when he only slumped at the kitchen table, in no condition to fight back, she'd acted almost as if she were guilty for what Cookie had done, saying, "Oh God, what was my sister thinking?"

He looked at Annie now, at the tension in her lean, muscular cheeks. Cookie always talked about how, of the two of them, Annie was considered the better looking one by their mother. He couldn't see it. Her features were strong but almost too strong, like her personality.

She took a spoonful of her fruit salad. "Well, you know I didn't come all the way up here to talk about nothing."

He folded his arms across his chest and waited.

"My cousin Denny went on a vacation and swears he caught a glimpse of Cookie," she said.

A fist knotted up in Warren's stomach. "Really? Whereabouts?"

She stared at him hard. "What makes you think I'd tell *you*? So you could go after her and stab her back?"

Warren held up his hands, palms out. "No," he said, "I mean her no harm."

But Annie only continued to stare, unconvinced.

"When was this?" Warren continued.

"Just a couple of weeks ago, beginning of August."

"What made him think it was her? He talk to her?"

"He tried to, but she vanished, must have snuck out of the place they were in. Some small town rinky-dink museum he and his wife were visiting. He was looking at some old photos when he glanced up and saw a woman exactly like Cookie. He went to get his wife to take a look, but by the time they returned, she was gone. They asked a blacksmith behind the museum if he knew Cookie Wagner, but the man just looked at them as if they were crazy and said, 'No one by that name here.'

"The blacksmith was holding up a red-hot poker and pointing it at him in a way Denny found threatening."

Warren felt excitement building, and his wound suddenly began to ache, but with Annie's eyes on him, he tried to keep breathing normally.

"So there," she said, as if she had bested him in golf.

"I did find out there was evidence she'd bought a ticket to Canada," Warren said.

"Yeah, well, this *was in Canada*, but Canada's huge, as you know."

"So, are you headed up to look for her?"

"Are you kidding?" Annie asked, leaking sarcasm. "To seek out my sister who, in five years, hasn't given me the courtesy of a post-card to let me know she was alive?"

"Well, she could hardly afford to," said Warren.

"She could have found someone coming back to the States to mail it."

"Maybe she didn't want to be found."

"Obviously."

They sat in silence a moment, strange companions, the swirl of the river ringing in Warren's ears. Where its rushing flow had been comforting the night before, it now seemed to communicate urgency. Annie was waiting for something from him and keeping as quiet as he had ever seen her.

"I'd think *you'd* be the one interested in going after her," she said.

"Well, I might be, if you were telling me where she is."

She rolled her eyes. "Remember Denise, my partner who was a cop? I learned a lot from her about what goes on behind closed doors. I was onto you even when Cookie wouldn't let on you'd ever laid a hand on her. I could see her get jumpy if we were even a minute late getting home. *Oh my, what'll happen if I don't have dinner on the table when Warren gets home?*"

He bristled at her mocking him but forced himself to sit still, working through the riled up feeling in his chest. Finally, he shrugged and, lowering his shoulders, said, "I hope you can see what a different man I am today." Her eyes stayed hard but he went on anyway. "Sober five years but I could lose it in a minute so I put a lot of effort into keeping it. And I went through a six-month research program for batterers."

He could tell that surprised her.

"A lot of deep stuff. Maybe from Denise you know the same statistics I know, about how hard it is to break the patterns, but I'm still working on it. As you saw last night, I've got a new woman, and I don't want to lose her . . . I went down far enough . . ."

She looked at him with greater interest now. "Good for you, Warren," she said, for once sounding sincere.

"I'm only sorry I tried to take Cookie down with me. She never deserved a moment of that."

"I know," she said, lowering her eyes. "There were times when we were little . . . and Cookie was so sweet. It was easy to be mean to her."

Warren felt as if sparklers were going off all around them. His hands tingled. What was she saying?

Annie gazed out on the creek. "It still goes against my better judgment, though, so I'm not telling you where Denny thought he saw her."

Warren shrugged. "I couldn't go running up there right now anyway," he said. "I'm fully booked until first frost. But I'm glad to know, *if that was her*, that she's okay."

But to himself he was singing, *Canada, oh Canada*. For the first time since the time he'd foolishly traipsed off to Montreal, he had some direction, and surely there was some way to narrow down where the little bitch had landed.

After canvassing the job site to be sure the work was going well, he stopped off home for lunch. Melinda was out working and he was glad of that. Found some sliced turkey and made a fat sandwich and couldn't sit to eat it, he was so agitated. Because he had already decided he would present himself to Denny, whom he'd met once years before. He'd find out where Denny had gone on vacation. And strike out from there. And when he found her? *Damn! He needed a drink!* He stuffed his face with the sandwich instead.

Cookie suddenly formed before his eyes. "What the fuck, Cookie?" he said. "You very nearly killed me. Ma's right. Why should I let you get away with that?" He dropped the last of his sandwich on the counter and his fists curled and uncurled. His jaw clenched and his vision grew blurry. He was just about to hit the wall when his eyes lit on a photo on the TV shelf, of him and Melinda.

Just then, the phone rang. Rattling with energy, he picked it up.

"Son?" his mother asked.

"Who else, Ma?"

"How come you're not at work?"

"How come you're calling at this hour?" he demanded.

"Psychic," she said. She was right there. Her timing was so good, despite knowing he should keep it to himself, he blurted out he'd had breakfast with Cookie's sister.

"What was her name, I forget."

"Annie."

She forgot a lot these days, but as she often said, why not, she had to make room in her ninety-five-year-old brain to fit some new things in it. She hadn't forgotten Cookie, though. His mother was the one person who regularly reminded him Cookie had gotten away with murder. Then she'd correct herself, saying, "Well, you know what I mean. Just because you're strong as an ox and pulled through, but not for a minute should that let her off the hook."

She paused, then went on, "Did her sister hear from that little bitch?"

"Ma, please."

"Well?"

"She didn't really hear from her. All she knows is she's in Canada."

"So let's go get her!" she exclaimed, her voice rising with vigor.

"Ma, I'm trying to move on. You know, Melinda . . . we're doing good, gonna have a baby. Remember?"

His mother had always acted as if Cookie were an intruder to their small family circle but had taken to Melinda and seemed glad he had a new girlfriend. Maybe she was realizing she wouldn't be around to watch over him forever. She'd always tried to compete with Cookie and, rather than pushing back, Cookie had only stepped herself out to the sidelines.

"Oh yeah, that's good, you're finally going to make me a grandma," she said now. "I like that Melinda, but call the cops, tell them to go after Cookie. Get 'em to take you with them. You're no wimp, Warren. Go after her and bring her back and make her serve her time."

He should never have spoken a word; now she would not let him rest.

"That little bitch," she said again in a raspy whisper.

"Ma, let's cool it," he said. "You've already had one heart attack."

"So, if you don't want me to have another one, go get her, Warren," she said. "I don't forget for one minute what she did to you, and don't you dare forget it, either!"

Chapter 18

"Hold on, I'll be there in just a minute," Edith called out, when a rap on her front door caught her lolling in bed. She leapt into sweat pants and sweatshirt she had left at her bedside the night before, only to discover it was Janie, the librarian's daughter, with her baby, the fat-cheeked, redheaded boy of less than a year whose picture was displayed on the library checkout desk.

"Janie, how nice to see you!" she exclaimed.

Janie nodded shyly. "Hello, Mrs. Biddle. Mom said *you* said to come over and bring Jason to meet you."

"Indeed, I did," said Edith, going on to herself, *but not before I've had a chance to brush my teeth.* "Come on in, and I'll make us a cup of tea."

While the water was heating, she rushed into the bathroom to wash up, and by the time she came back, Janie had removed the whistling kettle from the flame and was gazing out the kitchen window.

"I miss it," she said.

"What?"

"The wildness up here. The waves crashing. The huge rocks."

Edith smiled. "Yes, it's rare."

When the baby pounded on the bar of his stroller, Janie lifted him and held him to face the sea. "Look at that," she said. "It'll fill you with dreams."

They took the tea out to the little French table on the patio, and Janie arranged the stroller so Jason was looking at the sea alongside them.

"You're a good mother, I can see," said Edith.

Janie shrugged. "I got lucky. He's an angel."

"You've been very productive since you left here, just as I expected," Edith went on.

"Well . . . did you see my book got published?"

"I not only saw it, I read it."

Janie colored slightly.

"And enjoyed what I read, too."

Janie covered her mouth with her hand as if to hide the smile brought forth by Edith's approval.

"But I don't know when I'll ever get to another, given this little one." She reached over to rub the top of Jason's head, which set him to cooing.

"Well, he's certainly part of your being productive," said Edith.

"I guess so," said Janie, as if she hadn't thought of that before, and the two women laughed and Jason laughed, too.

Just then Edith saw Molly descending the stone steps and called out to her. "Please, come say hello to one of my former students."

Molly came onto the patio and shook the young woman's hand.

"Molly lives up in Doc's cottage and it's really nice for me, having her up there," Edith explained. "And Janie, here, is one of our former stellar residents of Seal Cove, just back from Halifax for a visit."

There was a lull in the conversation, broken by the baby shrieking with joy over absolutely nothing, which led to Molly dropping down to where he bounced up and down in the stroller.

When he grabbed at her watch, Molly made a clicking sound with her tongue and said, "Tick, tock, tick, tock," and the baby broke into a huge grin, which, in turn, brought forth a rare, wide smile from Molly.

"He likes you," said Janie.

Molly looked up.

"I remember seeing you around town a couple of years ago when I was home from college," Janie continued.

Molly went quiet.

Edith moved another chair up to the table and invited her to sit and have a cup of tea with them, but Molly declined, saying she'd promised Butch she'd be at his place about now, to look over some of the damage to the nets.

"Ah," said Edith.

"Where do you come from, Molly?" Janie asked.

"The States."

"Your family all there?"

Molly nodded. "What's left of them."

"I'm sorry," said Janie.

"No problem." Molly caught herself biting at the skin around her thumbnail and quickly stuck her hand into her pocket. "Is yours all here?"

"Oh, yeah. Except for me, because my husband got a job in Halifax as a computer programmer, so for now, that's where we'll be. The big city."

Before Janie could ask another question, Molly reiterated she had best be on her way. Edith didn't protest, only took her elbow as she walked her to the top of the path, telling her Janie had been one of those kids she'd wanted to see get out of here because of her smarts and her native ambition. "And I wanted to thank you for what you've been doing for Chrissie—teaching her to drive and having her help at the museum. It's been great for her, and I'm so pleased to see her putting a little meat on her bones." Then she added, "Stop by any time. You know I'm always glad to see you." She let go of Molly's elbow and turned back to Janie.

As soon as Molly was out of earshot, Janie tilted her head and asked, "What's her story?" The directness flummoxed Edith. Janie, the "insider" expecting Edith to collude with her about the "outsider."

"Molly's really taken to us," Edith replied. "She's been working with Butch during lobster season, and he's taken a shine to her. And it's lovely for me, having someone up in the cottage."

Janie narrowed her eyes. "But where'd she come from? Didn't she just up and appear one day?"

"Right. She's circumspect about where she came from, but that doesn't bother me. She's a really good person," said Edith.

Janie nodded. "I heard you thanking her for teaching that girl to drive. Is she the anorexic girl?"

"Well, yes, Chrissie's thin, but let's not label her."

"Well, you must know it's her father who's always trying to find out where Molly came from. He drinks down there at the veteran's hall with the Mounties when they're off duty, and he's been trying to get them to bring her in for questioning."

"For what?" Edith asked, struggling to hold her anger in check.

"That's what *they* say. They can't call her in unless they have something on her."

Thankfully for Edith, Jason let out a loud squeal just then. Janie carried their cups to the kitchen, took him out of the stroller, and changed him right there on the café table.

"Well, best be going before I need another diaper," Janie said, and Edith was glad to see her pack up her diaper bag and go.

She wanted to say, "You can take your insinuations with you," wondering, Was this attitude of hers what Halifax had done for her young protégée?

But after she left, Edith couldn't stop thinking. Who was she kidding, saying it didn't bother her that Molly didn't talk about her past. It blocked her from getting past the surface of Molly, even though Molly was definitely not a surface person. She must return to what she'd started at the library. There was something so vulnerable about Molly, and if only she knew its source, maybe she'd be able to help her.

That very afternoon, she found it—a picture of Molly, although her name was Carol Wagner and the article said she went by the name "Cookie." It was on the front page of the June 15, 2004 edition. In the headshot, she was much younger; it might even be her high school graduation picture. There was also a picture of her husband, a handsome, robust-looking fellow named Warren. It was alleged she had stabbed him. He'd been taken to the hospital in critical condition, and she had vanished.

Someone took a seat at the next computer over. Edith quickly scrolled down so the picture was not showing. She carefully moved back to the beginning of the text and read it again, her breath stopping. So this is what had brought Molly to Cape Breton. Goodness! Was it really her? She glanced to the side to be sure her neighbor was busy, then scrolled back up to the picture. The young woman had long hair pulled back in a ponytail, strong, inquisitive blue eyes but with a defensive squint to them, a shine in her smile. It sure did look like Molly. Furthermore, it made sense why she had arrived with that blunt haircut and harried look.

Edith sat in shock. Close it, she told herself and clicked to close the screen and sign out. Then she was sorry she hadn't looked through the rest of the paper to see if there was more. Some description of this woman, Carol Wagner. Had she had a restraining order? Was there some history? But she could not go back and look again, not now. Someone in the library might pass by and recognize Molly, just as she had.

She perused the shelves to find another mystery to check out. Another Agatha Christie would be good. Now, in her sixties, with her no longer sharp memory, except for a few favorites, she was never sure which ones she had read. This could be seen as a blessing of getting older, she guessed. You could read your old favorites again. But her head was capable only of thinking about Molly. My God, how had she gotten away? With murder? Or had her husband survived? They'd said critical. She'd have to go back and read the next week's edition. Not now, though. She squeezed her forehead, trying to think straight, though nearly faint. She took a chance on one of the mysteries she wasn't sure of and headed for the desk to check it out.

"Janie was thrilled to see you," said Dottie. "She only hoped she hadn't dropped over too early."

Edith shook her head. "We had a lovely visit," she said, controlling her voice. Her feelings for Janie had changed, but she didn't want that to show. Besides, she thought of herself as one of the sharper tacks in the community, which meant early to bed, early to rise, and she didn't want anyone thinking she was becoming a late sleeper just because Doc was gone and school was out for summer.

Back in Seal Cove, she avoided the diner, where she usually stopped for her late afternoon snack and cup of decaf. She wanted to be home alone, to mull over this news. But once there, she rather wished she had followed her usual routine. *Her* life hadn't changed; it was Molly's. But *this knowledge*, if only it could be put back. She wished the picture didn't stand so strongly in her mind, of Molly in a ponytail with a broad smile, Molly before. She thought of the rolled-up hank of hair she'd found in the cottage. How was she to behave as if nothing had changed, as if questions were not going loop de loop in her mind? Questions like, should she be afraid of Molly? She stopped where she was preparing her supper at her kitchen counter and stamped her foot. Certainly not, she's as gentle a soul as ever I've met, she told herself.

Did Butch know? She was sure he didn't the day Molly took off and he found her out on the highway. Should she tell him?

What about the legal situation? Was she putting herself in jeopardy by housing someone who might be a criminal? How could she have known? She wouldn't even know now if her curiosity hadn't gotten the better of her. And how she wished it hadn't!

Chrissie's father had it in for Molly from the start. If he knew enough to look up the same newspaper as she had, it would be a disaster. She should have listened to Chrissie back then, when she said her father thought Molly was an evil witch. But how could she regret bringing Chrissie and Molly together when it was Molly who, quite literally, had saved her, getting her to eat again with simple tea and cookies, while the two of them put together a 1000-piece puzzle. Sure, the girl still had problems, but she was going to be alive to deal with them.

Edith ate too fast and got the hiccups. She needed to resort to the way she'd learned to be able to hold the secrets of people and yet still relate to them. Separating these special pieces of knowledge from her daily knowing of them, so they could relate as townspeople and neighbors.

She and Martin had shared this. People told him all sorts of things behind his examining room door, and he left those secrets there. Every once in a while, she or Martin would speak of these underside nuggets of information, without mentioning names. Just sharing some particularly distressing bit, like when Martin told her about one of his teenage patients, a young girl with a particularly tender appearance, who had revealed she thought she was meant to be male and wanted to have her breasts removed. She had raised her eyes to him and with a hopeful voice, asked, "I already look more like a boy than a girl, don't I?" just as he was thinking he could see nothing but the girl in her. He'd not told Edith who it was, and she'd run through the students she knew but not come up with a clue.

She missed Martin now, wished he were sitting here telling her what she should do in this situation. "First thing," he would say, "let it settle, no use holding onto anything so tight."

Well, he was right. She was doing just the opposite, clenching this to her breast.

Since she'd missed her visit to the diner, she put on water for decaf, and staring at the same view as Janie had earlier, saw a head bob into view as Molly ascended the path. She almost ducked, as if there were a reason Molly shouldn't see her, but caught herself. And lo, Molly didn't just pass but came right up to her door.

"Hello," she said. "I'm sorry I rushed off this morning. Don't know the work I had to do with Butch was really urgent, but I told him I'd be there. So I thought I'd stop back by now."

Edith was momentarily speechless but opened the door wide and welcomed her. "Just in time for a cup of decaf," she said.

"Great," said Molly, looking radiant, pink-cheeked from her walk up the hill in the brisk breeze.

"How're the nets?" asked Edith, at a loss for what was safe to talk about.

"Amazing," said Molly. "You can't imagine how huge a hole a seal can make. They don't look that big when you see them out there rounding the point in the sea."

"No, but I know they are."

"They chew through those strong nets and then it looks like they must get two of them, one on either side of the hole, and say, 'Okay, pull!' and split the thing farther apart. They wouldn't have to do so much damage just to take the bait, now, would they?" Molly laughed.

Edith shook her head no, all the while thinking, wasn't there a milder way to stop whatever your husband was doing to you than to stab him? Like walk out? She set down a cup in front of Molly and realized she wasn't holding up her end of the conversation. "So, can you salvage those nets, after the seals have been wiggling around in them?"

"Oh, sure," Molly said, "but with a lot of work and a lot of hemp."

"And a lot of time," Edith added.

"Well, that we have," said Molly. "We're looking ahead at a long fall and winter."

"I hate to think of it," said Edith.

"Me, too."

There was an interlude of silence in which they sipped their coffee, then Molly asked Edith what she had been up to today.

"Well, you met Janie. I visited with her, and then I straightened up a bit. Janie's mother is the librarian, so seeing her reminded me I had a book overdue, so I went to the library and exchanged it for another." Her face felt hot, as if she might be blushing, though she was not blushing, just lying by omission.

"Another mystery?" asked Molly. They sometimes spoke about the books they were reading, and in fact, Edith often passed onto Molly the books she had checked out before taking them back.

Edith nodded, then looked away, realizing she had been staring at Molly, comparing her face to the image in the picture.

Molly looked at her quizzically.

"Do you need me to pick up anything for you tomorrow?" she asked, falling back to her role as the tenant who lived in the cottage in exchange for doing some cleaning and errands.

"Oh, no," said Edith. "I've got plenty of time to shop for myself as long as school's out."

Molly fiddled with her cup. "Did you get to see your doctor

when you went to Montreal?" she asked.

"Indeed, I did," said Edith, "and he declared me totally fit, except for vitamin D, which none of us this far north can get enough of. Especially once you're in or past menopause. Evidently, it's important to your body taking up calcium to keep your bones strong." Edith paused. "Ever have yours tested?" she asked, then immediately realized of course Molly wouldn't have.

"Never knew much about it," Molly said.

"Well, never mind, you're young and healthy, and you get in a lot of walking. That's what my doctor told me I need to do—get out in this good sea air and walk a couple of miles every day."

Molly nodded.

"I should get started with a good habit before school begins again," Edith added. "First thing in the morning. How about you? Seven-thirty? Shall we take a walk together on the high road?"

"Sure," said Molly. "Why not? As long as I go home now and get to bed early."

Edith breathed easier once Molly was gone but wondered why she had made a plan to get together again so soon when she didn't seem able to put this startling information into a box and get it to stay closed. She went in the bathroom and checked her looks in the mirror, expecting to see hives or some terribly revealing expression but saw only the way her mouth fell when she relaxed. It made her look unhappy, though she wasn't unhappy. She remembered when her mother had been the age she was now, sixty-two, and Edith had noticed her mother's mouth doing the same thing and decided it must be a manifestation of some underlying depression. Of course she'd hurt her mother's feelings by telling her. Bunk, she thought now, it was purely the effect of gravity. She wished she could have her mother back for a moment, to tell her she stood corrected. But that was not to be, just as, from now on, she could never *not know* about Molly's plight.

Chapter 19

M olly had been to Butch's for dinner and met his sister Lil for the first time. They'd all gotten a little high on the bottle of wine Lil had brought from New York, and now Molly had gone home.

Lil had once lived in Italy, on a communal farm, developing her taste for Italian food and wine, so Butch freely turned his kitchen over to her whenever she visited. She was the baby of their family. When his mother had hauled them all up to Canada, of course she'd been forced to move with them, but after high school, like so many young Canadians, she'd decided to have her year abroad, only it had lasted four, before she'd come back to Canada and then gone off to college in the States.

Butch sat out under the stars with Lil, happy to have the sense of family she exuded, her shoulders wide like their mother's, an expression of contentment on her face as she leaned back and took in the wide sky. He patted his belly and complimented her on the meal.

"A hell of a challenge out here," Lil said. "Your grocery store was nearly empty and what was there cost double what it ought to."

"Yeah, well it's a long way to ship anything up here. You can't forget that," he said.

"At least you've got the good fish."

"Right. Can't beat it." He had gone down to the fish market, which was only open for a few hours after the local catch was brought in each day, and gotten a good piece of flounder, which Lil had cooked for him and Molly.

They were quiet a moment, then she asked, "Is Molly a good cook?"

"Not bad," he said. "She makes a good spaghetti sauce. But she's not the cook you are."

"She seems like a very nice woman. I like her," Lil said.

Butch nodded. "She *is* a very nice woman, and I'm glad you two have finally met."

"She's quiet," Lil said. "Seems deep. Seems like a good match for you."

"She is. She's saving me from being an aging hermit who was getting sick of his own company."

"Well, bachelor brother of mine, are you going to marry her?" she asked with that talent she had developed as a child for raising a single eyebrow.

Butch took a deep breath. He grabbed Jimbo's snout and brought it up to his nose and said out loud, "What do you think, Jimbo, shall I marry her?" He was churning inside, a mix of desire to tell Lil everything and a big stop sign he could almost see Molly holding up in his mind. He'd been doing his best to stay in the present and not think about what she had told him, not think what would happen if someone were to come searching for her. But ever since Molly's cousin had come to the museum, he'd been scrambled. They'd spent a week with her scooted down in the seat whenever they drove through town, scared her cousin might still be here, though Butch had repeatedly checked the various tourist houses where he might be staying and never found a trace of him.

"What's the matter?" Lil asked. "You hooked and don't want to admit it?"

"What about you? You and Bonnie could get married now. Not New York yet, I know, but you could come up here and get married in Canada, but I don't see you racing into it."

"We might," she said, "but no hurry. Bonnie and I hardly need a wedding to know we're committed. Most lesbians don't. And what do we need with a bunch of wedding gifts when we live in a too-small apartment that's already clutter city? Why support the wedding industry? I'd sooner put my dollars behind helping battered women get away from the fists of their husbands."

He hadn't meant to get her started, had forgotten how impassioned she became on this topic. She reminded him of their mother railing against the war in Vietnam, the loss of "our good young men" and the harm to the civilian population, and for what? The way she saw it, women had much wiser instincts when it came to peace and the protection of life, and they had to pass these on to men, starting with their sons, if the species were to have a chance of evolving or even surviving.

"You sound like Mom."

"I'll take that as a compliment," Lil said, looking up. "May she rest in peace."

"Right here over Cape Breton," he added, looking up to the sky with her, "even though she died in Vancouver."

"Amen," said Lil. "She had a good death. *You* know that. I'm so glad you got there. Just sorry Ian didn't."

Lil had gone home to be with their mother and passed those final days with her, holding her even as she left the planet. She'd rung up both the brothers and told them to come quickly, but given how stalwart their mother had always been, Ian had convinced himself it would take a major storm to carry her out, so he took his time leaving San Francisco, and the result was, he'd gotten there only in time for the funeral.

Raising one eyebrow again, Lil reminded Butch he hadn't yet answered her.

"It's not that I'm such a committed bachelor," he said. "I *would* like to marry Molly. In fact, I always regretted losing Janet because I was too lost in myself then to realize she wasn't going to wait forever . . . "

"So," said Lil.

"We didn't really have much of a role model for marriage in our family, did we?" Butch said. "I mean we had a good mother, and she made sure we stood up for each other as siblings, but Dad, well, he always seemed more like an appendage. Coming and going. Mostly going."

Lil shrugged, tilted her head. "True, but then there was Uncle Charlie, Mr. Stability, who hardly spoke a word. But Aunt Gladys touted him as a good husband. Personally, I'd rather have our dad. At least he wasn't boring."

Butch chuckled and admitted that he would, too.

"So?" Lil said again with a grin when he didn't go on.

"Can you promise me you'll hold what I tell you entirely in confidence?" he asked.

"Course," she said, sounding suddenly alert.

"I did propose," he stated flatly. "After six months of our seeing each other, but Molly freaked. She can't get married. She ran away because of something she did, and that's why she's up here, but there's no way she can become a citizen or do anything official."

Lil's eyes popped. "What'd she do?" she demanded.

"Really, really, you must keep this a secret."

Lil nodded soberly.

"About five years ago, her husband came at her one time too many. He had a habit of pushing sex on her and then beating her to a pulp, but she grabbed a butcher knife near her and . . . We assume he's dead, because she thinks it went straight into his heart. They lived out from Woodstock in the country and there wasn't anyone around to rescue him. She hightailed it out of the U.S. and has never gone back."

Lil's mouth dropped open in an "O."

"He had been abusing her for years," Butch added.

"*That* I already guessed," Lil said. Lil was a paralegal and worked with a lawyer who had a reputation for taking on cases of battered women. "Yikes, that's some story," she added.

Butch put his head back and closed his eyes. "It sure is," he said. "Just don't forget you're the only person who knows it besides me."

"Man, oh man," said Lil, "it's just too common. There's a whole string of women in prison because of it."

"Thank God Molly's here and not one of them."

"Right, good for her. But look at how her life's compromised. There's no real getting away."

"What do you mean?"

"Well, she can't marry my terrific brother, like I'm sure she would like to."

"True."

Butch let out a sigh. It released him to no longer keep this to himself, and as he relaxed, a bone-weary tiredness came over him and he wanted nothing but to lie down and invite a sound sleep. But Lil was warming up for action. She had started out as a child demonstrator in the lap of their mother during the Vietnam War, and gone on to become a radical lesbian feminist, standing up for women's causes, gay rights, whatever was the next human rights' issue. She didn't hang out at the edge of the crowd but was always up front, carrying a banner. The only problem with having told her was she would want to do something about it.

"Look, as soon as I get home, I'll do some research."

"What do you mean?"

"I mean, like, for starters, did the man die?"

Butch squeezed his forehead. It would be nice to know, but he didn't want to get Lil started. "Okay, but no more," he said. "I don't want you getting involved here. It's true, Molly has to keep a low profile, but this is a good place to do that. Hardly anyone ever comes here; she's well known now in the community and accepted. Even though people originally wondered where she came from, I don't think they even trouble themselves anymore."

Lil raised a single eyebrow again.

"We have a good life. I'd marry her if I could, but I can live without the formalities. She's made me a very satisfied man."

Lil was nodding. "I hear you," she said. "But, if the man's dead, you're in a much more serious situation."

"Right," he said. "Well, I'm pretty sure he is, so it might be best to leave it at that."

Lil stared hard at him and he could tell she was thinking of every possibility. He remembered when they were kids how she would outlast him and Ian at almost any game, especially the imaginative ones. As the big brothers, they would start the games and then she would take over.

"Stop thinking," he said, "please."

"Are you kidding?" she said. "You tell me a shocking story about your new girlfriend, who happens to be a lovely, gentle woman I can see you are crazy about, and who's saved you from becoming a grizzly old bachelor, and she's in deep shit and you want me to put it on the shelf?"

"That's right," Butch said, nearly whispering. "I just wanted you to know."

She brought her hands up over her ears. "Okay," she said. "I'll try to pretend I didn't just hear what I heard, but it's not going to be easy."

They sat in silence then, and he looked up and started pointing out the constellations, something he had often done when they were kids. The sky was clear and downright sparkling with its light show, enough to make them giddy as he went on, and she chimed in with her speculations about what might be what—most often incorrect—and pretty soon they were laughing and Jimbo was bouncing up and down as if he might like to jump to a star, and Butch thought, okay, and was glad he had told her.

The next morning, they went down to the diner for breakfast and, as planned, Molly came along. She'd been out early, walking the cliffs with Mrs. Biddle, accounting for her rosy cheeks and overall spitting-good, healthy look.

"That's what I should be doing," said Lil, patting her somewhat thick belly. She was a big woman, might even qualify as obese in spite of how well she carried her weight. "Especially as I was just contemplating ordering bacon with my eggs here."

"I wouldn't have done it on my own," Molly admitted. "But Mrs. Biddle is trying to build up her bones, so the doctor told her to walk every day."

Butch, side by side with Molly in the booth, put his arm around her, drew her close and sniffed in a strong breath, saying, "You've got the sea in your hair. Smells good."

Muriel, the waitress, greeted Butch and Molly warmly, then Lil, too, when she was introduced as Butch's sister. "Oh, yeah," she said. "I know you; he talks about you."

Lil looked up at her.

"All good stuff," she said.

"He's not such a bad guy himself," Lil said, before putting in her order.

There was a lull in the conversation, Lil putting together what she had learned about Butch's girlfriend with the sweet-looking woman across from her. She wished Molly knew she was aware of the tragic event so they could make a plan together. She could go home and speak with Bronwen, the main attorney she worked for, about how best to pursue her case. She could research her odds for getting off with a plea of self-defense. It would mean everything to the woman if she could clear her name, wouldn't it? But then she saw the way Molly's smile lit up when she gave Butch a playful punch, goading him to walk with her the way Mrs. Biddle had. Maybe Butch was right. Leave well enough alone. Here at the end of the earth, they did already have a life. Yet, she couldn't leave it alone completely.

"Do you have any siblings?" she asked Molly. "Any family still in the States?" Her eyes never left Molly's face.

She saw Molly's hesitation, and Butch's squint that usually gave him a look of cheer, grew fixed, as if warning her to cool it. But her eyes remained on Molly, and then Molly cleared her throat and spoke over a frog in it, saying, "Yes, one sister is all. But we're not in touch."

Now Butch's mouth formed into an "O."

"What's her name?"

"Annie."

"Older or younger?"

"Older."

"Were you close as kids?"

Molly nodded yes.

"I always wanted a sister," Lil said. "Even though I loved having brothers."

Molly dropped her shoulders about an inch. "I always wanted a brother," she said.

"How come?"

"To protect me."

"Protect you from whom?"

"Oh, the bigger boys at school. Sometimes, maybe my father. And sometimes from Annie."

"But you said you and Annie were close," Lil said.

Molly looked down. "We were, but she had a mean streak."

There was the smell of bacon cooking and the occasional ding of toast popping up in the toaster, and they were actually having a real conversation, Butch thought, amazed at his sister's ability to bring Molly out. Had she actually lied to him about having a sister or had he never asked, or if he had asked, not held to her as closely as Lil did, so that she'd been able to lie without him seeing it.

"What was your father like?"

"Well," Molly slowed to a stop as if she had left them for a moment, "I liked him better than my mother, but he drank too much and then it was hard to predict how he'd be."

"Sound familiar?" Lil asked Butch. "Our dad was fun until he wasn't, but you never knew when that might be."

Butch nodded but then narrowed his eyes at Lil, sending her a look of caution.

"And did Butch put himself on your father's side, like my sister did?" Molly asked, gazing sideways at him.

Lil shook her head in a definitive no. "That was my other brother, Ian. Butch stood up for me, no matter what."

Butch's eyes came into a squint again, but this time with his playful look. "And believe me," he said, "sometimes Lil got me in a lot of trouble." They all laughed.

The waitress slid their plates onto the table, and when she returned with a fresh pot of coffee, they seemed to feel the warmth of the room as the steam rose up from the coffee pot. Lil wanted to go back to asking about the sister, but she'd seen Butch's expression, as if to say, "Stop and eat your food." And so she left it alone, for now.

Chapter 20

The day after Lil left, Cookie and Butch took the morning to go out to Cape North and do some final tidying up of the museum to prepare for fall closing. While Butch went out back to clean up the tools, Cookie worked on covering up some of the exhibits with plastic. She didn't know what compelled her, since rarely was anything to be found in the mailbox, but after a while, she went out to check it and the shock she got sent volts clear down to her knees. There, on top of the weekly circular for the hardware store, was a small envelope, addressed, in a flowery script with a shakiness in the letters—or was it just her eyes were jerky with surprise—to:

> *Cookie Wagner*
> *c/o: North Highlands Historical Museum*
> *Cape North, Nova Scotia.*

Oh my God! She took it out of the box and flattened her fingers to hide the name as she walked back to the museum. Who had sent her something? Cousin Denny? She started to shake so badly she had to sit down. She put the envelope in her pocket and looked out the side window to make sure Butch was still busy. Sitting down at the reception desk, she took out the envelope and looked at it again. No, she thought, you can't open it. What if Butch comes in? She returned it to her pocket and tried to transport herself back to the pleasant breakfast they'd had with Butch's sister the day before. Anything to get her mind off what was in her pocket.

She'd liked meeting Lil and having a prism through which to know Butch a little better. She wished she could meet Ian, too, the problem guy. And what a strange coincidence that she and Butch both had sisters who were lesbians, though she hadn't revealed that to Butch and Lil. This was the first time she'd even admitted to anyone up here she did have a sister, and she'd seen Butch's long ears open to listen for more. It made her realize, once again, how unfair she was to keep everything about herself so hidden.

She needed to get away from him, go home, and open this envelope and see what was inside as soon as possible. This was her business, hers alone. Her stomach grabbed, but she couldn't rush him off when they'd hardly just gotten here. It wasn't far, only about 25 kilometers, but on the narrow winding road, the drive took well over half an hour. She'd have to put in at least an hour or two of the work they'd come to do.

Finally, after complaining about not feeling well and Butch reluctantly agreeing to go, he'd dropped her off at the bottom of her stone stairs, making her promise if they weren't going to see each other later, they'd at least spend Sunday together.

She placed the envelope on her coffee table and sat rigidly on the sofa staring at it. In spite of it still being sealed, it seemed very much alive.

She studied the handwriting. The letters were sort of heart-shaped, old-fashioned like her grandmother's handwriting. Flowery. But also in places with squiggles, like the person had been nervous enough to have a little tremor or shook when writing.

Thinking whoever mailed this knew exactly where she was made Cookie's heart whir like a motor. Her hands went clammy and her head spun with vertigo. My God, how much more of this could she stand?

The panicky feeling always came on fast and hard and gave her a deep feeling of dread.

It was five years now, would be five years and three months tomorrow.

She saw herself again grab the knife and plunge it into Warren's chest with the strength and fury of a caged animal. Going for the soft spot below his breastbone. How could she have made that thrust? She could see the picture, yet couldn't reach that part of her. And she needed to, because beside the horror in the memory, there was a moment of secret triumph hanging just out of her reach.

She went to the window and looked far out onto the sea. Watching its mammoth proportions always made her feel small, and right now, small seemed good. Whitecaps crested and she imagined going under them and not coming back up. The image gave her enough relief for her hands to start feeling like hands again, instead of appendages covered with thick bandages or boxing gloves, and separate from her.

But as soon as she looked away from the ocean, her eyes pulled to the envelope again.

She went back to the couch and, for the first time, examined the postmark: *Woodstock, New York*. It had been mailed over a week ago. Did mail take so long to get to Canada, or had it been sitting in the mailbox a while? Maybe another museum volunteer had discovered it and just left it there, not knowing any Cookie Wagner. Her hands shook as she tried to slip a finger under the flap and pry it up neatly, until finally she gave up and just ripped the envelope open and drew out the card.

It was a picture of a hummingbird, its beak deep into the throat of a fiery red daylily. Inside, the note, in the same flowery, shaky writing:

> *Dear Cookie,*
>
> *Don't think you got away with murder, that's one thing you can be sure of. We know where you are now. Someone's coming after you.*

No signature. No hint of who had written it. Was it someone who knew about the hummingbird feeders in her backyard? She smelled the paper. Maybe a slight aroma of kitchen. Her heart raced again. She couldn't bear another of those dreaded panic attacks. She went to the bathroom, threw cold water on her face, and looked at herself in the mirror. Her eyes were crimped and her mouth was clenched; yet, she looked soft. Not like when she'd had such a monstrous look on her arrival in Seal Cove.

Then someone called out, "Hey, Molly?"

She forced herself out of the bathroom. It was Chrissie, coming up the steps. She'd forgotten all about the plans they'd made. Chrissie was getting ready to take her driver's test for the second time and, since it was Saturday, Cookie had promised to take her out to practice at 4.

"Just a minute," she called, returning to the bathroom. Her cheeks were extra red, her eyes wide open. She turned up her hands and saw her palms were redder than usual, too, but her heart was no longer going like a motor. Well, good, since she had no choice but to carry on in spite of this threat, it might as well be with Chrissie, whom she'd grown very fond of.

"Can we practice parking, too?" Chrissie asked, as Cookie tossed her the keys along with a chair pillow to raise her up higher in the car, and opened the passenger door.

"Long as you promise not to bump anyone, fore or aft."

This was pretty much a joke because the only parallel parking spaces in Seal Cove were those with the never-in-effect meters in front of the diner, and they were so spread out they were no challenge. The only way for Chrissie to practice parallel parking was for them to set out the cones like the motor vehicle office did.

The car was a 1995 Honda Civic hatchback, blue inside and out, stick shift with four forward gears. It got great mileage so Cookie only had to fill up once a month, since she walked everywhere in Seal Cove and rarely left town. But now, when Chrissie suggested they drive out in the direction of Meat Cove, she agreed and added, "Maybe stop off for a walk on Silver Beach," thinking a walk might help her with her suffocating feeling.

Chrissie drove with her eyes straight ahead, full concentration on the road.

"How's it going in school?" Cookie asked. It was the end of September and school had been going for a few weeks.

"Pretty good. I like my English teacher," said Chrissie. "And Mrs. Biddle came to homeroom to talk about how, if we want to go to college, we need to start looking at schools now that we're juniors and decide where we want to apply."

"Wow, already!" Cookie said. "So are you going to do it?"

"I guess," Chrissie said. "Mrs. Biddle says I should. But I don't think my dad wants me to."

"Why not?"

"He doesn't want to pay."

"How about trying for scholarships?"

Chrissie stopped at a temporary light strung up to hold traffic to one lane because of roadwork. She turned to Cookie, a look of bafflement pursing her mouth. "You really think I could get one?"

"Why not?'

"There're a lot of kids smarter than me."

"I doubt it," said Cookie.

"How would you know?" Chrissie challenged.

Cookie laughed. "You saying I'm not smart enough to know who's smart? Look how fast you learned all the history and stuff at the museum."

"Oh well, that was easy. A lot of it I knew already."

"Still, you can't know if you can get a scholarship unless you apply."

"True," Chrissie said, allowing her smirk to turn into a smile. Her light blue eyes seemed to match the sea. She had light skin with freckles that gave her a softness and cuteness rather than beauty. Especially since she had started eating again and was filling out from the skeletal form which had scared Cookie the first time Edith brought her over.

When the light turned green, Chrissie returned her concentration to maneuvering the narrow lane they traveled, the shoulder falling off treacherously to their right. She didn't speak again until they came out past the construction. Then, still looking straight ahead, she asked Cookie if *she'd* gone to college.

"Junior college," Cookie said.

"And did you have to apply for a scholarship?"

"Sort of. Student aide. Something like a scholarship, but you had to pay most of it back later."

"I wouldn't mind that," said Chrissie, "long as I could get a job."

Cookie almost agreed with her. Take loans and pay them back was the better way to go. But then she thought of how her life might have been different if she'd had someone to encourage her. Her mother had wanted her to go on with her education, but her father seemed almost jealous. Like, since he hadn't gotten the chance to go to college, why should anyone else? He'd been stingy, too, like Chrissie's dad. Well, she could hardly blame him; he was already working overtime to support them all. Her sister Annie had nevertheless managed to get herself into a state school and left home to go there, even if it was only an hour and a half away. Annie had worked part time in the school cafeteria, and eventually got herself a degree.

With Cookie's long silence, Chrissie seemed to have dropped the subject, but as they pulled into the parking lot of Silver Beach, Cookie firmed up her voice and spoke with more authority than she thought herself capable, saying, "Well, chances are you'll need loans, too, but you should try first for scholarships."

They got out to walk, Chrissie pulling a scarf from the pocket of her jean- jacket and winding it around her neck, Cookie zipping up her windbreaker and pulling up the hood.

"Kind of scary when you've grown up in a tiny town like Seal Cove, to think of ever leaving here," Chrissie said, her voice made small by the wind whipping at their faces. "Even if you want to."

"Of course," Cookie said, "of course it is." She took a deep breath of the sea air. The wind whipped the ocean, making the water frothy. "But you can't stop at fear. Lots of things are scary."

She sensed Chrissie looking at her, waiting for her to explain, and searched for a way to say what she meant.

"You just have to keep going after what you want."

"You think?" said Chrissie.

"It's not that the next scary thing won't come along." Cookie saw the note with the flowery script sitting on her coffee table. "It surely will . . . but you have to keep walking through," she said with growing conviction.

Chrissie stopped and looked out over the ocean and Cookie stopped beside her. "I guess," she said, her voice barely audible above the wind. "I guess I can try for whatever."

Walking back to the car, Chrissie asked if Cookie'd had a dog when she was growing up. Cookie told her about Goldie, their golden retriever mix who'd been the one to come in her dreams and lick all over her face and neck after Warren beat her. She didn't tell this to Chrissie, though. Nor how, after her father spanked her and she ran up to their bedroom, Annie might be right there, ranged out lengthwise on the other twin bed, leafing through a fashion magazine, and if Annie looked to see if Cookie was okay, she made sure to do so when she wouldn't be caught looking. But their golden retriever would lengthen her body and flop up against Cookie's back, soft against the sting of her butt, sopping up the grayness, which made Cookie feel so ragged and small.

"I want one so bad," Chrissie said, "but my parents say it'll cost too much to feed, and who'll pay the vet bills?" She went on, rolling her eyes. "I swore to them I'd get a job, even though I don't know where."

Cookie and Chrissie both knew there were no jobs for teens in Seal Cove; the only kids who had them were the ones whose parents owned the grocery or the gas station or the lobster shack, who worked summers and after school, but most likely didn't get paid.

Later, back in town, Cookie set up the cones for parking and Chrissie knocked one of them over the first three trials.

"Drat," she said, when the third orange cone went rolling away. "So stupid. I do the same thing wrong over and over."

"Never mind," said Cookie, "you'll get it. Just hang in there."

And on the fourth, Chrissie succeeded.

But as Chrissie pulled out to drive back up the hill to Cookie's cottage, a police car came up behind them, and Cookie's heart dropped. What if he stopped them? Chrissie looked so young, like a child driving. She had a proper restricted license but they'd ask Cookie for hers, and all she had was an expired New York State driver's license. They'd put her in a computer and then . . .

She found herself pinching her fingers together hard, glancing back to see if he was still following.

"Yikes," Chrissie said, "A policeman is following us."

"Just keep up your good driving," Cookie said, doing her best to keep her voice even. "You're not doing anything wrong."

Maybe it wouldn't be so bad if she were to get caught. It might be better than constantly living with worry and panic. But when Chrissie turned up High Street, and the policeman didn't follow, Cookie sighed with relief.

Saying goodbye, Chrissie gave her a quick squeeze and blushed, thanking her for the driving lesson. When Cookie returned the hug, she hung on for a second, patting Chrissie's still-too-frag-ile back. The girl had no idea how much being with her was allow-ing Cookie to let her heart open a little.

"You can come up and play with Jimbo any time," Cookie called out as Chrissie headed down the driveway. "Butch doesn't mind."

"Thanks," Chrissie said, but Cookie knew this was not what she wanted. She wanted a dog of her own who would wait for her at home.

She wished there was a way she could help Chrissie get a dog. Just the other day on their walk, she'd suggested to Edith, "I could put aside enough money to help her buy dog food, if that's what's stopping her parents." But Edith had suddenly taken on the cold, stern look of an old-fashioned school marm, holding up her hand, a clear *no*. "That father of Chrissie's . . . I don't want you getting involved." And then she trailed off and Cookie didn't dare ask her to explain further.

Had Edith sussed her out? Or Chrissie's father, Logan? Ever since Denny had spotted her, it seemed like everyone was on her tail.

She walked into her cozy home and her eyes immediately trav-eled to it—the note on her table.

We know where you are.

Self-defense, she wanted to cry out. Wasn't there some way she could explain she had stabbed Warren in self-defense and get herself freed? Her sister would probably know. If only she could trust Annie. Her sister had once come to visit when Cookie could still count on one hand the black eyes Warren had given her. Yet Annie had gotten onto him and deliberately provoked him, shaking her fist in his face as she told him about some woman who had shot her husband point blank and then gone before the jury, declaring she'd done it in self-defense. "It was a big case," she said, "because before that, lawyers were always too scared to go for that defense; they'd settle for a plea bargain or something less, fearing if they lost, the woman might be in prison for life."

"Well, was he coming at her with a gun and she was a better shot than him?" Warren had said laughing and tilting back his chair, pretending hilarity, as if he had little sympathy for the man for being a bad shot.

Annie glared at him. "Not at all. She shot him while he was sound asleep in their bed."

Warren brought his chair back down hard. "So what's it going to be, open season? Is that what you women's libbers want? The Wild West all over again?"

Unperturbed, Annie merely pointed her pistol finger at him, as if perhaps not only did *he* deserve to be shot but all men did, and said, "That woman had endured his beatings for nineteen years. You can't say he got any less than he deserved."

Cookie had shrunk in her chair, expecting Warren to spring up and do something, but he had merely harrumphed and turned away from Annie to ask Cookie what was for dessert. But later, after Annie was gone, he told Cookie her sister was a first-class bitch.

What Cookie could not remember was whether Annie had said, in the end, the jury found the woman guilty or not. She wished she could, because knowing that would mean so much to her now.

She woke in the middle of the night, tangled in the sheets, and couldn't stop seeing the note on the coffee table. *Don't think you've gotten away with murder. We know where you are now.* It wasn't the police. Nor Chrissie's father. Nor Denny. *Some woman.* Not

Annie. Why would some woman want to come after her? Maybe she should go somewhere else and start over, this time knowing better than to get involved with people like Butch and Mrs. Biddle.

But how could she do that to Butch? He was so patient with her panicky spells, though he might also be the cause of them. Because she had not had them those first couple of years when she'd had so little contact with anyone but Mrs. Biddle. But the more she'd gone outward, as if she might live a real life, the stronger they'd come on.

She grabbed the side of the bed to stop the feeling she might fall out of it. She had come to the far end of the earth already. Now she was coming to the far end of her mind. She held tight as her heart started up like a motor, and she anticipated a thimbleful of dread about to spill into her chest. She grabbed the edge of the bed tighter and followed her breath all the way up and down, as it passed across a rough ladder of cartilage in her center. What was it except a feeling? A feeling that was not going to kill her, only make her wish that she was dead.

What had she told Chrissie? "You can't stop at fear but don't expect it to disappear either."

She curled her back the way she had as a girl and imagined Goldie pressing her warm, furry body against her.

Chapter 21

When Warren proposed the trip, Melinda jumped right into researching Cape Breton, the place where the cousin had thought he'd spotted Cookie. She was good on the net. Right away, she located the museum Denny had spoken of: North Highlands Museum. She also found a great little cottage for them to spend a few days in and sent off a deposit. But, from the start, Warren wondered if it was such a great idea for them to go up there together. After all, his real purpose was to find Cookie, and then he didn't know what would happen.

Not that he had bad intentions. He wanted to see for himself if she was all right; he wanted to show her he was a changed man; he wanted to—as they repeatedly harped on in the program "make amends." Though he couldn't picture what he was going to say because his anger still flared when he thought of what she'd done to him. Yeah, he'd been a guilty party, but why hadn't she just yelled at him like Ma had always yelled at Pa and held him off? Worse yet, he harbored a feeling of such deep offense, it made him want to go in swinging. The offense not so much her striking him down, but her abandoning him so utterly after all their years together. They'd had fun times, serious times; she supposedly had loved him. So how could those feelings disappear in an instant? How could she be that cold?

One night at the dinner table, when Melinda was going on and on about all the things she wanted them to do when they went to Cape Breton, getting excited as if it was nothing but a vacation, he put up a hand and said, "Whoa, wait a minute. You need to remember my main purpose in making this journey all the way to goddamn Timbuktu—not somewhere I ever wanted to go—is to see if I can find Cookie."

Melinda's face went blank and some of the color left it.

"And I'm going to have to spend some of my time up there looking for her," he continued, "so you'd best understand that before we take off."

That's when she sprang on him. "Well, thanks for telling me now instead of later. I don't get why you want to go after the little bitch, anyway."

"She was my *wife*," he said in a measured tone. "Don't call her that."

"Your mother does. 'The little bitch' is all she ever calls her."

"Well, she's my ma, which gives her special license."

Melinda leaned in over the table. More than two years together and he had never seen her like this.

"I bet *the little bitch* is gone from there by now, anyway. Your mother wrote her you were coming."

"What do you mean my mother wrote her?" He was half out of his chair.

"She asked me to get her the address for the museum from the internet."

"And you did?"

She gave him one slow nod.

"Damn it," he said. "That was none of your business."

"It *is* my business," she said, her eyes dark with fire.

"You should have asked me," he said, matching her fire. "You had no business . . ."

Melissa lifted her nose in the air and threw back her head as if he had delivered a punch. "Don't try to boss me around," she said.

"I'm not bossing you around."

"You are," she said, glaring then, "with *that tone* in your voice."

He shrugged. "What tone?"

"You know what tone. The one that puts you in charge . . ."

He shook his head, trying to remember what his voice had sounded like. True, he was anxious, not really looking forward to this mission, thinking he would like to find Cookie right at the start and get whatever this was going to be over with.

"Come on," he said, "I didn't mean anything."

But Melinda only continued to glare at him, not speaking.

He felt a meanness about her he had not known before. It made his stomach queasy. What was he supposed to do now?

"Maybe we're both a bit nervous," he mumbled. "Maybe I should have planned to do this alone."

Suddenly she was half yelling and half crying, saying, "I'll be perfectly happy to bring up this child alone, if I need to, but I'm never going to be with someone who bosses me around again, so you want a woman you can boss, you might as well take your wife back, *if* you can find her. I don't need to go chasing after her with you. I was looking forward to us taking a vacation. But if you're only going up there to see if you can spy on that woman who once tried to kill you, forget about it."

She got up and started clearing the table, but over by the sink, she suddenly grabbed her belly and folded over. It scared him silly. He could only think, is she losing our baby? And suddenly, it was distinctly theirs. He was down on his knees at her feet and knew how deeply he was in, no matter what he would find in Cape Breton. Why was he in such a hurry to find a woman who had stabbed him, anyway, when, meantime, he really *really* wanted this? That came clear in a flash, and he was begging her to look at him, to forgive him for trying to boss her, for whatever had come out in his voice.

It was his father's voice, his father who had lodged in him and was always seeking a way out. He heard muscle-man Sam, the counselor, rattling off the odds of guys like him returning to their old behaviors, eighty-some percent, saying, "Those of you who don't will be the exceptions," and Warren had taken the vow to be the exception.

Melinda was still furious, her lips tucked tightly against her teeth, her eyes cold. She looked down upon him as if he were a stranger she didn't recognize, but she had straightened back up and was no longer clutching her stomach. And in some exotic way, her face was more fully formed and sculpted in her fury than he had ever seen it. He was pierced by her coldness. She was a mile apart from him; yet, as her eyes slid away, he wanted even the coldness of them back.

"Please," he said, reaching to take her hand. She left it in his but as if it were detached from her. "I didn't mean to boss you," he said. "Are you okay? The baby . . . I saw you bend over . . ."

A softer light came into her eyes and she touched her belly again, cradling it and nodding like the baby was okay.

He got up then and didn't know where to place himself, so he went to the table and brought over the rest of the dishes.

"I'm not going," she said. "You go on by yourself. I'll stay home."

He could tell she was simmering yet but no longer boiling, and even though she had lost the warmth he'd grown to count on, she was still with him, and this was her style of fighting.

The leaves turning color lit up the road, even the interstate, which Warren didn't like to travel on, because there was so much same old, same old. Same gray road surface, same wide shoulder, same embankments and green exit signs, and then the occasional *Rest Stop 5 Miles*. He remembered his father refusing to travel the new, boring highways when Warren was a child, taking the two-lanes, even when it meant many extra hours to get somewhere. But he was making pretty good time, bouncing along in his truck.

They had planned to come in Melinda's Honda Hybrid, since the gas prices were so high, and he'd figured, why not, since she was smart enough to have one. But plans changed after the fight.

He had finished up all the jobs he had for fall. A remarkable thing in itself. How had the economy fallen into such a sinkhole? Maybe it had been coming on for a while, but no one had really

anticipated it. Who knew when there'd be any work of conse-
quence coming in. All the construction guys could be found hanging around at the deli in the mornings, not grabbing an early coffee
before they got started, but literally hanging out to complain. No
work. How long until the first snowfall when they'd get in a little
snow plowing? How foolish so many of them had been through
this economic bubble, not thinking it necessary to save, since they
couldn't finish one job fast enough to satisfy the customer who was
waiting for them on the next one. Gave everyone a false sense of
security. Now most of the men in construction were saying it was
a good thing the wife had a job. At least that meant they could
pay the rent or the mortgage. Warren had always been a saver, so
he wasn't in bad shape, at least not yet, though this was a first for
him—finishing up his fall jobs before the ground froze, which was
what usually stopped his work for winter.

Sly Annie had thought she was leaving him with just enough
information to frustrate him, not giving him a clue which direction
to head in Canada. But he'd found Denny's number in Cookie's
old address book he kept buried deep in a kitchen drawer where
Melinda wasn't likely to come upon it. Denny had been shocked
to hear from him, but not so guarded as Annie, when Warren told
him he'd heard he might have seen Cookie.

"Whereabouts?" Warren asked, making his voice friendly.

"Far out the Cabot Trail," Denny said, "Ingonish is the biggest
town, then there are several tiny hamlets nearby, fishing villages."

"Thanks," Warren had said, and then swore he could feel the
tension coming over the wire.

"Hey, man, you're not looking to hunt her down, are you?"

"Only to tell her she can come on back if she wants to, and I'll
leave her alone."

There was a long pause from Denny, but then he let out a deep
sigh and said, "I've been feeling bad I didn't go back and look for
her the next day, tell her if she was in legal trouble, we'd try to
help her. But my wife wanted to see some places over on the other
coast, and we went across on that steep, curvy road . . . Man, I had
no idea what an intense road it was . . . and my wife has a real fear

of heights, so she didn't want to come back across it."

The leaves became more brightly colored the farther north Warren went in Maine. He made it up near the Canadian border before stopping for the night, where he had a hardy but cheap meal of fish 'n chips and fell into bed. He called Melinda and told her he missed her but figured she'd have been exhausted by so many hours on the road, since she was the one carrying extra.

She gave him a lot of silence, enough so he could tell she hadn't totally gotten over their fight. But he hung on anyway, talking about stuff like how little traffic he had encountered.

The next day he zoomed through New Brunswick, which seemed to offer nothing much but major forestation, with pine trees and blueberry bushes lining the road, and when he got into Nova Scotia, he deliberately left the interstate and took some two-lane roads so he could see what sort of country he was passing through. Melinda had wanted them to go to Louisbourgh, a place on Cape Breton where the French had built an extensive fortress, then lost it to the British. She had a touch of French in her background, which she tended to make more rather than less of, and he suspected, if she were with him, she'd be reading the signs out loud with a fake French accent. So, as he drove toward Louisbourgh, he made a feeble attempt to imitate the sounds he thought she would make, but the nasal voice he came up with only fell off into a void.

Driving for such a long time led to thinking too much. He hoped he hadn't blown it with her. He had to get used to the idea women could get just as angry as men. Well, wake up, he thought, look at Ma. She's the one, after all this time, who's never given up on being furious at Cookie. And may even have sent her a warning I was coming.

The cottage Melinda had found for them was a small, two-bedroom structure plunked down no more than twenty feet from where the land dropped off to a pile of stones, constantly battered by the sea. There was a small cove below it, a few boats in the water, and a point, around which whales were sometimes spotted, according to the landlady. The wraparound porch, practically smack on the sea, had entrances from the both the bedroom and the living room, and Warren stood out there a few minutes, excitement mounting.

So here he was in Neil's Harbour, a small hamlet just beyond Ingonish, the bigger town most likely Cookie lived in, if indeed she was around here. Of course, she *could* live right here in Neil's Harbour, for all he knew, or the next town out, Seal Cove. Each hamlet was only a few blocks long, a smattering of houses along the perimeter road that followed the coastline, the Cabot Trail.

He deposited his suitcase on the bed and the food supplies Melinda had packed for him in the kitchen and went back to the main house to pay the rest of what he owed.

Earl, the man of the house, had come home by then, and when Warren said how much he liked the cottage, Earl bragged he had built it with his bare hands. Didn't surprise Warren; he had already taken note of the unconventional foundation, adequate enough, but he'd have done it differently.

"What's your plan?" Earl asked. "Where're you heading first?"

"Looking at the map, I thought I'd drive out to Meat Cove tomorrow, stop off at that historical museum on the way out."

"Not sure the museum's still open," said Earl, "but Meat Cove's worth the trip. Go find out why they call it that." He added with a wink, "I'm not telling."

Earl's wife, Kelly, a nurse at the local hospital, chimed in, teasing. "What's the big secret, Earl?"

Earl shook his head at her interference and said, "Just let the man find out for himself."

"The hours'll be sketchy now," she said, "but you might find someone at the museum, if you're lucky."

"Is that right?" Warren said, backing toward the door. The prospect the museum might still be open and he might find none other than Cookie there shot an alarm jangling through his body. Nice as these people were, he needed to get back to the privacy of the cottage and figure out what he was going to do.

Chapter 22

Cookie and Butch often went down to the diner on Sundays for supper, and if they were early enough to find Mrs. Biddle there, she'd invite them to join her.

On just such a Sunday, with the chill of fall coming brisk, basking in the warmth of the overhead lights, they were telling Mrs. Biddle the good news about Chrissie finally passing her driver's test on the second go-round.

"What happened the first time?" Mrs. Biddle asked.

"She knocked over a cone, parking," Butch said. "She was so embarrassed she turned a scarlet red, and I'm betting the color of her face scared the instructor more than he was worried she'd whack someone's bumper." He chuckled. "So he failed her."

Mrs. Biddle laughed. "Well, even though Lord knows how she'll get a car, it's great that you two have given her the independence and confidence that comes with being able to drive."

Cookie nodded, remembering the morning she'd gained that feeling herself. "My sixteenth birthday," she said, "I begged and cajoled my father into driving me down to the motor vehicle bureau to take my . . ."

Suddenly, the door to the diner swung wide. Had Cookie been standing, she would have fallen to the floor, because there was Warren, holding the door open and taking in the room. She turned toward Butch, whose mouth opened in a question. Mrs. Biddle, too, looked alarmed.

Butch pulled her up against his chest, as if to hide her, as the well-built man approached.

"What?" Butch murmured.

"Warren," she said, barely audible.

The tall man now stood over their table and said, in a voice quivering with barely-controlled emotion, "Cookie? Is that you?"

Cookie raised her head. My God, what was he doing here, if not coming to get her and take her back? She started to shake.

His eyes, brought out by his bushy dark eyebrows, held steady on her, but not with the glare they always took on when he was about to hit her. His whole face was open, the way she remembered him when he'd been young and awkward, asking her to go to the movies for the first time, *if* she would like to. He'd asked it with enough hesitation so she'd know he wouldn't be toppled if she said no. But it worked the other way. She'd sensed he *would be* toppled, and so had said yes, not wanting to disappoint.

She brought her hand to her forehead, as if she had to protect her eyes against looking at the sun, and more fully took him in. *He is not dead, he is not dead*, kept repeating in her head, loud enough to overtake fear. She gulped. "I'm so surprised," she managed to say.

"Me, too," said he.

"What are you doing here?"

"Hoping to find you."

Butch sat up fully erect, angling his body toward Warren at the end of the booth. He cleared his throat and asked, "Just what is it you want of her?"

"No, no," Warren said, holding up a hand. "I don't want anything from you, Cookie, but can we talk? I'm staying a few days in the next village out. I could come by and pick you up tomorrow or meet you somewhere."

No, no, no, repeated inside her. I'm not going anywhere with you. "I work with Butch," she said tersely, "and we're working tomorrow."

"Well . . . after work."

She couldn't speak but her head was signaling no to make up for her muteness.

"I need to move on," he said, his eyes imploring her. "And now that I found you . . ."

"How about down at the dock," Butch said to Cookie. "If I come with you and stay nearby, hang out over at the fish shack with Jimbo?"

When Cookie nodded yes, Butch went on to describe where and when Warren could meet them.

Muriel came to ask Warren if he'd like a table and Warren had the grace to say no, he'd be going, and suddenly, as quickly as he had materialized, he was gone.

"Don't worry, I knew," said Edith, into the silence left by Warren's exit.

Cookie arched her eyebrows. "Knew what?"

"About the unfortunate incident with Warren."

Cookie's mouth came open but no words came out.

Oh, she thought, is this why Warren knew where to find her? And why Edith seemed so remote lately? She began to feel the numbness in her hands that came with her panic attacks. Did Warren know where her cottage was? Her safe haven, where she could see who was coming before they saw her?

She dropped her face forward into her hands, hoping to stop the near vertigo. She stayed in this position, paralyzed, until she felt a warmth on the back of her hand and looked out from her fortress to see Edith had reached across the table to touch her.

"Does he know where I live?" Cookie asked meekly.

Edith shook her head. "I don't think so," she said. "I only found out from going back to the newspapers from New Paltz, where Butch said you'd lived. And I saw your picture there."

"I lied to you," Cookie confessed, her head still in her hands. "I never lived in New Paltz, just close enough to know something about it."

"Don't worry about that," said Edith. "The question is, 'Do you want to see him tomorrow, or should we be working on a plan to hide you away?'"

"Oh, dear," Cookie said. "I don't know. I thought he was dead."

"Me, too," said Butch.

"Well, he's very much alive," said Edith.

Warren was alive. It was good to hear this fact spoken out loud. Cookie took a deep breath, raised her head up, and sighed. She was so exhausted. If she could rest her head on Butch's shoulder, she could fall asleep in less than a minute. "Did I say I would see him?" she asked.

"Down at the docks tomorrow," Butch said, putting his hand to her cheek, "but that's entirely up to you. We can change that if you don't want to. Me and Jimbo can handle him. Jimbo's out of practice, but he was bred to be a guard dog and he picks up my vibes just fine."

"No," Cookie shook her head. "I'm in shock but not freaked out. It probably sounds odd, but I'm more relieved than you can imagine." She looked from one of them to the other. "I might just be able to sleep tonight without nightmares."

There was a cheese omelet in front of her, only one bite taken out of it, the toast growing cold. Butch had resumed eating his supper and now touched her elbow and pointed at the food, as if he didn't want to ruin her appetite with words.

"What about eating?" he suggested. "I'll ask Muriel to warm this up."

"Maybe I should try to eat," Cookie agreed.

Mrs. Biddle kept quiet but Cookie could tell she was fully concentrated on what all this meant.

Muriel brought the plate back with fresh toast, and Cookie dug in and finished off her omelet. Then, she broke into a wide smile. "He's alive," she said. "I was so sure I had killed him."

"You didn't," said Edith.

"I didn't," she repeated, "and he doesn't even seem so scary anymore."

"No," Butch said, "but we're not trusting anything until we make absolutely sure he's not come thinking he can hurt you or frisk you away."

Chapter 23

Warren had cased the strip for another place to eat but didn't find one, so he'd gone back to the cottage and put together a sandwich from the food Melinda had packed for him. He'd had his main meal at lunchtime, at a picnic table at the Meat Cove Lobster Shack, the wind whipping so hard he had to hold down his paper plate and eat with one hand, the sun casting shadows on the range where it curved out into the sea. He'd been glad of the wild wind, though, hoping to let it blow away his nerves. He'd been half relieved and half let down when he'd found the museum closed.

At least he'd discovered what Earl had been withholding—that they called it Meat Cove because that's where, when the seals came in to breed, the fishermen would lie in wait to slaughter them. *Slaughter.* The word got to him, making him remember how close Cookie had come to slaughtering him. How he had clutched the rug to his chest, his blood pouring out of him. Seeing Cookie in the diner, though, he had only seen the shock lighting up her face, not the Cookie who attacked him.

He brewed coffee and sat out on the porch to watch the ocean, relaxing with the magnitude of how far he could see. After a while, he moved in to the big, comfy bed but left the patio door open so he could hear the sea sucking the shore while he tried to decipher the jumble of feelings running in him. Cookie was five years older and, surprise, surprise, had found herself a home. She was smaller than he had remembered her, small enough it was hard to believe he could have mishandled her. He remembered her squinting around a shiner as she made breakfast the next morning, or clutching a sore shoulder, and him teasing. "What's a matter? You ran into the fridge door or what?"

And her giving him a look that said she wasn't going to bite at his pretending he didn't know what he'd done, when he damn well knew he'd been drunk the night before. He *did* know it; yet, he wasn't lying when he said he couldn't remember. He'd never heard of a blackout until he went to AA and, when he finally opened his ears long enough to learn what a blackout was, it put a lot into perspective.

He shifted from side to side in the bed. "You mother-fucker of a lout," he said out loud. "Supposed to be fearless, but you're fucking scared." How could he say he was sorry, when even thinking the words made him feel like lashing out? He flung himself back to his other side. But she fucking stabbed me and didn't care if I bled to death. Damned plush mattress, he pummeled it with his fist. It seemed to want to swallow him up.

Act *as if*, his sponsor had told him. As if what? As if he was a decent human being when he wasn't? But Melinda had a baby on the way and he was running out of time to learn how to be one.

Unable to sleep, Warren wrapped himself in a blanket and went back out to the porch. Leaning back in the Adirondack chair, under a startling array of stars, he remembered when he and Cookie had met, how her mouth puckered something like a rose when she was frightened, and how, in the beginning, this look always made him want to take her in his arms. My Cookie, he thought. He'd meant to take such good care of her. Not harm her.

His heart grew heavy as a stone as he realized how far he had fallen from his intentions. Like the distance between him and those stars he was looking at now. Did intentions count for anything when they had only ever served him as excuses? At least maybe it counted for something that he was admitting this now, even though it pained him. He found himself pressing his hand hard to his chest, like he'd tried to do the night he was bleeding out. But then he laughed. What kind of irony would that be, huh? If he had a heart attack working up to telling Cookie he was sorry. Or whatever the hell he was going to do, if he couldn't get this stone to melt before they met up?

Chapter 24

Cookie stepped down from the passenger side of Butch's truck the same time as Butch came out the driver's side, and by the time Butch signaled Jimbo to jump down from the truck bed, Warren was ambling across the parking lot toward them. Cookie didn't know if Butch gave some subtle signal to Jimbo or Jimbo just sensed this was all happening too fast, but when Warren was about twenty feet from them, the dog lay down, squarely blocking him. Warren stopped short and stared down at Jimbo, a wary look on his face until Butch called out, "Okay, Jimbo, you're done," and Jimbo rose slowly and came back to them.

"Thanks," Warren called out.

Butch extended his hand and gave him a handshake and Cookie spoke a quiet hello.

"Why don't you two go sit on the bench there by the water, while I get us some coffees over at the fish shack. That okay, Molly?" Butch said.

Cookie nodded and Warren said sure.

"You take cream and sugar?"

"Just black."

Warren followed Cookie to the bench and they sat, one at each end, silent, the water lapping in a soothing rhythm against the wooden structure beneath them. Cookie tried to breathe deeply in and out and calm herself the way she often did when she came down to sit here, but Warren's presence was overwhelming.

Peripherally, she took him in, then finally her eyes moved directly up and down him. He was not six feet under like in the picture that had so often haunted her. "This is making me speechless," she finally said, shaking her head.

"I can see that. But you knew I was a tough old bird."

She nodded but then looked away. Her voice a bit hoarse, she asked, "Who found you?"

"Guys from the rescue squad. They got an emergency call and couldn't figure out why they couldn't reach me, so Davy came looking. Just in time."

"I'm so sorry," she said, hit with the full brunt of what she'd done, her hand coming up to her mouth.

"Sorry he saved me?"

"Oh, Warren, no. Of course not. Sorry for what I did. I still don't know how I could have done it."

Butch came back then with three cups of coffee in a cardboard tray and made eye contact with Cookie. "You okay?" he asked. When she gave him a slight nod, he took his coffee and went down to the dock but stayed fully in sight.

"Where were we?" Warren asked, once Butch was out of earshot.

She shrugged.

"Look, it's me who's sorry," he said, his voice low and gravelly. He sat with his knees apart, his long legs slightly wobbling. "I was one mean son of a bitch. I don't know why you didn't leave me way before that night."

"You don't remember saying you'd kill me?" she blurted out. She looked up for a second, then away.

"You knew I didn't mean it."

"Hard to tell, when your hand was up, ready to wallop me."

Warren reddened. "I was blasted half the time. I know it's no excuse, but most of the time I didn't even know what I was doing, didn't hardly believe I had hit you, even though the evidence was there."

Cookie's face fell apart as memories flooded into her of times Warren had used that "can't remember" excuse to pretend he couldn't be sure he was the one who'd turned her black and blue. She remembered how he'd mock and tease her, challenging her to find a witness, prove it. It was her word against his and he was the big guy standing over her, shrinking her.

Only suddenly now, some kind of backbone came into Cookie and she sat up straight, on fire. She shook with the same fury that had mounted the night she'd grabbed the knife. She was not going to let Warren control another moment of her life and render it not worth living. When she opened her mouth nothing came out, but she didn't let him speak either. She held up her hand like a traffic cop when he started to, all the while shaking her head no.

"I loved you, Warren," she said when she was able to, her voice reverberating as if it were coming out of her on a tight wire, "and you took advantage of my love. You started out just scaring me enough so I'd walk circles around you, tiptoeing, hoping to keep you assured you were in charge." She kept her eyes on him like an animal straining for the upper hand and her voice grew stronger. "You acted like you didn't know what you were doing, and like a fool, I bought it." She made her voice singsong. "He doesn't know what he's doing. He doesn't know his own strength. He doesn't have any idea how drunk he was last night!"

She drew in a deep breath and went on. "I wish *my memory* was more faulty, but I remember everything you ever did to me, Warren. The blows are alive in my body and play over and over. You didn't want me to live outside of you . . . of us. You pushed me into a corner until my love turned to hate. Why do you think I didn't leave you?" She shook her head slowly back and forth. "This is something I've asked myself over and over. Always the same answer." Her voice dropped from hard and sharp to a sorrowful whisper. "I was too scared you'd come after me and kill me."

She sighed. She thought maybe she had left her body, but then she heard the waves lapping below and knew where she was. She was here on this bench in Seal Cove and she was finished with that life; she would never cower to Warren again. Her face was hot, her hands tingled, but not with fear.

With life.

She could see Warren was stunned. He closed his eyes and dropped his head like a shamed child. When he looked up again, he said, "Cookie, you were nothing but good to me. I . . . I was out of my mind."

She waited for the but . . . the excuse. But he surprised her, leaving it alone. Finally, he brought his hand up to his chest. "There *was* some good that came out of me being nearly six-feet-under, though. Because it stopped my drinking."

She looked at him again and this time didn't look away.

He took a sip of the coffee.

She could see he did not look as haggard as he had always looked with a hangover, but she didn't know what to say. Eventually, with little expression, she got out, "You do look good, Warren."

"You, too," he said, and they sat looking at each other as if they were strangers.

After a while, he said, "Your sister Annie wants you to get in touch."

Cookie reeled, as if struck by a strong blast of wind. "My sister?"

"She came all the way up to Woodstock to tell me she knew you were in Canada. She wouldn't tell me where, though."

"Cousin Denny," Cookie muttered.

"Right."

She shook her head. "How come she didn't come herself?"

"Offended, I think, that you haven't made contact."

"How could I? Everyone would have known where I was then."

"Of course."

Cookie hated to even ask, but the question came out automatically. "How *is* Annie?"

"Seems fine. Still in North Carolina. New girlfriend, though. Some kind of basketball coach for the women's team. She still looks fit, like she jogs daily before the sun comes up."

Cookie chuckled. "She stay with you at the house?"

"You kidding? She stayed in the Lodge out in Mt. Tremper. In fact, I ran smack into her when me and Melinda, the woman I've been seeing, were having dinner there. Kinda like I ran into you yesterday. Seems like it was meant to happen."

"Yeah," she said, "only it's not so odd in Seal Cove or Neil's Harbour, where you see just about everyone who lives here in the course of a day."

They went on about Annie for a minute, then the subject turned to Butch.

"I don't live with Butch here; I work with him," she said.

"But isn't there more than that between you?" Warren asked.

Why this friendly talk? She only turned up her hands. She didn't want to give him anything he might use against her.

"I'm with Melinda a couple of years now," he said.

"Is that who you put up to send me that card with the hummingbird?" she asked, her eyes taking on a razor-sharp look.

"What card?" Warren shook his head.

"The card that said, 'Don't think you've gotten away with murder. We know where you are.'"

His head shook harder. "No," he said, "no way I put anyone up to that. I . . . I don't know anything about it. Could it be your sister?"

"Hardly."

He looked at her, waiting for more.

"You said yourself my sister's so mad she wouldn't even come looking for me," Cookie said. "Besides, I know her handwriting."

"I'm sorry," Warren said. "I had nothing to do with it, but really, I'm sorry."

Cookie saw Warren ball up his fist and looked to where Butch was throwing a stick for Jimbo.

"Melinda did look up the address of the museum for me," Warren went on, "but I can't believe she would have sent that."

Cookie gave him a look that could cut. She shook her head slowly back and forth, ready to be done with this.

But Warren didn't seem finished. He cleared his throat and said, with a sheepish look, "Must have been all the booze that didn't let my sperm rise when we were trying for a baby, 'cause right now Melinda's pregnant." He shrugged his shoulders and snuck out a grin. "That's one reason I'm thinking it would be good if we got a divorce. So I could marry her, and you won't have to worry about me no more."

Warren was telling her they should get a divorce as if they were two normal married people whose lives had merely changed. And he was saying he was sorry. Something Warren didn't do. "I don't bend. I stand here strong, like the tough, unyielding tree that's been standing in our front yard for over a hundred years, and I'm not about to weaken myself with namby-pamby apologies," was the excuse he always used.

This Warren was more like the guy she'd thought she was marrying way back when she was twenty-five. Not that she wanted him back. He would never have the generous nature of Butch, nor could she ever drop the vigilance with which she was charting his every expression, each variance in his tone, with every word he uttered. Her skin was tuned to read him, her brain on high alert, and yet, some part of her was growing lighter by the second as she waited for him to leave. Because he didn't seem to want to charge her with anything. And if she got a divorce and was not wanted by the law, she would be free to return to the States and see Nita, and even her sister. She could get a passport. Open a bank account and put away money for her older years. Be a real person. She could sleep through the nights and walk in the mornings with Mrs. Biddle and tell her the truth when Mrs. Biddle asked, as she always did, "So just how are you doing this fine morning."

"Divorce," she said now, testing out the word. "I'd like that. What would we need to do?"

"Well, file, I guess. Get a lawyer. In New York State I think you can request a separation, and then, after a year, it goes on to become a divorce. Maybe if we say we've already been separated five years, that would count."

"Would it be on the grounds of what happened?"

Warren shrugged. "No need," he said. "Just plain incompatibility."

Cookie gave him a quizzical look.

"What is it?" he asked. "You don't believe me?"

"No," she said, "I mean yes, but even if I believe you, whoever sent that card . . . someone is still after me."

Warren sucked in air. He looked out over the water. "I can't blame you, Cookie," he said finally, sitting up straighter and touching the spot where Cookie had put the knife into him. "But I did not send that card, and I'd like to convince you I'm not the same guy who took the wound. I'm using my stubbornness to stay on the right path and not go bonkers every time I get angry."

Cookie swallowed hard. Why couldn't he have done this when they were still together? And spared her the agony of the past five years.

"I'm sorry about us," he said, his voice a rasp.

She tried to say something back but couldn't find words. She was sorry, too, but it wouldn't come out of her. Not right then. Maybe sometime later, she'd be able to say it to him.

"I'm hoping someday you'll forgive me," he went on, hesitantly. "They tell me there's no point in not forgiving myself, so I hope to do that, too, eventually."

It didn't sound like Warren. If Cookie believed this was really Warren talking, maybe she could melt the rock-hard coldness she had to speak around. "I don't know what I feel," was all she managed. She didn't want to go back and remember all those times he had made her feel like a helpless doll who couldn't get away from him.

When he reached out his hand as if to touch her, she jerked back. It took all she had not to rise up from the bench and run. She shook her head and then found the word she wanted and spoke it out loud. "*Divorce*. That sounds right." She spoke very slowly, almost as if she were someone simple. "That'll be a place to start."

As they stood to depart, she thanked him for coming, but when she saw he was inclined to come toward her again, she deftly stepped to the side of the bench, and he took the hint and stayed in place, his hands going into his pockets as if trying to find something to touch.

Butch appeared with magical timing, wishing Warren a pleasant stay. "It's even better here in summer," she heard him say, as Warren was about to walk away.

Warren took a hand out of his pocket and, holding it up with his keys dangling, his eyes intently on her, gave her a sort of wave. She swallowed over a lump in her throat. She felt badly about not being able to even offer to shake his hand, but she only held up her hand in the same sort of semi-wave and went to Butch's side.

Chapter 25

I n his truck, once Warren drove away, Butch took her in his arms. He didn't tell her not to cry when she began to weep, just whispered, "You're all right, everything is going to be all right," and held her until she had wept out the trauma of seeing Warren again.

Before they went into Butch's, they stood a moment, looking out from his patio. The ocean was vast as always, but Cookie no longer seemed so dwarfed in the face of it.

"How about a beer?" Butch said.

"Yeah," she said, smiling for the first time. "We have something to celebrate! I'm getting a *divorce*." The word which had held her aloft through the end of that awkward hour with Warren sounded so sweet.

They went in and Butch cracked open a beer for each of them and Jimbo stood on his hind legs as if he wanted to dance with her, and she put on one of Butch's CDs, some light jazz, and they danced around the room, first individually and then together and with the dog, like silly children. She remembered Annie and her dancing like this, at moments of great relief, like when their father had finally passed out so deeply they were sure he wasn't going to re-erect himself until the next day. They would jump on their beds then, or race away from each other, playing chase, but the point was for one of them to catch the other and with a quick "got you!"

actually give her sister a fast, tight squeeze of a hug, a signal say-ing, "We made it again, and don't let anyone think we care about a thing, but we can go to sleep now."

"Tell me word for word what he said," Butch said, after they wore themselves down with celebrating and went into the kitchen to chop some things for dinner.

Cookie was fixed on two things. One: the notion she was not the murderer she had believed herself to be for the past five years. Seeing Warren in the flesh had affirmed she should be able to relax about that, yet, as she let go of the tension she'd been holding tight for these five years, a great sorrow came into focus, about how much she had punished herself for thinking she had killed him. And two: how she had told him clearly to his face what he had done to her. The feeling of glory which had come from that, she was going to hold close!

Beyond that, it was hard to absorb how Warren didn't seem like the man she had stabbed. When she told Butch how changed he seemed, he chortled, "Sounds like he would have been better off had you stabbed him long before you did," and they both laughed.

"What about your legal status?"

"He doesn't want anything but a divorce."

"But does he know if that's okay with the State?"

"He didn't seem to think there'd be a problem, but he wasn't sure about how we should proceed. 'See a lawyer in New York State,' I think was what he said."

"My sister," Butch said. "She works for a lawyer who does a lot of work with battered women."

"Great," Cookie said. "You're not going to believe this, but I have a lesbian sister, too. I wanted to tell your sister when she was here, but I was too scared. My sister used to poke around, ques-tioning me, as if she had guessed what was happening, but I still couldn't tell her what was going on with Warren."

"Why not?"

Cookie shrugged. "Too ashamed, I guess."

"Oh, Molly," he said, touching her chin, directing her mouth upward and planting a solid kiss on it. "You've had to keep so much to yourself. Does she know you're here?"

Cookie nodded. "She does now. Because of Cousin Denny. She's the one who told Warren I was in Canada. She didn't come herself because she's so mad I didn't find some way to get in touch."

Butch harrumphed. "A lot easier for her to expect than for you to do."

He convinced Cookie to stay over again. He wasn't sure if it was distrust of Warren, because he seemed too good to be true, or because Cookie seemed more fragile than ever, in spite of the things they'd learned these past few hours which might make her free. Or was he just having *his* applecart upset by her freedom?

They made a fire in the bedroom fireplace after supper, and with the room good and toasty, came together with all their mixed-up feelings until they nearly wore out the bedsprings, and Jimbo came and asked to be let out. Spent, Butch nearly fell asleep waiting for Cookie to come back from the bathroom. But when she slipped in behind him, spooning him, the small heave in her chest brought him alert enough to turn over and hear the little hiccup noises she made as she wiped away tears with the backs of her hands. He didn't ask why she was crying, only cradled her.

"It's just so much change at once," she said. "Don't worry. I'm not really sad."

And he knew what she meant. He'd been having a spooky feeling of loss himself. The kind of imbalance he had when he drove over the high curves on the mountain, where the road had been cut into the steep cliffs, with the rugged sea crashing below, so the car hugged the earth as he leaned in to help it cling against gravity pulling it down into the ocean. He was ecstatic they no longer needed to worry about someone arriving with a warrant. Nor would Warren come and snatch her back. And if Warren didn't want to press charges, there was probably no one else to motivate New York State to do so. Yet he and Cookie had settled into a routine. They spent some nights together, her staying at Mrs. Biddle's cottage the rest of the week. While he'd rushed her with a proposal because he didn't want to take a chance of losing her the way he'd lost Janet, it had worked out so he still had the satisfying parts of his bachelor life and yet enjoyed her company several nights a week. Because they weren't underfoot all the time, they didn't take each other for granted, the way a lot of married people seemed to. He remembered Lil saying she didn't need to get married to prove she loved her girlfriend. Maybe this was true for him and Molly, too.

Or was he getting the old proverbial "cold feet"? Did a man not know himself until there was no longer an obstacle in his way, and he had to *make a choice*, even if it frightened him? He remembered his dad, the sway of his rambling walk, the holding forth with his loud voice about how a man needed freedom. "Don't try to tie me down, woman," he would say to his wife, throwing back his head, his thick head of hair flopping loosely as he brought it back, and then bent forward in a theatrical gesture, to slam any table nearby with his fist. "A man cannot be truly tamed and be who he must be!"

So much bunk. Their mother would roll her eyes and Lil and Ian would see she knew it was bunk.

And he did know it. But had he absorbed more of his father than he thought? Almost as if he were a sponge which couldn't help but expand when presented with a liquid. Whatever. He had become a man of habit and routine and found that reassuring. The rhythm of the seasons, the busy summer, the fall devoted to putting the boat back into perfect shape, saving the net repairs for winter, the work a sort of meditation, and then the spring, coming in slow, too slow, his eagerness for summer having to be tamped down. The time of year his father would not have been able to tolerate, he thought. They would come home from school and he'd have launched out on a trip, gone prospecting, whether to Colorado, panning for gold in small streams, or off to Alaska with a big rifle on his back and a plan to bring home a caribou to quarter and put up in the freezer. Of course, he'd never come home with anything larger than a bear tooth strung on a necklace, most likely purchased in a shop.

No, he had never been anything like his father, yet it was strange how a parent infected you. As if one part of him *was* his dad. DNA he understood, but besides that, something else, a sort of scrim living behind his exterior.

Maybe he was just scared to get too relaxed now that it seemed entirely possible that he could marry.

Cookie, she had said she wanted him to call her.

He thought of the night she'd run away. He wouldn't have had a real name to give the Mounties. He'd have told them Molly, and they would have been looking for Molly, and no one would have known her real last name.

A wash of relief came over him, same as he'd felt when he'd spotted her on the roadside. She was here. He had found her. And he was not going to do anything to jeopardize holding onto her if he could avoid it. Go for it, kid, he told himself. Let's get this divorce underway. And make another stab at proposing as soon as you can.

Chapter 26

B ack in the cottage, Warren heaved back the recliner and studied the ceiling, riled, trying to calm himself. He wanted to call Melinda and dump this on her, but thought better of it. *Don't mix your women* was the line running in him. Anyway, he was mad at Melinda for helping his mother. It had to be his mother who'd sent that card, and he could still see Cookie bristling when she'd asked about it.

He took a deep breath and a loud sigh escaped him. Damn, he needed something to drink. This was an occasion to be celebrated, at least saluted in some way. He, the man who prided himself on never apologizing, had said I'm sorry. More than once. So why didn't he feel great? He didn't feel anything. When was his reward for good behavior supposed to click in?

He cracked his knuckles. When they wouldn't crack again, he tilted his neck until it cracked, but the sum total of what this did for him was nothing.

He still had the cottage for another two days. Should he take off and barrel down the highway? Surprise Melinda by arriving early. No, that was stupid. He'd paid good money and ought to at least get a night's sleep. Maybe look around for a place he could go fishing in the morning.

But then he felt the flatness again, and the insult of Cookie not even touching his hand when they'd stood up to part. A little hug is all he'd wanted. A little reminder, *Oh, yeah, it's you, Warren, my husband of quite a few years*. But she'd backed away, as if he were dirt.

He heard the ocean slapping the shore, only now, rather than consoling him, it created more turbulence. He ought to go out and sit on the porch like he had the night before, but he didn't have the energy to move from the recliner. Instead, he beat his fists on its thick arms, rallying for a fight. He heard his mama in one ear, "Go up there and get her, Warren, and restore your manhood! Don't let her get away with murder! Or near murder!"

Then, in the other ear, he heard Sam, the muscle man, taunting him. "Only twenty percent don't go back to their old ways, Warren, and you think you're going to be one of them? Not too likely, man, unless you shut your mouth and open your ears."

"You let her go once," said his mama. "Now you're going to let her go again?" Was he? He'd been nearly offed by a not particularly strong woman and was he going to say that was okay, and take it?

Sam, with his hard hat AA program, had a whole different notion of letting go having to do with trusting the universe. Now, how could you put your finger on that? What a load of crap! Especially when you felt like he did at this moment—totally exposed.

He got up and looked in the kitchen, thinking some previous renter might have left behind a bottle. They'd left ketchup and mustard, olive oil, even a little coffee in the cupboards. It didn't have to be a full bottle, just anything would do. But damn it, he opened and slammed shut each of the cabinets but found no alcohol.

If there was a bar in Seal Cove, he hadn't spotted it, but he had noticed a liquor store in Ingonish as he'd passed through. No one would have to know. No one but Melinda and his mother even knew he was up here. He could tie one on and yet sober up and start for home in the morning. Melinda wouldn't even have to know he'd gone off the wagon.

You're as sick as your secrets, he heard Sam saying.

But a few drinks would help him think more clearly. Should he let Cookie go, once and for all, or take her down? "The little bitch" as his mama called her.

Yeah, he'd not been good to her, but for her not to give him even a smidgeon of a hug after all his apologizing? His mama was right—she was a bitch.

He shook his clouded head. Big Sam would say his thoughts were off the charts, yet he couldn't get them to stop, nor could he straighten them out, and there wasn't anyone here to help. So maybe he was doomed to fall back to his old ways with the eighty percent.

But when he went to grab his keys, he caught sight of the thin, local phone book, which reminded him of when he'd gotten out of the hospital in Montreal, and Danny had driven him back to Bearsville, and damn it, he'd hated doing it, but he'd opened the phone book and there it was. AA. Right at the beginning. Well, here he was in Podunk. What were the chances of a meeting right now, tonight, when he needed it? But when he opened the phone book, there it was again—the AA number, right up front. Exhaust all resources, he heard Sam saying in that grainy voice.

He called the number and a man answered, no French this time, just "AA hotline, how can I help you?"

Warren gave up little of himself and his mission. Only said he needed to know if there was a meeting in Ingonish.

"Seven o'clock," came the reply. "Ingonish Community Hall. Eight-sixty Cabot Trail."

"Tonight?" he asked, hoping the fellow would say, "Not until the end of the week."

But the scratchy voice came back. "Yes, tonight, seven o'clock."

Damn. What a wrench this put in his plan. Warren hung up without really thanking the guy.

He went out and sat in the Adirondack chair a few minutes, listening to the sloshing of the sea. He didn't have to go anywhere, but the sound no longer consoled him; it was just riling him up more. He grabbed his keys again and heaved up into his truck.

He'd head for Ingonish and see. Maybe the AA place wouldn't be easy to find, but he had a map in his mind to where the liquor store was, exactly.

Chapter 27

Six thirty a.m. As the sun rose over the water, painting red sky as far as she could see, Edith stepped out onto her terrace to meet Molly for their morning walk. Only Molly wasn't there. Suddenly spooked, she pulled the wool scarf tighter around her neck, realizing almost anything could have happened to Molly the day before. But surely Butch would have called if the not-dead husband had caused trouble.

The wind came up stronger, and as she turned to put her back to it, there was Molly, coming up the stairs, calling out a cheery good morning.

"I was wondering where you were," Edith said, relieved.

"Wouldn't miss it. Besides, for a change, no nightmares! I slept right through the night at Butch's and was up and raring to go at five thirty."

They started up the high road, walking east, the sun rising higher until its rays penetrated nearly straight into their eyes. When the road flattened out, Cookie glanced sideways at Edith.

"I want to thank you," she said.

Edith gave a slight shrug. "I don't know what for."

"You must know," said Cookie, looking at her fiercely. "First, for scooping me up and putting a roof over my head when you had no idea who I was," she halted in the path, "and then for not giving me up when you found out what I'd done."

Edith shook her head. "I knew what I read was only one side of the story, and *your* side was the one I was on, even if I didn't know exactly what it was."

Cookie let out a huge exhale. "I sure got lucky when I went into the diner. Either it was luck, or some force I don't even know if I believe in, was watching over me."

"It's not all one way," Edith said. "I thought I'd never get over being depressed about losing Doc, and then you showed up. I needed *someone* up there in the cottage, and you were the perfect one to have."

They walked on as the red faded from the sky, replaced by blue sky and pink clouds. The gulls swooped and dove above them. "So how did it go yesterday?" Edith finally asked.

Cookie's voice turned shaky, the confidence with which she'd greeted the morning gone. "Warren was more like he used to be back when I first married him. Still . . . it was really hard to see him."

"How old were you when you married him, Molly?"

"Cookie," she corrected.

"Yes, of course, Cookie."

"Not that young. Twenty-five."

"He's a handsome man."

"He is," Cookie nodded. "When I first met him, I couldn't take my eyes off him. Plus, he had the sort of strength needed to counteract my dad."

"What kind of strength?" Edith asked, deeply curious. So many of the girls she counseled fell into the marriage trap instead of taking up the options she presented to go further with their education and get out on their own.

"That hard, burly chest, a strong voice, a firm idea of who he was. At least on the outside."

"No clue he might be an abuser?"

"None at all. The only thing I knew was how much he wanted me. He treated me like I was a precious piece of gold and no one had better hurt me. And we had a few years in the beginning like that."

"Must have made you feel protected," Edith offered.

"More than I'd ever felt in my life."

"You feel all that protection," Edith said, shaking her head, "but then when the protector turns, there must be an enormous sense of betrayal."

"There should have been," Cookie said, "but the first time he hit me, I couldn't believe it. He'd picked a fight. I was pummeling his chest, almost like a joke, telling him to leave me alone but hurting my hands more than I was hurting him, when he hauled off and whacked me on the side of my head with the heel of his hand. I saw stars. But then, when the whole side of my face turned black and blue, I convinced myself it had happened accidentally."

Edith listened intently.

"I did anything to convince myself it was my fault. *If it was my fault*, I guess I was able to think I was in control."

"False assumption," Edith said softly.

"Yes, it sure was."

Edith thought back to the shock of seeing him walk into the diner. She held back from asking more. Let the woman give out her story piece by piece, as she was ready. It had become fully light, and Edith had a moment of regret as she always did, wishing the transformation from darkness would hold on a little longer.

"He started off as a good man," Cookie went on. "His daddy beat him as a boy, and it was like that was stored up in him, looking for a target. He started to drink more and more and he was always drunk when he came at me. The morning after, he'd shake his head like—'Who the hell'd you run into, girl?' Like it didn't make sense." Cookie's voice grew thin with emotion. "I'm filling your ear," she said.

"No, no," said Edith, "I'm glad you're talking."

"Yesterday, he was . . . he started with that 'don't remember' stuff again and I reared up and laid into him and I can tell you that felt good. He apologized and said we could get an ordinary divorce. I wasn't scared like I used to be, but it was still hard to be right up close to him. Seeing him in the flesh brings back so much. Even though I'm glad he's alive," she added. "So glad."

Edith held silence.

"Butch wants us to get married," she said after a while, looking straight ahead so that Edith couldn't see what was in her eyes, "but first I have to see if there's anything in the way of my getting divorced."

"And do you want that, too?"

"Well, he's such a good man, and I feel so lucky to be with him."

"But marriage?"

Cookie shrugged. "When I was young, it was all I wanted. Maybe not exactly marriage, but it seemed like the best way to not belong to my father was to belong to someone else. So I jumped into Warren's lap." She spoke with a quiet, almost tender voice.

They walked along without speaking for a few minutes. Then Cookie broke the silence with, "Did I always seem like a total mystery?"

"No, no, the you I've gotten to know never seemed false; I was just aware of missing the dimension of your past but sensed it was better not to ask about it."

Cookie nodded.

"But you helped me stay in the present that way," Edith went on, "which wasn't all bad."

"Funny," Cookie said. "I remember one time we had a talk about having children, and I was so tempted to tell you about Warren. How upset he'd been when his sperm count tested low. Stuff like that would set him off and I'd end up knocked around and . . ."

Edith stopped and turned to catch the soft blush heightening Cookie's skin.

"Never mind." Cookie's face was pinched with pain.

"Did he do more than beat you?"

Cookie swallowed hard and then breathed out slowly. "He took me anyway he wanted to," she said.

Edith turned toward the sea and Cookie turned with her. Edith put her arm around Cookie and drew her close and said she was sorry, how painful that must have been.

Tears rolled down Cookie's cheeks and she wiped them aside but let herself be held by Edith while they both kept their eyes on the sea.

After a minute, she pulled out of Edith's embrace. "But that's all over now," she said. "I want to go on from here, not always looking back. And I didn't let Warren know this, but a lot of my wounds have started to heal already, just from being here in your cottage."

"Yes," said Edith.

"And Butch, I *do* want to marry him."

"Here, here," said Edith, "I'm all for the two of you."

"And I'm happy to have my real name back, even if it's going to cause some talk in Seal Cove."

Edith gave her a thumbs-up and they started back down the high road.

"What do you think about forgiveness?" Cookie asked at the first switchback.

"I think it's a good thing, if and when you can do it."

"When Warren asked me to forgive him, I didn't know what to say. I'd like to, but my heart still feels hard as this rock." She kicked a stone out in front of them.

Edith nodded with understanding.

"*He* seems to have forgiven *me* for my one big strike, so I guess I should try."

"You need to forgive yourself," said Edith. "Because what you did, you did in self-defense."

Cookie hadn't thought this until Edith said it, but it seemed right. She kicked the stone again and it went off the trail and picked up speed, rolling down the hillside.

"Did *you* forgive Doc for forging ahead with building the cottage and moving up there?"

"I didn't think I had to because he didn't really hurt me."

"No?"

Edith looked over, her eyebrows raised.

"Well, it seemed like you had hurt in your voice when you told me about it."

"Maybe you're right," said Edith. "Maybe I should revisit that."

As they came to the place where the descent started, Cookie asked Edith to tell her the story again.

"Like what?"

"Like how come Doc moved up above and you stayed below?"

"Oh," Edith said, picking up speed. "Even there in the big house I didn't have enough room for all my nice things, and Doc wanted me to move everything up there, so what was I going to do? Take them back to the auction house? We had a big row. We both liked our privacy, right from the start. I set up the guest room more or less as my separate room, and when Martin snored, I'd quietly slink over there in the middle of the night and sleep like a baby. We kind of had a precedent for being together but also being apart. I never could understand how people merged into one being in a marriage. Do everything together, maybe the wife gets her privacy by keeping the kitchen to herself, but that comes with always being in there preparing food or cleaning up."

Cookie nodded.

"I never believed there was anything wrong with being married but keeping some space between you and your husband. Once we fought it out, I got up the next morning and said to Martin, 'You go right ahead with your cottage and your plans to move up there, but just know I'm not leaving this house. I'll come up and visit and you can stay here whenever you want and we'll be close enough to wave at each other . . .'"

Cookie laughed. Then asked, "Was Doc okay with that?"

"Yes, it seemed to suit him, too. I mean, at sixty, we weren't exactly jumping around in the bed like rabbits." She looked over to see how intimate she could be with this Cookie who had nothing to hide, and Cookie looked remarkably open, eager even.

"Between you and me, I even wondered from time to time if my husband was bisexual. Not that he had a problem being with me, but his interest never seemed so much sexual as intellectual and more like I was a person who matched up with him in plenty of ways."

Cookie's eyebrows went up. "What made you wonder?"

"Just little clues. It's not like he brought men home with him. But sometimes he went to medical conferences, and after the first few years, he stopped asking me to go with him, and sometimes when he came home, he seemed extra pleased with himself. And once I found a tie I didn't recognize in his suitcase. And another time, a picture of him in a bar with his arm around a fellow who looked a bit fey. And Martin grinning ear to ear."

Cookie shrugged, amazed but hoping to conceal her amazement. She was thinking you never could tell much about people from what you saw on the outside. She'd thought Mrs. Biddle such a totally straight arrow, as if she were a character from a book. Now she'd suddenly sprung out of her role and was swooping to and fro in Cookie's mind like those gulls she could see playing the winds over the shoreline.

"I guess, even though I enjoyed having so much space for myself, maybe I did feel a bit abandoned when he moved up above, and again when I found that photo and the tie. And if he hadn't been up there, maybe I wouldn't have had to lose him so early." Edith wrapped her arms around herself and stopped for a moment. "Maybe there is a bit of forgiveness I owe him."

Then she drew herself up to her full height and, taking Cookie's hand, said, "Onward!" and Cookie echoed back, "Yes, onward!" and they moved at a clip down the hill.

Chapter 28

After Cookie had taken off for her sunrise walk, Butch called his sister. Her voice squeaked, she sounded so surprised to hear from him. Understandably, since he'd never called her at work before.

"Everything okay?" Lil asked.

"Fine and dandy."

"You sound light."

"I am, but how you can possibly hear that?"

"Acute hearing," she said. Then, "What's up?"

"Molly," he said. "The husband came up here and found us, but the good news is he's still alive, and it seems like he's not after anything but a divorce."

"I'm not surprised," she said, "at the alive part, at least. I did some research after I got back, but I was still looking for a way to tell you, so you wouldn't be scolding me about staying out of your business."

"You found him?"

"Their story was all over the local papers a few years back. It was a huge thing for a small town, plus he was Mister Community with a big role at the rescue squad—the guy who fixed anything wrong with the machinery, a natural born mechanic."

"What about his role as a wife beater? Was he famous for that, too?"

"Seems that was kept pretty much in the dark, although after the stabbing, a few people said they'd noticed Cookie having more than her share of bruises and black eyes. Your girlfriend's sister was one of them. Said she'd seen her sister bruised but hadn't been able to get her to admit whatever was happening."

"That so." Butch shook his head, hating the reminder of Molly—he meant Cookie—being battered.

"So, are you going to marry her now?" Lil asked.

"Well, first she needs a divorce, which is why I'm calling. Can you ask your lawyers if she would have to worry about being charged even if her ex doesn't want to go after her?"

"Sure can."

"That would be great."

"What else?"

"How long will it take to get a divorce?"

"No problem, I can find that out for you."

"Can we use your lawyers to represent her?"

"Sure. I could just about walk her through a divorce myself."

"No fault?"

"No fault, my ass. I'd like to see her rake his ass through the mud and then get half of what he earns for the rest of his life."

"Down, girl," Butch said. "She stabbed the man. He could mean big trouble, but if he's willing to walk away, she is, too. She just wants to get this behind her."

"Okay," Lil said. "Let's take it one step at a time, but I'm looking forward to another trip up there to see my brother get hitched."

"I promise," he said.

She laughed and said she had better get back to work, and he could imagine her putting down the phone and jumping right in.

Later that afternoon, when Butch called to let Cookie know he'd started some inquiries and she didn't answer, he realized she must have taken his suggestion and gone out for a drive with Chrissie. He poked up the fire and sat looking into it, following its flames, his feet up on the coffee table. The flames leapt and jumped higher and higher, and when an ember spit a chunk of fire up against the screen, startling him, he knew it was going to take a while, not only for Cookie, but for him, to settle down.

Cookie and Chrissie did go up and over the mountain to St. Ann's that afternoon, Chrissie driving.

"Now that I have my license, I only wish I had a car," Chrissie said, handling the curves nicely.

"I still remember the liberation of getting my driver's license, and even more, my first car," Cookie said. "It was a wide old Oldsmobile, with fins in back, and I called it the boat because it was so low slung and cornered wide and took up more than its share of the road." She remembered the peace that had come with sitting behind the wheel. Peace and control and ownership. "I even fantasized moving my clothes into it and telling my parents I was moving out of the house. Not that they were so bad," she added.

The road became steeper and curvier, and Cookie watched Chrissie concentrate hard on the driving. This was a scary road, for anyone. After you maneuvered past tons of hairpin turns, you came to Wreck Cove, and it was easy to imagine where it had gotten its name. Cookie found her breath catching as they went up and over the steep slope, her body involuntarily pressing her foot against the floorboard, as if her energy would be capable of keeping the car on the road, even though Chrissie was driving ever so carefully. "You're doing great," she said, wishing she were driving.

When they got to St. Ann's, they went in for an ice cream. At least Chrissie had one; it was too cool for ice cream to appeal to Cookie. She had a coffee and sat watching Chrissie catch the drips as they came down the sides of her cone. It still thrilled her to see Chrissie eat, period, and even more, with enthusiasm.

They sat in silence, Cookie trying to think of a way to explain she was no longer going to be Molly, without going into more about her past. It was good to be away from the smallness of Seal Cove, the town she had grown so familiar with, though St Ann's was only slightly larger town seventy kilometers away. It seemed to offer breathing room, yet she couldn't figure out a way to tell

Chrissie to start calling her Cookie.

"How're you doing with the college application stuff?" she asked instead.

Chrissie took a couple of quick licks, trying to get ahead of the melting ice cream. "Okay," I guess," she said, "at least with the parts like filling out all your information, but I have to write my essay about why I want to go to this or that college . . ." She hesitated and licked the cone, swirling it to catch the drips all the way around. "They want to know what I have to offer them."

Cookie nodded, "Yeah . . . what do you say?"

Chrissie shrugged. "I don't know what to say. Why do they ask that anyway? It's *me*, coming to get an education from *them*. So why do I have to bring something?"

"I see your point," Cookie said, "but you have a lot to offer. You just have to figure out how to put it into words."

Chrissie stopped licking a minute, held her cone over the saucer, and let it drip. "What do you mean?"

"I mean you're smart, you're curious. You can say you worked in the museum this summer and learned the entire history of Cape Breton. You have good grades. Your English teacher said you wrote one of the best essays she'd ever seen. Put all those things in."

"Oh," Chrissie said, raising her eyebrows. "That's the kind of stuff they want?"

Cookie nodded. "I think so." She'd only ever gone to community college and didn't remember anything more than filling out some papers so she was not sure she was giving the best advice. Still, she could see not having parents who made Chrissie out to be someone special, left her thinking she was not worth anything.

"You know what," she said. "For me and Butch, teaching you to drive and having you up at the museum with us this summer . . . we really enjoyed working with you and having you around."

Chrissie's face turned red and she licked with a ferocious speed, cracking at the cone with her teeth, pride mixed with embarrassment showing in her face.

"Not really," she said.

"Yes, really," Cookie insisted.

They looked at each other a moment, then Chrissie picked up the saucer where some of her ice cream had dripped and licked it clean.

"Me, too," she finally said, after she put the plate down. "I almost didn't get to do it. My mom and dad got in a big fight when you first came to Seal Cove, and my dad told us not to associate with you, even though he couldn't say why. But that's him. Thinks everyone's out to get him." She looked up and gave a little smirk. "But when it came to the museum, my mom said you'd been a big help. She couldn't believe you got me to have tea and cookies the day I came up to help with the puzzle, without even begging me to eat. She told my dad to just hush up and let me have the opportunity to work at the museum, even if it wasn't paid work. It would give me experience and help me get out of Seal Cove, if I wanted to go to college. 'We don't need *that* expense,' he said, but she just waved him away, like she was sending me, regardless."

"Good for her," said Cookie.

Then she took a deep breath and leaned forward and said, "I don't want to frighten you, but I'd like to set things straight." She forced herself to push on. "In part, your father was right. I did come here to hide from something I'd done. It had to do with my husband, who hurt me badly, over and over."

Chrissie's eyes were fierce. She looked so startled Cookie wasn't sure she'd heard what she'd said.

"What did you say?" Chrissie asked quietly, her eyelids hooding down the way Cookie suspected her father's did when he was suspicious. "I mean what did you do?"

"I don't know if I should tell you."

"Yes, you should," Chrissie said. "I'm not a child."

"I stabbed my husband and, rather than stay and get sent to jail, I ran away and landed up here. I just found out two days ago that he survived, because he came up here and found me."

Chrissie was breathing short and hard. "But you're the nicest person I know," she said.

"Probably not," Cookie corrected.

"He must have been really mean."

"He was. Not by nature, but when he drank."

Chrissie nodded as if to say she knew something about that. She looked down like she'd done the first day she'd come to visit Cookie.

"You're shocked," Cookie said.

"Yes," she murmured. She raised her eyes but only for a second.

"I'm still the Molly you know, but my real name's Cookie, so I'd like you to call me Cookie."

"You're the only one who made me feel like eating again. And I don't even know why."

"Maybe it's not important to know why," Cookie said. "Let's just be glad it happened."

Finally, Chrissie seemed to come back into herself, and she met Cookie's gaze. "Cookie," she said and cackled. "And your cookies made me want to eat again."

Cookie smiled. "Yes," she said, "hallelujah."

"Will everybody, I mean . . . people like my father, find out?"

"We'll have to see," Cookie said. "I'm not going to announce it."

Chrissie screwed up her face and soundly proclaimed, "Well, if he does hear of it, I'm not going to let him tell me I can't hang out with you."

"Good," Cookie said, though she knew it was not going to be easy as Seal Cove received this news. She brought her hands up to either side of her face and touched herself, amazed she had gotten this far. Then, suddenly overcome with a desire to get back to Butch, she inclined her head toward the parking lot and told Chrissie they had best get going.

Chapter 29

Cookie and Butch made a nice supper. They took out some fish from the freezer and Butch put together a salad and nuked a couple of baked potatoes while Cookie breaded the fish.

"Where'd you go with Chrissie?" he asked.

"Up over the mountain to St. Ann's," she said, and told him about revealing herself as Cookie, and Chrissie's shock.

"I wondered when I saw that blue Honda in the parking lot at the ice cream shop," he said.

"In St. Ann's?" she said, all agog.

"Right."

"What were *you* doing there?"

"Giving Warren an escort off our beloved island," he stated frankly.

Cookie's mouth opened wide. "You did?"

Butch grinned. "I wanted to make sure he wasn't lurking somewhere, so I drove over to Neil's Harbour. Sure enough, he was getting ready to depart, so I hid out until he was ready to take off. And then, it was so much fun, seeing him leave, I just kept following him until he crossed the bridge past St. Ann's, and I tooted a big good riddance and watched him fade."

Cookie clutched for a second, thinking of Warren passing right by where she had been. What if he'd stopped in St Ann's? But then she gave Butch a wide smile. "So he's gone," she said.

"Yes, he's gone."

He poured Cookie a glass of wine.

"To your divorce," he said. "I have to call my sister and see what she's found out."

"To my freedom," Cookie said, holding up her glass. "And to Warren—may he live a long life . . . far away from me." She wondered for a moment how he was with his new woman. Was it possible he could make her a good husband? I hope he's able to become a different man, but I don't need to know, she thought, and then she said this out loud to Butch.

"To us," Butch said, raising his glass. "To the best thing that ever happened to me the day you were hanging out on the dock and I was looking for a good hand to go fishing with me, eh?"

Cookie flushed. It would take some time before she'd trust anyone completely again. She'd been on high alert 24/7 since the horrible night five years ago. She could still see vividly those stark walls topped with double or triple rolls of razor wire she had passed riding the bus to Montreal.

She got up from the table and patted the fish filets into the flour and seasoning on top of the butcher block. Flipped them and patted some more. Hesitated, but then flashed a smile back at Butch, who had his eyes-nearly-closed squint because of the width of his smile. "I still get nervous about all this freedom," she said, "but be patient, I'll get there."

"I know," he said. "No hurry, no worry. Let's just enjoy our evening without thinking about the future."

She dusted the flour off her fingers, then leaned into his shoulder and felt the warmth of his chest against her as her heart cracked open, her own resilience touching her, as well as the gift of Butch's gentle spirit.

"I want to get you a present," he said, his voice just above a whisper. "Something to celebrate that you've come through this in one piece."

She shook her head; where had this generous man come from?

"What shall it be? What would you like if you had your druthers?"

"Anything?" she said. "It could be anything?"

"Anything," he echoed.

She closed her eyes and thought for a moment, like she'd done on birthdays when someone said, "Make a wish." Her thoughts had always been clouded with the fear she would ask for too much.

Then it just floated into her. "Do you think Jimbo would mind if we got another dog, a golden?" she said. She was remembering the dream in which a golden retriever had her back, lying up beside her, soaking up her sorrow. Besides, she thought, she could share the dog with Chrissie.

Butch didn't hesitate, only gave her another wide smile. "No worries. I predict Jimbo will love a new dog just about as much as I love you."

As if he had been called, Jimbo gave out a musical moan, as Butch steered Cookie to the window, to see the golden sun coming to rest on the sea.

the end

Acknowledgments

I would like to extend my deepest thanks to those who helped with careful reading and other support during the writing of this novel:

Bob Bachner, Priya Doraswamy, David Foster, Aaron Hamburger, Susie Hara, Martha Hughes, Jillen Lowe, Carol March, Robin Martin, David McConnell, Elin Menzies, Debra Moskowitz, Carol Rosenfeld, Mina Samuels, Rebecca Shannonhouse, and Jackie St. Joan.

And to Virginia Center for the Creative Arts, the late Ann Stokes and Welcome Hill Studios, and The Writer's Room, for providing inspiring spaces for writing.

Also to Michele Orwin, Lorraine Fico-White, Lorie DeWorken, and Al Pranke for their fine work in the publishing of the book.

And for all, a special thanks to Martha Ellen Hughes.

About the Author

Maureen Brady is the author of seven books, including the novels, *Folly* and *Ginger's Fire,* and the short story collection, *The Question She Put to Herself,* as well as the nonfiction *Daybreak: Meditations for Women Survivors of Childhood Sexual Abuse* and *Midlife: Meditations for Women.* Her stories and essays have appeared in *Sinister Wisdom; Bellevue Literary Review; Just Like A Girl; Southern Exposure; Cabbage and Bones: An Anthology of Irish American Women's Fiction; Conditions; Lesbian Texts and Contexts; Intersections: Banff Writers, among others.* Her short story, "Basketball Fever," won the 2015 Saints and Sinners short story contest.

She teaches creative writing at NYU, New York Writers Workshop, and the Peripatetic Writing Workshop, and has received grants from Ludwig Vogelstein, Tyrone Guthrie Centre in Ireland, Money for Women, NYSCA Writer-in-residence, and NYFA, and has served as long-standing Board President of Money for Women Barbara Deming Memorial Fund. She co-founded the press Spinsters Ink in 1979 and was a co-founder of New York Writers Workshop in 2001.

She divides her time between New York City and Woodstock, NY, where she lives with her partner of 22 years and one sweet pup named Bessie.